# Running Scared

## by

## Desiree Holt

*Guardian Security Book Four*

**Running Scared**

Contact Information: info@thewildrosepress.com

Cover Art by *Diana Carlile*

The Wild Rose Press, Inc.
PO Box 708
Adams Basin, NY 14410-0708

Visit us at www.thewilderroses.com

Publishing History
First Scarlet Rose Edition, 2017
Print ISBN 978-1-5092-1768-7
Digital ISBN 978-1-5092-1769-4

Published in the United States of America

**Waking with a gun in her hand and no memory,
she is…running scared.**

"Someone blew up my house?"

He nodded. "I'd say it's pretty well destroyed. Whoever set the explosives did a good job. These people are playing very, very rough." He let out a long slow breath. "Even *this* house may not be safe enough for you if they get any idea you came to me."

"Zak—"

"It'll be okay. I'll make it okay. But before I do anything else, I need to wash off this junk. Then we'll talk." He reached out to touch her, then drew his hand back. "Everything's gone. I am so sorry."

"Gone?" She took in a steadying breath. This was no time to fall apart any more than she already had. She swallowed and clenched her fists. "It's nothing that can't be replaced. Even the laptop, as you pointed out. At least you're alive. Go take your shower while I make some fresh coffee." She tried on a weak smile. "I think I still remember where things are."

"Coffee sounds terrific. I don't think we'll be getting sleep any time soon."

Without warning, his head lowered and his lips lightly brushed against hers. She was totally unprepared for the spike of electricity that jolted her system.

From the look in his eyes, so was Zak. He stared at her, heat in his eyes, then backed away and walked upstairs to the master suite.

## Dedication

To everyone who helped make this series so successful—my dedicated cop Joseph P. Trainor, my fantastic beta reader Margie Hager, my son, Steven who lets me bounce logistics off him, and my incredible editor, Diana Carlile, who makes all my books sing.

# Chapter One

Zoe Lombardo wanted to open her eyes, but her lids felt coated in cement. Immovable. She shifted her head only to discover a percussion orchestra had taken up residence inside her skull and a huge bubble of nausea was stuck in her throat. Exerting a superhuman effort, she tried lifting her eyelids again, but her vision blurred, everything swimming as if she looked at things from underwater. The only shape that distinguished itself was the outline of the tall window on the opposite wall with the blackness of the night shimmering like waves.

*Oh, God. What's wrong with me? And where the hell am I?*

The room had a vaguely familiar feel to it, but her head was pounding so heavily she couldn't properly focus. She blinked once. Twice. Slowly, the image of the room began to sharpen, and she looked around.

Okay. She was wearing a jeweled cocktail dress in the paneled den in Nate Dunning's—her partner's— very palatial home.

*Cocktail dress? High heels? Had there been a party?*

And where the hell were her shoes?

Aware that she was lying on a couch, she turned her head to the side carefully and with great difficulty, scanned the room. Familiar enough, considering the number of times she'd been here. Nothing unusual. Until shock sliced through her like a steel blade.

She nearly threw up at the sight of Nate's tall, muscular body lying on the floor. Dressed in a tailored shirt, with an entwined ND on the breast pocket, and black boot-cut slacks, no jacket or tie, the pristine white of his shirt was covered with blood. And he wasn't moving.

Zoe closed her eyes again, fighting back the nausea that surged forward again and waited for the dizziness to settle. Her skin felt clammy, and when she lifted a hand to wipe her forehead, she realized she was holding something.

A gun.

*Gun?*

*Holy hell!*

She didn't even own a gun, so where did this one come from? She stared at it stupidly.

*Don't panic. Just don't panic.*

*Right. Easier said than done.*

Gritting her teeth, she dragged herself upright and pushed to her feet. Still holding the gun, she walked unevenly across the room and forced herself to kneel beside the body. She pressed two fingers to the hollow at Nate's throat to feel the carotid artery. No pulse. Nothing. Not even a faint thump.

Nate was definitely dead.

What had happened here tonight? And why was she here in the first place? As far as the evening was concerned, her mind was a total blank.

Another wave of dizziness hit her, and her eyes threatened to slam shut again. Biting her lip hard enough to shake off whatever was working in her system, she rose on shaky legs. How had she ended up in Nate's den with his dead body? And this gun?

Walking unsteadily to the door and cracking it open, she listened for sounds of anyone else in the house. Any activity. No voices or sounds of movement, but in the distance, she heard a thin wailing sound. Even in her foggy state, she identified it as the sound of a police siren, no doubt headed for this house. Her stomach twisted itself into a huge knot.

*Think, think, think, think, think.*

A cold sense of dread settled into her stomach. She might not remember what happened, but she couldn't forget how upside down her life had been since she'd confronted Nate about some strange accounting information. First, her house had been broken into and her den ransacked. Two nights later in a blinding rain, her car had nearly been run off the road, leaving her shaken and terrified.

The police had been absolutely no help. There was no evidence of another car, and they blamed it on poor driving conditions. There was no evidence of the break-in at her house, and she could tell they wondered if she'd somehow done it herself.

No, the police were not going to be her friends. Whoever had her in their sights had set her up. With Nate's dead body.

Her brain, which had been on freeze frame, suddenly shouted at her to stop thinking and get moving. The sirens came closer, nudging her to move faster.

Taking another wild look around the room, she spotted her purse on the polished walnut surface of the desk and her high heeled sandals lying on the floor, peeping out from behind a chair. She thought about putting them on but realized for damn sure she wasn't steady enough to wear them without breaking her neck. Okay, barefoot it was.

Grabbing her purse, she stuck the gun in it, snatched her shoes, and opened the French doors that led to a patio.

All the outside lights were on, so she crept along the thick shrubbery bordering the yard, staying in the shadows. Still dizzy, she nearly fell twice, catching herself against a chair with her hands. She wondered if the security sensors were still active along the perimeter, then decided it didn't matter. She had to get the hell away from here.

The quiet, residential street that ran behind Nate's house was wide and lined with old trees that formed a partial canopy over the road. The houses were set well back from the street, most of them surrounded by ornate, wrought iron fences. All but a few were made of natural Texas limestone, and every one of them flew the obligatory Lone Star flag. Texans were unlike any other breed-a nation unto themselves.

The only lights Zoe saw were from the fancy streetlights. No one seemed to be moving. Some of her clients lived in this neighborhood, old Texas money that loved working with a homegrown business. She had to make sure she avoided them.

She paused at one of the lights and squinted at her watch.

*One o'clock on the morning? What happened to the rest of the night?*

She backed away from the light and leaned against a tree. Whatever she'd taken—or been given—was still making her head pound, her vision blurry, and her balance questionable. She took a deep breath, trying to center herself.

Now what? She couldn't just wander around dressed the way she was, barefoot. Certainly, the police who had arrived at Nate's house would be canvassing the area for anyone. For *her*. Why had she been the only one left in the house? She'd bet a month's profits an anonymous caller had given them her name, setting her up. Too many strange things had been happening lately, things to which Nate hadn't wanted to give her answers.

Someone had gone to a lot of trouble to set this up, so going home wasn't an option.

Not only didn't she remember much of the evening, but other details eluded her, such as what she did with her car. Not that she could drive in her present foggy condition. Besides, the cops would be on it before she was.

Somehow enough of her brain was working that she managed to make her way through the quiet streets, not stopping until she had put four blocks between herself and Nate's street. Walking barefoot wasn't the most fun she'd ever had, but it beat falling on her nose. One more block and she reached the cutesy little upscale neighborhood shopping center. With its faux Texas architecture and manicured greenery, it blended discreetly into the very expensive neighborhood.

A slatted wooden bench with Texas stars embedded in it sat decoratively at one end of the little sidewalk, and Zoe gratefully collapsed onto it. Wiping her hands on her dress, she tried to force her thoughts into some semblance of reason.

She couldn't just sit here all night, nor could she call a cab. Cabs could be traced.

The pain of the rough cement scraping the bottoms of her feet helped her shake off more of the fuzziness and force her brain into a more lucid condition. She needed someone to come and get her. Yes. She knew that. Someone who could help her figure out what had happened and how she was involved. Someone who probably wished her in hell but maybe, just maybe, might be decent enough to at least listen to her.

She pulled her cell phone out of her purse and hit speed dial for a number she'd never erased. She hadn't called it in two years, but it flashed at her like a lifeline. The one person who, no matter what happened between them, she could always trust.

She prayed he wouldn't hang up on her.

****

The ringing of the telephone cut into Zak Delaney's sleep-fogged brain. At first, he thought he was dreaming it, but its shrill insistence wouldn't stop.

"Damn." He fought his way up through the mists of sleep, pushed a pillow aside, and reached for the offending instrument on his nightstand.

"This better be damn good," he said to whoever was on the other end of the line. Clients seldom called him at home, especially well after midnight. That's what he had assistants and agents for. He squinted at his watch. "Do you know what the hell time it is? It's after one in the morning. Who is this, anyway?"

There was a slight pause, then a soft voice said, "Zak?"

His stomach clenched as if someone had punched it. This was one voice he hadn't heard in two years, not since their last screaming argument, and hadn't ever expected to hear again. He'd carefully avoided any and all places where they might run into each other. Now, here she was, out of the blue, calling him at this ungodly hour. It couldn't mean anything but trouble.

"Zoe?" He asked it as if he couldn't believe it was her. In truth, he wondered if someone was in fact playing a cruel joke on him.

"You have every right to hang up on me," she said quickly, "but I'm begging you not to."

The edge of fear in her voice was very clear, even across the telephone connection. Zak took a deep breath, held it, and let it out slowly. In another moment, his pulse had almost kicked back to normal. After two years, what reason could Zoe Lombardo possibly have for calling him? In the middle of the night?

"Zak?" Her voice was thready. "Are you still there?"

"I'm here. What's going on?"

A sob caught in her throat. A sob? His heart pinched. Zoe Lombardo hardly ever cried. This must be some serious shit.

"I have no right to ask this," she went on, "but I don't have any place else to turn. Something terrible's happened." A pause. "I need your help. Can you please come and get me? Right now?"

His first inclination was to say no way in hell and slam the phone down. But that sob had been like a knife in his heart. Zoe never, ever shed tears. Something had to be terribly wrong. And there was something about the way she spoke… Real panic laced her voice, a terror that jumped at him and blocked the bitterness he'd been carrying around all this time.

*I am such a sucker. I am so going to be screwed.*

"Where are you?"

"In the little center where The Edibles Boutique is. Do you know where it is? Can you come?"

"What's wrong?" God, he didn't want to do this. But every protective instinct stood at attention at the thought of Zoe in some very bad trouble.

"I'll tell you when you get here. Can you just please come right now?"

Yes, that was definitely panic in her voice, but more than that, dread and shock. Very unlike Zoe. If nothing else, curiosity would have piqued his interest. What could traumatize the coolest person he'd ever met?

*Damn, damn, damn. He was letting himself get sucked in.*

"All right. I'm on my way."

"Th—thank you. And Zak?"

"Yeah?"

"Turn off your lights when you get close and just pull into the center. I'll be watching for you."

*Turn off my lights? What the hell was this?*

"All right. But you'd better have a damn good reason for this."

"I do. And thank you. Again."

He disconnected the call and began to pull on his clothes.

*Hell's bells. What am I doing, anyway? My partners would tell me I'm crazy, and they'd probably be right.*

He had met Zoe four years ago at a party, and he'd been very impressed with the extremely bright software programmer who left corporate security to start her own business. They'd had their first date a week later and, in less than a month, were living together.

But the last time he and Zoe had been together, they'd thrown bitter, hurtful words at each other. Words meant to wound, and they'd done just that. Two years of love and passion, of plans for the future, disappeared in a firestorm of anger. The ashes continued to smolder in the secret place where he kept them tucked away. He'd loved her almost to distraction, and she'd turned away from him to chase a dream he'd tried to tell her was tainted.

Maybe he should have kept his mouth shut. But hell. It had been her future. *Their* future. He'd seen nothing but disaster ahead in her decision, and she'd simply thrown his words back in his face.

Now, she was reaching out to him after this long silence. Whatever trouble she was in, it had to be pretty bad for her to call him. That was uppermost in his mind as he drove to where she told him she'd be.

Zak turned the corner from Main Street onto the side street where the little upscale center was, cutting his lights and coasting into the parking lot. Riding the brake, he scanned the area carefully, trying to distinguish a person in the darkness. When a sharp rap sounded on his passenger window, his foot slipped and the car lurched forward. Slamming on the brake, he jerked his head around.

Zoe's face looked like an apparition in the darkness, ghostly white against the blackness of the night.

"Unlock the door," she mouthed.

The minute he hit the unlock switch, she yanked the door open and tumbled into the seat.

"Go," she ordered, breathing as if she'd run a mile. "Now. Please. Get out of here fast."

"I don't suppose—"

"Now, Zak!" Her voice rode the narrow edge of hysteria. "And make sure no one's following us."

That was an exercise second nature to him. With his lights still off, he glided back to the corner and rolled through the stop sign. When he turned back onto Main Street, he checked his rearview mirror. No one behind him.

He gave fervent thanks there wasn't much traffic at this time of night. In a moment, he turned the headlights back on and picked up speed. He spared a quick glance at Zoe, and an unexpected wave of heat and desire swept through him. Her long, smooth blonde hair was swept up into some complicated arrangement, but half the curls had come loose and were hanging haphazardly around her face.

Her face!

God, that face with the porcelain skin, the wide blue eyes and the dark lashes that had been permanently burned into his brain. She was thinner than the last time he'd seen her, and she hadn't had much to spare then, but it was hard to really tell in the dark and with her sitting down.

All the old feelings came back just as if the last two years hadn't happened. She was in trouble, she needed him, and whatever resentment he'd hung onto began to dissipate.

But what had she gotten herself into? Before he tossed his heart into the shredder again, he needed to know what the hell was going on and how much danger she—and he—could be in.

She sat stiff as a board in the passenger seat, hands clenched in her lap. In the lights from oncoming cars, her face looked chalk white.

"Where's your car? Hot date leave you high and dry, princess?"

"My car?" Her teeth chattering, she repeated the words as if he spoke a foreign language. "You want to know where my car is?"

"Yes, your car. Damn it, Zoe."

*No. Calm down, Zak. Anger solves nothing. And there's definitely something very, very wrong here.*

He hauled in a deep breath and let it out. "Okay. We'll worry about your car later. How about telling me what this is all about? I have to say, you surprised the hell out of me with your call."

"I—I have a problem." She sounded as if she was dragging the words out of her throat one syllable at a time. "Is…Is anyone following us?"

Zak checked again in both the front and rearview mirrors. He had enough experience in spotting a tail, and he was pretty sure they didn't have one.

"No unwanted company," he assured her, hanging onto his patience. "A problem. Okay. What kind of problem? It's got to be pretty bad for you to call me, of all people. After two years, by the way."

"I… That is… I mean…" She unclenched her hands and rubbed them over her face as if wiping cobwebs away. "I keep hoping this whole thing is just a bad dream. That I'm really home, I'll wake up, and it will all be gone."

"*What* will be gone? Damn it, Zoe. Spit it out."

"All right, all right, all right." She rubbed her hands over her face again, then twisted her fingers together. "I've had…some problems lately."

Zak cocked an eyebrow. "Problems? What kind of problems?"

She fisted her hands so tightly her knuckles looked white. "My—My house was broken into and my den torn apart. Then two nights later, someone tried to run me off the road."

"I would think you'd call the police," he pointed out in a flat voice.

She snorted. "Yeah, right. They couldn't find where anyone had broken in, so they told me I probably just forgot what a mess I'd left in the den."

"And the other thing?" he prompted.

"There was a heavy rain that night. They chalked it up to highway hazard and careless driving." She reached over and gripped his arm so tightly he could feel her fingernails digging into him. Whatever was happening, she was about to lose it. "But I know what happened, Zak. I swear it."

"Okay, okay." He waited a moment to see if she'd say more, wishing he could get inside her head. "But that's not what prompted the call tonight, is it?"

"No." She shook her head, took a deep breath, and said, "Nate Dunning is dead. Murdered. In his den."

Zak's neck always itched when real trouble was about to visit him. Right now, he felt as if a million insects were dancing on it.

"Dead." He glanced sideways at her again. Her body was so rigid he thought it would shatter. "Are you sure?"

"Yes, I'm sure," she snapped. "He was covered in blood and not breathing." She drew in a shuddering breath.

12

"That's usually a pretty good indication someone's dead, I'll grant you that." His hands tightened on the wheel. Dead. Serious shit indeed. "Exactly how did you happen to be with his dead body?"

"I—I don't know."

*Shit. Double shit.*

"Okay. Let's try something else. Do you know how he was murdered?"

He heard a click as she opened her small purse.

"With this."

When he saw the gun in her hand, he almost drove up onto the sidewalk, straightening the car at the last minute.

"Put that back in your purse," he ordered. "Do the police know?"

"Yes. I heard sirens coming down the street. After the last two episodes, I didn't figure I had much chance to explain my way out of this, especially since I had the gun and can't remember a thing."

"All right." He sighed. "Obviously, this isn't something we're going to solve over a cup of coffee."

"W—Where are we going?"

"My house. Where you're going to tell me the entire story, and don't leave out one single detail. Am I clear?"

"Will you help me?" She sounded fuzzy now, and he wondered if she'd been drinking.

"Did you kill him, Zoe?"

"I...I don't know. I don't think so, but I can't be sure."

"You don't know." The invisible insects scratching at his neck had now invited an army of their friends to join them. Trouble in capital letters. "Well, that's

13

interesting. You've lost your car, and you aren't sure if you did or did not kill your business partner. And you don't remember a thing about the evening."

"Zak, please."

He could hear the panic rising in her voice again. "All right. First, I want to hear everything you have to tell me. And I mean everything, Zoe. Then we'll go from there."

## Chapter Two

"Come on. I think we need some coffee."

Zak took her arm, the touch sending instant tingles through Zoe. He led her through the living room into the kitchen with its familiar granite counters and gleaming appliances that were a testament to his talents as a gourmet cook. Zoe tried not to remember all the meals they'd cooked together in there.

She hadn't been in his house for more than two years, and the last visit certainly had been far from pleasant. Their argument had taken on a life of its own, escalating until there was no turning it around. It ended finally when she'd yanked Zak's house key off her key ring, tossed it at him, along with her engagement ring, and stormed out of the house. And his life.

If only he hadn't been so arrogant about the whole thing. So...so...dictatorial.

*If only I hadn't been so stubborn. I'm afraid to tell him how right he was.*

Tonight, when he'd pulled up in his car, all the angry memories from the past had disappeared like smoke. It had taken every bit of restraint she'd had left not to throw herself into the comforting circle of his arms and let out the hysterics building inside her.

Settling herself in a chair at the kitchen table while he fiddled with the coffee maker, she took her first good look at Zak after all this time. Soft jeans and a black T-shirt molded to his tall and lean body. He still moved with the grace of a jungle animal. Maybe a lion, with his thick shock of sun-streaked brown hair that just tickled the edge of his collar. Longer than before.

When he turned to look at her, the familiar square-jawed face with its high cheekbones, the light scruff he always wore, and whiskey-colored eyes framed by thick lashes was like a punch to the stomach. She could try to deny it all she wanted to, but she was far from getting him out of her system.

He looked at her critically. "Coffee will be ready in a few minutes. I think we can both use some."

"Thank you." She rubbed her arms nervously. "Coffee would be nice."

"So other than this, how are you?" he asked as he worked. "Lombardo Simulations has really made a name for itself."

"I wanted to be able to convert the sims to games we could sell and expand the market. Remember?" She stared at him, hoping he'd remember how important her dream had been to her. "Nate provided the funding I needed and the marketing know-how. And we've been lucky."

"Nate Dunning makes his own luck. I tried to tell you that if you recall." Then he remembered why she'd called him. "Or at least, he did."

"Zak—"

"Okay, okay. I'm sorry. I'll back off."

The silence filling the room was palpable, and all their unresolved issues sat between them like a bloated elephant. Would they have to get all that garbage out of the way before she told him what happened tonight? Zoe hoped not. Her head still throbbed like the inside of a bass drum, and while most of the fuzziness had disappeared, the nausea hadn't. She concentrated on taking deep breaths while the coffee dripped and Zak pulled cups out of the cupboard.

If she'd had anyone else to call, she would have. In her bones, though, she knew Zak was the only person who would respond the way he had. Anyone else would either tell her she was crazy or insist she wait for the police. And Zak might still do that. Somehow, she had to get past the wall between them and convince him to help her.

She felt his eyes on her and looked up to find his gaze raking over her.

"Nice threads," he commented, looking at her dress. "Doesn't look like something that came off the rack. Lombardo Sim must *definitely* be doing well." He raked his gaze over her, his eyes cold and unforgiving. "So. Were you at another one of Nate's fancy shindigs tonight?"

"Zak..." If he would just stop poking at old wounds... Although she probably should have expected it. But she needed his help desperately, and she needed him to not be angry with her. Resentful.

He held up a hand. "Sorry. I'll be good. Why don't I wait until the coffee's done? Then we'll talk."

Lost in thought as she tried to create a story with some semblance of coherency, she was startled when Zak put a mug filled with hot liquid in front of her.

"Drink this. You look like you could use a good jolt of caffeine."

"Thanks." She picked the mug up with two hands, but they were shaking so badly, the hot coffee sloshed over onto her skin and the table. She put the mug down quickly, more liquid spilling over the rim. "Oh! Oh, Zak, I'm so sorry."

He looked at her shaking hands and the puddle of liquid. "Don't worry. Hold on a sec."

He snagged a paper towel from the holder on the counter, mopped the table, then gently blotted her hands. When she curled her fingers into her palms, trying to still the trembling, his hands closed over hers. They were firm and warm, and the heat from them seeped into her system more than the hot coffee could ever have done.

"Zoe?" The deep sound of his voice cut through her panic. "Zoe, look at me."

She forced her eyes to meet his. "What?"

"Take a deep breath. Good. Another one." Air whooshed out of his lungs as he released her hands and sat down opposite her. "So before you tell me what this is all about, I want to know something. Actually I *have* to know it. Was tonight's call too personal because we were…whatever we were? Apparently, it was more to me than to you." He held up his hand when she opened her mouth to speak. "Or is it strictly business because you're in trouble. Do you want to hire our security services? If that's the case, we have a number of good people we can assign to you."

The jackhammer in her head had finally eased, but she still had trouble focusing, putting the pieces together. And the cold, impersonal tone in his voice wasn't helping. God, if only she could think straight. But this was a fair enough question. Which one *had* she called?

She was aware that a year ago Zak had merged with the much larger Guardian Security Corporation, becoming a partner with Reno Sullivan and Nick Vanetta. Guardian was considered one of the largest operations in the country. It provided a wide range of services for both its corporate and individual clients, occasionally doing under the radar work for the government.

When she'd made the call, she hadn't given a thought to how Zak's partners might feel about this. Would they object to him helping her? Or he might not want to involve his partners at all. Maybe he wouldn't even *want* to help her. He might still resent her for the way she'd ended things between them. How should she answer him?

"Both, I guess," she admitted at last. "But…mostly, um, you. Personally." God, she hoped it wasn't a mistake telling him that.

A mixture of surprise and…something else— caring?—flashed across his face, then disappeared so quickly she wasn't even sure she'd seen it.

"That's a shocker, I gotta tell you." He shoved his hands in his pockets. "We didn't exactly part on what you'd call the best of terms."

*Well, she guessed he had to say it.*

The nausea rolled up out of her stomach. She was terrified, and he was her only hope, but what if he couldn't get past everything that had happened before? If all he wanted to do was throw ancient history at her and then call the police, what would she do? She couldn't think of anyplace else to turn.

"Zak, listen…"

He rubbed the back of his neck. "Sorry. Knee jerk reaction." He turned and looked at her, studying her face as if he expected to read the answers to his unasked questions written in indelible ink. "I really am sorry, Zoe. I'm being a jerk. I realize you'd have to be pretty desperate to call me, so let's cut to the chase. You've got to tell me what happened if you want my help."

*Was that a trace of leftover affection in his tone? Oh, god, she hoped so.*

Zak added fresh coffee to her mug, then folded his fingers around hers while she took a sip. The shock of the contact sent a jolt of electricity zapping through her body. The chemistry between them was certainly still there, and when he moved his hand away, she wanted to reach for him but forcibly stopped herself.

"All right, now?" he asked. "Can you hang onto it?"

She swallowed hard and nodded. She felt him watching her while she took a few more sips of the strong brew. Finally, she put the mug down, her hands steadier.

"Better now," she told him. "Thank you. I can't believe that someone who is supposed to be so smart could be dumb enough to get caught up in a situation like this. Where's the brain I'm so proud of?"

"Still there, just clouded over at the moment. Fear and panic can make even a genius do dumb things and behave not so smartly." He studied her with eyes darkened almost to chocolate. "My first question should probably be, where did you get the gun and did you shoot Nate Dunning. But I'd rather ask you to tell me exactly what's going on that made you call me. Especially—as I said earlier—considering the way things ended between us."

Zoe really didn't want to get into the argument that

still haunted her. She'd only been wearing Zak's engagement ring for two weeks the night she announced that Nate Dunning was buying into her company, and Zak had exploded. She'd never forgotten the scene that followed.

\*\*\*\*

*"You're making a big mistake, Zoe." Zak's voice was hard. Angry. A big change from the sensuous tone he'd used only moments before when they made love.*

*"Then it's my mistake to make," Zoe threw back at him, pulling on her blouse and shorts.*

*How had this turned so bad? She'd thought their relationship was so perfect, everything she wanted. She'd thought Zak had been glad she was getting her wish for her company. But since the first time she met with Nate Dunning, he'd been picking away at it. It seemed that for the past few weeks that was all they'd talked about. Argued about. The harder he pushed, the harder she pushed back. He had to understand he could not control her.*

*She thought they'd finally gotten past that tonight, making love that exceeded anything in the past. Apparently not.*

*"Nate Dunning is a slime ball of the first order. A user. A crook."*

*She glared at him. "You keep saying that, but do you have proof?"*

*"I'll get you all the proof you want, but everyone knows beneath that suave exterior he's nothing but a crook."*

*"A pretty successful one," she snapped. "He's got money he hasn't even counted yet."*

*Zak banged his fist on the bedroom dresser. "Is*

21

*that what appeals to you? Money? That's all you're interested in?"*

*"You know I want to expand the business," she pointed out. "A rich partner is better than the banks."*

*"If you wanted a partner, I could have gotten you one. Make that twenty." The rage rolled off him in waves. Even stark naked, he looked formidable. "You could have had your pick. And all reliable and properly vetted."*

*"By Delaney Security?" she sneered. "No, thanks. I didn't want you to find me someone. I wanted to do it myself. Why can't you understand that? I want my independence."*

*"At least my people are trustworthy." He grabbed her wrists, pulling her closer to him. "They aren't well-dressed scum."*

*"How juvenile. For god's sake, Uncle Ivan recommended him. He's one of the law firm's clients. And my uncle is a major player in San Antonio. Well respected, a feat for a Russian immigrant in a Texas environment. He's so clean he squeaks. And family is everything to him. He wouldn't steer me wrong."*

*"Oh." The word was heavy with sarcasm. "So it's okay for your uncle to find you a partner, but not the man you plan to marry? And let me tell you, Uncle Ivan isn't so squeaky clean, either. This is my business, Zoe. I know what kind of people these are. Why won't you listen to me? This is a huge mistake."*

*"So now you insult my family, too?" Rage surged through her like a tidal wave. How had she never seen this side of him?*

*"You'll regret it. I promise you."*

*Something cold dropped into her stomach. "Is that*

*a threat I hear?"*

*"Just the truth." His voice was getting louder and louder, unusual for Zak.*

*"Nate travels in some pretty stiff social circles, and he owns an international corporation. A very successful one," she emphasized. "I'm flattered he's even interested in someone as small as I am."*

*Zak's eyes narrowed. "Maybe he has personal reasons for wanting to get involved. Nate Dunning is not only rich, he's good-looking and charming. A ladies' man, or so I'm told. Is that what sold you, Zoe? His looks? His charm? Did he sweep you off your feet?"*

*Now she couldn't hold back the rage. The anger, or the sick feeling it created.*

*"That's insulting. If you don't trust me" she yelled, "maybe we should rethink this marriage business."*

*"Maybe we should," he shouted.*

*Zoe took a deep breath and clenched her fists. "Maybe you're right. Trust goes both ways."*

*The anger in his eyes had muted to something else, and he took a step toward her. "Zoe, listen, I—"*

*"I'm done listening." Without thinking, she yanked the diamond solitaire from her finger and tossed it on the counter. "Here. You can have your damn ring back. And here's your key to go with it."*

*"Zoe, wait." His voice was softer now. "I didn't mean—"*

*"I know exactly what you mean." She glared at him. "I thought you were different from other men, but you're just as controlling as every male in my family, not to mention every one I've ever met."*

*"That's bull, and you know it."*

*"Are you jealous, Zak, because Nate Dunning is so rich and good-looking? Is that it? Don't you trust me to work with him?"*

*"What?" His eyebrows hit his hairline. "Where is this coming from?"*

*"What kind of a future would we have if you had to make all the decisions? If you exploded in anger whenever I did something you didn't like? That shows me you not only don't trust me, you don't respect my decisions. We're done, Zak. Finished. You're out of my life."*

*Grabbing her purse and car keys, she slammed out the front door. As she cranked the ignition, the door opened and Zak came running out, barefoot, in jeans and T-shirt.*

*"Wait," he yelled, racing toward her.*

*She shifted into reverse, backed out of the driveway, and laid rubber as she peeled out into the street.*

*And that was the last she'd seen of Zak Delaney until tonight.*

\*\*\*\*

"Zoe?"

Zak's deep voice shook her out of her mental meanderings.

"Sorry. I was—"

"So back to square one," he said. "Just out of curiosity, why not call your uncle or your cousin? I'd think they'd be your first choice."

"First of all, they aren't criminal attorneys. At least my brain is working enough to know I need someone who specializes in this." She flopped a hand. "Whatever this is."

"Neither am I," he reminded her.

"But they... But I... But you..."

He tilted her chin up with the tip of one finger. "Say it, Zoe. Just say it, and we can move on."

She licked her dry lips and looked down at her lap. "Because I didn't know who else I could turn to. No matter what happened between us, Zak, I don't trust anyone else. Just you."

"Me," he repeated.

"You're the only person I could ever really trust completely. The only one I was sure would help me no matter what. And because..."

"Okay, I get it." His voice was flat. "Just go on with your story. Tell me everything and start from the beginning."

She inhaled and let her breath out slowly. "I told you about the break in and the incident on the road. They just happened a couple of weeks ago. Tonight...tonight scared the hell out of me after what's been happening. I woke up in the den and...and... She waved her hands in the air. "There was Nate. I mean his body, and...and I couldn't remember anything. Nothing. Not why I was there or how I had the gun in my hand. Then I heard sirens coming closer to the house, and I was afraid..."

She dropped her head into her hands.

"Afraid you'd really killed him?" He shook his head. "Zoe, I don't think you have it in you to just murder someone. Okay, let's have the rest of it."

That didn't take long, because there wasn't much she knew or remembered. Just the image of Nate's blood-drenched body stretched out on the floor.

Zak rubbed his neck again. "Let me see if I

understand. You woke up in his den, holding the gun, his body just lying there? Dead?"

Zoe nodded, then wished she hadn't as the movement made her stomach flop. "I'm guessing there was a party there, and I must have been talking to Nate in his den for some reason. Otherwise, why would I have been in there? God." She scrubbed her hands over her face. "I'm glad the people who call me a brilliant programmer can't see me now. They'd laugh their asses off."

"I don't think so. Like I said, fear changes everything up." His lips curved in a hint of a smile. "Even for brilliant programmers."

"It's possible someone put you there to be found with the body," Zak pointed out. "Anything else?"

"I have a pounding headache, which still hasn't gone away, and incredible nausea." She tried a weak grin. "I hope I don't throw up in your kitchen."

"Let's check something out." He moved to stand behind her, his fingers gently sliding through her hair as he probed her skull. "No bumps, so nobody hit you. Okay. What did you drink?"

Zoe tried to think, but her mind seemed to have taken a vacation. "Just wine. I'm pretty sure because it's usually the only thing I drink." She rubbed her forehead. "God, Zak, I don't remember. It's all a big blank."

"What *do* you remember? Anything at all?"

She drew in a steadying breath. "Getting dressed for the party. Driving there. Talking with people in the early part of the evening."

"People? Like who?"

She shrugged. "Oh, you know. Business friends of

Nate's. Some were people who wanted to talk to me about creating simulations for them."

"What's the very last thing you remember?"

She squeezed her eyes hard against the tears starting to leak down her cheeks and raked her hands through her hair, dismantling what was left of her fancy hairdo.

"Talking to some friends of Nate's. Someone handing me a fresh glass of wine. And that's…that's all. Nothing after that." She looked up at him, the panic rising again. "My brain is like oatmeal. What's wrong with me? Why can't I remember anything else? I don't even know what I was doing in the den."

"Don't sweat it. Things will come back to you. Let me get you some aspirin and water and see if we can take the edge off that headache. When you settle down, I'll see what I can pick out of your brain."

She swallowed the aspirin gratefully, the water cool gliding down her throat. "Now what?"

He pulled out his cell. "First I'm getting someone here to draw some blood. Guardian has a couple of techs on call twenty-four seven and a lab that will do us favors."

Her eyes widened. "My blood?"

"Zoe, there's a real good chance you were drugged, probably in that last glass of wine. I want to be sure and also find out what kind of drugs you were given."

She waited while he made the call, her stomach tied in knots at the possibility.

"Okay." Zak hung up. "He'll be here shortly. You're sure you were alone in the house when you woke up?"

She rubbed her forehead. "I didn't run around

looking, if that's what you're asking. But when I opened the door to the hallway, I didn't hear anyone. And there was no one else in the den."

He sat down across from her again. "Can you remember anything at all about the evening? About what you were doing there? Who you talked to? The way you're dressed it obviously wasn't a casual evening."

She looked down at her dress. "Like I said, there was a party, but I can't remember what it was for or who was there. I know that sounds stupid."

Zak ran his hand over the stubble on his jaw. "Somebody will know about it. His secretary. Maybe even your uncle or cousin. There are ways to find out. It just needs to be looked into properly. And quietly."

The cold knot in her stomach began to dissolve. "Then you'll help me?"

She seemed to wait a century before he answered her.

"Yes. I'll help you."

She didn't realize how tense she was, waiting for his answer, until every muscle relaxed. "What about your partners? Won't they object? Guardian is a huge agency with a long list of corporate clients. They might not take kindly to you helping a possible murderer."

One corner of his mouth turned up in a reluctant grin. "Believe me, Reno and Nick would be the first to jump in and help you. Remind me sometime to tell you how Nick snuck a witness out of the hospital right under the nose of the Department of Justice."

"Really?" She clutched the water glass. "They'll be okay with this?"

"They'll be fine." He paused. "But there's a big

stipulation here."

"Oh?" She clenched her teeth together against the coffee threatening to wash back up from her stomach into her throat. "What's that?"

"You'll have to do exactly as I say. And I mean without exception. That's the ground rule. Do you trust me enough for that?"

She didn't even have to think about the answer. "I trust you for anything."

Blinking hard against the tears forming in her eyes again, what little discipline she'd been able to hold onto left her. She buried her face in her hands, fear and panic and relief all mixed together inside her. "I'm so sorry about everything, Zak. Sorry, sorry, sorry. I was so incredibly stupid. You were right. Everything you said was true. I was a fool for not listening to you."

He moved closer to her, and when she raised her eyes, he was crouched in front of her again, pulling her hands from her face and handing her a paper napkin. The heat between them was like a lit match, and the look in his eyes showed how it affected him before he tamped it down.

Okay, he wasn't ready to forgive and forget, and how could she blame him? But he was going to help her and that was a big start.

"We'll get into that later. But being right doesn't always get you points. It doesn't make me feel good to hear you say that. It means whatever I suspected about Nate Dunning may have been the reason he's dead and you wound up with the body and the gun."

"If only I could make my brain work." She sniffled and pushed her disheveled hair back from her face. "I hate feeling like this. If someone drugged me…"

"The most logical assumption is, it was dropped in that last glass of wine. That would account for the physical symptoms as well as the loss of memory." He cupped her elbows and lifted her from the chair. "I'd love to let you sleep, but we really don't have any time for it. The cops will be all over this one like white on rice, but I'm not letting you talk to them until we get the results of the blood test."

Zoe felt as if she might throw up any minute, and it wasn't just from whatever was in her system. "God."

"I'm also going to have you checked for gunshot residue."

"What?" Her heart tightened. "Please tell me you don't really think I shot him."

"No, but I want to have all our ducks in a row when we need them, that's why we need that test. So just hold tight for a little bit, okay?"

"Thank you," she whispered, reaching to put her arms around him, wanting to feel his familiar warmth.

The ringing of the doorbell startled her. Her hand jerked, and she nearly spilled the coffee she'd just picked up again.

"It's okay," Zak assured her, switching the television screen to the feed from the security monitors he had installed. Two men stood on the front porch. "It's the tech I called. Just hang tight for a minute."

When he came back into the room, a short, thin man was with him. Zoe didn't think he looked older than eighteen.

Zak caught her expression. "Don't worry. Kenny's old enough to vote. He's going to draw some blood from you and do the GSR test. Then, if you want to, you can take a shower."

God, that sounded heavenly. Hot water to wash away the disaster clinging to her.

She sat in the armchair, and Kenny went about his business with a quickness and efficiency that reassured her. He filled vials with her blood, then took swabs from her skin. Pulling out a sharpie, he wrote her name and date on each vial, sealed the box, and did the same with that.

"I need these yesterday," Zak told the tech as he packaged everything up.

"Of course." He flashed Zak a grin. "I think that's in my job description."

"I'm sure your bill will reflect it." Zak's chuckle had little humor in it.

"Just remember, these will only be preliminary. Just what shows up at first pass." He looked at Zoe. "I hate to ask, but it would be good if you could give me your dress, too."

She frowned at Zak.

"For lab testing," Zak explained. "You never know what we'll find that can help us point a finger. Or defuse someone's accusations." He helped her out of the chair and guided her to the downstairs powder room. "Go on into the bathroom and toss it out to me." He pulled off his T-shirt and handed it to her. "I'll do better once we get Kenny on his way."

Even in the stress of the situation, she caught herself drooling at the sight of Zak naked from the waist up. He was still as toned and buff as ever, a dusting of dark hair covering his lightly tanned chest and arms.

*Not now, you idiot. But maybe if you get out of this mess you can mend some fences.*

In the powder room, she yanked the fabric over her head, opened the door a crack, and tossed the dress to Zak. When she turned back to the mirror, the image she saw stunned her. She looked like a walking corpse. Her face was pale, and her eyes were sunken with dark shadows beneath them. And this had all happened in a very few hours.

*Well, I'm in better shape than Nate. He won't be walking at all.*

But the sight of her bedraggled state flicked a switch inside, and in moments, she changed from a frightened, helpless woman to someone mad as hell. How dare these people fuck with her life? How arrogant of them to think they could use her as a pawn, set her up to take the blame for Nate's murder, and she'd simply fall apart, just as she'd been doing. Her brain might not be hitting on all cylinders, but at least she still had one. And she had Zak, or at least his promise of help.

She held his T-shirt up and rubbed it against her skin, inhaling his scent from the fabric. The familiar aroma of male and citrus made her knees weak and nearly brought tears to her eyes again. What a mess she'd made of things. She probably deserved exactly what happened to her.

She slipped the T-shirt over her head, resisting the urge to inhale its scent again. When she came back out into the living room, he was holding a fresh cup of coffee for her.

"Drink this. Take it with you to the bathroom. The caffeine will counteract whatever's in your system."

"Thank you. I can use this."

He set her up in the guest bath down the hall from

his room and made sure she had enough towels and whatever else she needed.

"Take your time," he told her. "Come downstairs whenever you're finished. I have some calls to make."

She wrapped her fingers around his arms for a moment. "Thank you. I seem to keep saying it, and it seems so inadequate under the circumstances, but—"

He set her gently away from him. "It's okay. We'll get it all sorted out. Take your shower."

Zoe closed the bathroom door and leaned against it. What on earth had she gotten herself into? And how was she ever going to repair her situation with Zak?

# Chapter Three

The hot water felt so good on her body Zoe thought she might stay under it forever. She scrubbed every inch of her skin and shampooed her hair twice, trying to wash away not only the evening but the entire situation.

Zak had been so very, very right. Nate Dunning was unstable and difficult, and the things she'd inadvertently discovered gave her an unsettled feeling. Had she confronted Nate tonight with what she knew? Had they argued about it? Something tickled at the back of her mushy brain, but she couldn't bring it into focus no matter how she tried.

When she had rinsed off thoroughly, it occurred to her that she had nothing to put back on except Zak's T-shirt. Then she looked on the vanity counter and saw a San Antonio Spurs shirt along with a pair of shorts. With an aching heart, she recognized them as clothing she'd left here that Zak had never returned. Had he forgotten about them or had he wanted to keep something personal of hers so the connection wouldn't be completely broken?

Whatever the reason, she was more than grateful for them now.

The aspirin had helped marginally, bringing Zoe's headache down to a dull roar, and she had a renewed burst of energy fueled by her anger and the coffee she refilled her mug with.

Zak was in the living room, pacing as he usually did when he talked, the cell phone clapped to his ear. This was Zak in control. Zak in charge.

How many times had she seen him snap from casual and easy to the discipline of his business when working a case? Or when a client was in trouble? He was so good at what he did. No wonder the men from Guardian Securities had wanted to bring him in. If anyone could help her in this nightmare, it was Zak, and that steadied her wobbly insides.

"Yes," he was saying. "Anything you hear, anything you can find out. Anything at all. Whatever's shaking out on the streets." He paused. "Don't I always pay my debts? You get first call when I have something to tell you." He listened for a moment. "Okay, okay. Thanks."

He disconnected the call and studied her with those intense eyes of his, as if assessing her condition.

"I'm okay," she told him. "Really. Much better than before."

"That must have been some shower."

"No, I just got mad that someone is doing this to me. I'm angry that half my memory is gone and furious that they've screwed with my company, not to mention setting me up to take the fall for a murder. I'm not letting them get away with this."

He grinned at her. "That's my Zoe, the woman I..."

She had no idea how he was going to finish the sentence, because at that moment, his cell rang. He looked at the readout.

"Good. A callback from one of my partners." He placed the phone to his ear. "Reno? Sorry to wake you.

What? Oh, yeah, and whoever else is sleeping there. What? No. Got some serious shit going down and wanted to get you on board with it."

He wandered into the kitchen as he spoke, his voice low enough that Zoe had no idea what he was saying. She strained to hear if his voice raised, if he was battling objections, but nothing in the low murmuring indicated that.

"Okay," she heard him say as he walked back into the room. "Nick's still out of town on a case. I thought I'd leave him a message on his cell to call me back. Yeah? Okay, thanks. Yeah, yeah, I'll fill you in more in a while."

Zoe looked at him, eyebrows raised, but he shook his head and pointed to the phone.

He pressed the center button, obviously switching back to a second call. "I'm back. Thanks for waiting. Listen. Just keep it under the radar and consider this a personal favor, okay?" He raked his fingers through his hair. "I have what you might call a non-professional interest in this." He laughed. "Yeah, that's marginally different than personal. What? And to you, too. Anyway, I wouldn't ask this if it wasn't important. You know that. Okay. Thanks."

He snapped the cell phone shut. "Okay, I've got my feelers out."

"Who was that you were talking to?"

"A reporter who owes me a lot and a detective at SAPD headquarters I did a major favor for." He picked up his coffee and motioned for Zoe to follow him. "Let's go into the family room. The lab tech's on his way, and I want to check the twenty-four hours news channels."

He took her elbow and led her to a big easy chair. She had to grit her teeth against the zing that shot through her at even his lightest touch. Did he feel it, too, even after so much time had passed? This was neither the time nor place to think about that, not when she was in the worst trouble of her life.

"Would they have picked up anything about this already?" She eased into the soft leather. "It's a little soon, isn't it? And pretty local to get that kind of coverage."

"Nate Dunning is international news. You can bet some enterprising reporter caught it on a police scanner and called his news director, who got a direct link to one of the big networks. It's all about the scoop."

She felt his eyes on her as she carefully curled her legs under her, balancing her coffee mug.

"I won't pass out," she assured him. "I promise. I'm getting my shit together, and I promise not to pass out. At least I don't think I will. Apparently, I've already done that once tonight. I hope that's my limit. What did your partner say about this?" Zoe looked up at him eager for any information. "Everything okay there?"

"No problem. He said to do whatever I need to."

"Even though he doesn't even know me? Or what I might have done?"

"He knows me. That's enough for him. He was glad I'd gotten the lab tech over right away. Let's see if this has hit the news yet."

Zak punched the buttons on the television remote, and the flat screen came to life. On the screen, a male reporter was doing a standup in front of Nate Dunning's enormous McMansion in the city's northwest area.

"We're standing in front of the magnificent home of international businessman and multi-millionaire Nathaniel Dunning," the reporter droned. "Sources tell us he was hosting one of his famous cocktail parties tonight for a large group of people. But only an hour ago, police responded to an anonymous phone call and discovered Dunning's body in his den, dead from a gunshot wound."

"You're right," Zoe said. "Someone jumped on this right away.

"Shh." Zak held up a hand. "Let's hear what else he has to say."

"There's much speculation about what happened here tonight," the reporter continued. "No one we've spoken to knows exactly when the party ended. However, at approximately twelve forty-five this morning, someone made a 911 call. Police arriving at the scene discovered Dunning's body on the floor of his den. None of the party guests were still there. In fact, there was no one else in the house, and from what we've been able to discover, none of the help lived in. That leaves us to wonder who made the call to the police."

A voice in the background asked, "Any leads on that so-called anonymous tip?"

"No, not yet," the reporter answered. "The police are making no speculations at this time, either. However, I understand they're trying to contact Dunning's attorneys and his business partners. Of which, as you know, there are several."

"Do they think this was business-related or personal?" the off-camera voice asked.

"No one's saying anything," the reporter answered.

"The detective in charge of the scene said they'll be questioning a lot of people."

"So nothing definitive?" the voice persisted.

"Not at this time." The reporter looked straight into the camera. "That wraps it up for right now. We'll be waiting for further information…"

Zak muted the volume and turned to Zoe. "Someone wanted to make damn sure you were found with that gun. How unfortunate for them you woke up when you did." He raked his fingers through his hair and began pacing again. "All right. At least we know there was definitely a party there tonight, even if you can't remember it. That accounts for the fancy dress you're wearing."

Zoe squeezed her eyes. "I can't believe I've lost an entire night of my life, or at least a good part of it. How? Why?"

"I told you what I think about the how," Zak answered. "We just have to figure out the why. It would help if we could nudge your memory. Any tiny scrap of information, no matter how small, would be a help. Especially stuff about the people who attended the party, and if you'd met them before. Do you recall if Nate argued with anyone? If you heard them?"

"I told you." She bit down on her frustration. "Nothing, Zak. I mean, not a thing after I drank that last glass of wine. I swear to you. It's as if the rest of the night never existed." Zoe started to shake her head, then thought better of it as the movement hit her with another wave of dizziness.

"You know I wouldn't badger you if it wasn't important." He stopped pacing and crouched in front of her, taking one of her hands in his. "You said you drove to Nate's house. If you did, your car is probably around there somewhere, left for the cops to find."

She snapped her fingers. "There was a valet parking service. Does that help?"

"Only if they remember you. Otherwise the cops will say you moved it away from the house so you could leave quickly without going through the valet parking service. If that happens, it's another knot in the noose around your neck."

She pulled her hand away from his. "I don't—"

At that moment, the doorbell rang.

"Hold tight." He rose to his feet. "I'll be right back."

He headed to the foyer. When he walked back into the room, he was accompanied by a lean, muscular man, close to Zak's height, which made him at least six-four. A head of thick, black hair framed a ruggedly masculine face, and his dark eyes looked as if they could ferret out the deepest secrets. But what really struck Zoe was the aura of power he radiated. It almost vibrated in the air.

"Zoe, this is Reno Sullivan, the senior partner at Guardian Security." He turned to Reno. "Meet Zoraya Lombardo."

"Zoe," she corrected, standing to shake his hand. "I use Zoe."

Reno smiled, transforming his face into a warm expression as he held out his hand. "I'm very happy to meet you, although I'm sure we both wish it could have been under different circumstances."

"Thank you." Zoe shook his hand and looked at Zak, eyebrows raised.

"When Zak says something's important," Reno

said, interpreting her look, "it's *important*. I wanted to come here myself and see what I could do to help. And forget about that senior partner crap. We're equal partners at Guardian."

"Well, then." She wet her lips. "Thank you again for coming. I think I've dragged Zak—and I guess Guardian—into a terrible mess. When I called him, I didn't stop to think—"

Reno shook his head. "Forget that. Someone needs help, we help."

She gave him a rueful smile. "Even if they turn out to be guilty?"

He squeezed her hand before releasing it. "None of our clients are ever guilty. I can assure you of that. Now then. I'm glad we got the lab work taken care of right away. If someone did put something in your drink, we need to test for it before it dissipates completely, which a lot of these substances do."

"Oh. Okay." Once again, the thought that someone had drugged her hit hard and terrified her. Who could possibly hate her so much they would do this to her? And to Nate?

Reno gave her a reassuring nod. "We'll get to the bottom of this," he promised. "Zak will have all the resources of Guardian Security at his disposal. And our other partner, Nick Vanetta, will be back day after tomorrow if we need his input."

"I don't know how to thank you—"

"No thanks necessary. It's what we do for each other."

He left a short time later, and Zak went back to monitoring the news.

She tucked the wet strands of her hair behind her

ears self-consciously and nervously rubbed her hands on her shorts. "Zak?"

He looked up at her. "Would you like some more coffee? Or anything else?"

She shook her head. "No, thanks. Not right now." She paused. "Thank you very much. For picking me up. For bringing me here. For agreeing to help me. For your partner. For...everything."

"Hey," he said in a soft voice. "Didn't we agree it was enough with the thank yous?" Then his face sobered. "I could never turn my back on you, Zoe. No matter what happened between us."

God, what a fool she'd been, letting her temper get the best of her. When she looked at him now, it was hard to ignore the attraction still there, at least on her part. Her sex throbbed with the remembered feel of his hard cock, and her breasts ached for the touch of his hands, her nipples for his mouth.

Did he feel the same way? Was he hard for her, the way he used to be? Did he want to strip both of them naked, plunge himself into her, and fuck her with the heat and passion they'd once shared?

She took in a deep breath. "Yes. About that."

When he looked at her again, heat blazed in his eyes and a muscle twitched in his cheek. She did her best to keep her gaze from dropping to his fly to see if his shaft was hard and pushing to be released. But he shook his head at her words.

"Not now. We have business to take care of first. Reno and I think it's obvious someone planned for you to be the fall guy. Knocking you out and erasing part of your memory was the best way to do it. Hell, whoever it was could have killed Nate in front of you while you were passed out on the couch. They could even have pressed your fingers around the gun and pulled the trigger."

"Oh, my god." Zoe dropped into the big chair. "Someone's really out to dump this on me. Why?"

"Best guess? You're an easy target as CEO of Lombardo Simulations, and they want you out of the way. You're apparently too smart for them, and they don't want you to find out what they're doing. Whoever they are and whatever it is they're doing." He rubbed his forehead. "And I'm still worried about where your car is. We discussed all the ramifications of the cops finding it."

"My car?"

"Right now, unless you left something behind in the den—which I don't believe you did—the police can't connect you to what happened."

"What if they find my fingerprints in the den?"

He shrugged. "No big deal. The two of you were business partners. I'm sure you met there many times. Besides, you would have been at the party and could have had a perfectly logical reason for being in that room. No, fingerprints won't amount to squat."

"I still don't understand why the car is so important."

"If they find it obviously parked away from the house, not left with the valet parking service, it will look suspicious. They'll start trying to connect the dots."

He rubbed his jaw, the familiar dark shadow indicating the need for a shave. Zak had always shaved twice a day when they were together, even though she kept telling him how sexy the scruff was. She'd been after him to just trim it with clippers and not shave it off, loving the sexy feel of its roughness. Just remembering it made her wet, the pulse still thrumming in her sex and her nipples hardening to the point of aching.

*Oh God. Why did I have to think of that at this particular moment?*

With a major effort, she pulled in a deep breath and let it out. She refused to fall apart. She couldn't *afford* to fall apart.

"Normally, if I have a client that gets involved in something," Zak went on, "I have a friend at the San Antonio Police Department I can call and pump for information. Of course, my clients are usually surrounded by a football team of high priced lawyers and I'm the security guy trying to get information."

She stared at him, wide-eyed. "You have clients involved in murder?"

His grin was humorless. "Not usually, thank god. Anyway, this is a little different. I had to be very careful with my contact, make him understand no one can connect me to what's going on. If they do, this is the first place they'll come looking for you. And I'll have more cops hanging around my neck than I'll know what to do with. I won't be able to move."

She swallowed back the panic that threatened to resurface. She had to keep it all together. "So what do I do?"

"We have to make a plan to get more information. That means digging into everything about your relationship with Nate and his partnership with you. Everything about Lombardo Simulations that might mean something." He stood up. "We have a lot of work to do. Let me get some more coffee, and then I have a bunch more questions."

Zoe accepted the fresh mug of hot liquid gratefully. She sat on the edge of the chair, knees together, back stiff, sipping at the dark brew. "What do you want to know?"

"Start with some background information that may jar loose what we need to know. Have you and Prince Charming been getting along or has there been trouble in paradise?"

She looked away, trying to figure out how to answer. As much as he tried to hide it, she was well aware that Zak was still nursing the hurt she'd inflicted on him, and she didn't want it to get in the way of him helping her. He'd been right all along. He hadn't trusted Nate Dunning, which made him a lot smarter than she was.

And seeing Zak now, she wondered how she could ever have been so stupid as to walk out on him. But that was for another time, after all this was over.

She sipped her coffee, then cleared her throat. "We've been having…some…problems, Nate and I." She nibbled on her bottom lip.

He made his face expressionless. "Tell me about the problems with Nate. Business or personal?"

Zoe stared into her coffee mug. "Not personal. And just so you know, there was never anything personal between us, despite what you assumed. Not ever. But that's another story."

"All right, then. Business things. *What* business things?"

"Just…little stuff. It started a few months ago, so tiny I almost didn't notice it at first. But when I began to study the monthly reports, I had questions about some of our suppliers. Some of our customers. The accounting procedures."

"What about them?"

She nibbled on her lip again, tension coiling in her body as snippets of things came back to her. "When we signed the partnership papers," she explained, "Nate invested more than two million dollars in Lombardo Simulations. You knew I wanted to expand, hire more engineers, grow our overseas markets. With that kind of money, I could easily do that."

"Who drew up the partnership papers?"

"Uncle Ivan did." She shrugged. "Who else would I ask? After all, he's family and also Nate's attorney. And he's the one who introduced us."

"Oh, yes. Good old Uncle Ivan." A flash of something crossed Zak's face, gone almost as soon as it showed up.

"Zak, he's my mother's brother," she reminded him, "and he was wonderful to us after my father died. He's as good as they come. You know he's considered a leader in the San Antonio community. He would never, ever have anything to do with scum. He's the one who saw a great opportunity for me and advised me to take it."

"Okay, okay. I'll send him a medal. Who was in charge of all of that new growth? How did the responsibilities break down? Was it spelled out in the partnership agreement?"

"Yes." She forced herself to look directly at Zak. "I handled the design and development of the software. That's what I'd been doing before and where I felt the most comfortable. Nate took care of the international markets, overseeing the financial aspects and supervising the distribution." She took another swallow of her coffee, letting the hot liquid course through her veins.

"So how did that work out?"

"Really well, as a matter of fact, at least in the beginning. We were developing some innovative simulations for clients, then adjusted them to turn them into games. The orders were pouring in from everywhere. In fact, the business grew so much that Nate brought in a new accounting firm to handle it. One Caz recommended." She looked at Zak. "Do you know him?"

Zak's eyes narrowed. "Yeah, I know Caz Morgan. Nate's advisor, whatever the hell that means."

"I don't know what it means, either, but he's always—*was* always—hanging around Nate and whispering in his ear."

*Do I sound as stupid to Zak as I do to myself? I can't believe I was such a naïve idiot, ignoring what was obviously going on right under my nose. I deserve to be in trouble.*

"So let me guess." Zak took a sip of his coffee, then set the mug down on the coffee table in front of him. "That's when the problems started. With the new accountants."

Zoe dropped her gaze and ran her finger around the rim of her mug. "Yes. That's when it all began."

"Explain." He was all Zak Delaney, security specialist, now. "Give me details. Everything you remember."

"It had been months since I'd seen anything except a one-page financial summary. That's my fault, and I admit it. But I was so happy to have the time to do the things I enjoyed and not have to worry about the bank account." She twisted her lips. "I was deliriously happy in my fool's paradise."

"So what was the trigger that made you ask questions? I'm guessing that's what brought things to a head."

She nodded. "Nate didn't really have an office at Lombardo. He worked out of Dunning International, and I usually went there a couple of times a week to meet with him. Sometimes Max Detwiler, his partner in DI, would sit in with us to catch up on what was happening with Lombardo."

"I didn't think he had anything to do with your company."

Zoe lifted a shoulder and dropped it. "He didn't have an interest in the company per se, but since it was under the DI umbrella, he wanted to be kept in the loop. Nate was the major source of our financing so he felt what Lombardo Simulations did affected DI."

"Do you happen to know how Max and Nate hooked up to begin with? Just out of curiosity?"

She shook her head. "Not really. Uncle Ivan said they've been partners for years. Max owns a big cattle ranch south of San Antonio. He also made a ton of money in the oil boom. Apparently, he could light cigars with dollar bills, he's got so many of them."

"Zoe." Zak's face was set in a serious expression. "Oil hasn't boomed in Texas for a long time. If Detwiler has that kind of cash, he had to be making it somewhere else."

"I asked Uncle Ivan, who said Max has overseas interests that are highly lucrative. My uncle is very careful who he recommends and who he deals with. He is a senior partner in one of the oldest firms in Texas, and he has to be very, very careful."

"I know all about his law firm. I always wondered how your uncle came to be a partner with them. The others are all old Texas aristocracy. It seems like an unusual match."

She shrugged. "I don't know all that much about it. I seem to remember my mother saying they reached out to him when they needed help with an international situation. He was running a sole practice then. They were so grateful for his help they brought him into the firm. They wanted all his connections."

"Let's leave that for the moment. What happened to change your situation?"

"I got to DI early for a meeting one day. Nate's secretary wasn't at her desk and I didn't see Max so I just let myself into Nate's office. The monitor on his computer was turned sideways so it was easy to get a glimpse of the screen. When I saw the Lombardo Simulations name at the top of what looked like a financial statement, I had to look."

"And found what?"

"Customers I never heard of. Suppliers I knew nothing about. And while the company has quadrupled its sales, the numbers were nowhere near as big as what I saw on that screen."

She could see Zak registering everything in his mental computer, just as he always did. It was one reason why he was so good at what he did. No detail ever got by him.

Zak allowed himself a long moment to study the woman across from him. This was no act she was pulling. She was in big trouble. *Big* trouble.

And she'd called *him*. Despite everything, despite the way things were left between them, he was the one she'd called for help. He'd asked her if she trusted him, and she'd said yes. Maybe she'd have trusted him two years ago if he hadn't been a raving maniac and instead had tried to discuss the situation with her intelligently.

At least he had a chance to make up for that.

"Did you ever ask him about it?"

She nodded. "Of course. He told me that was just a list of prospects he wanted to discuss with me and new suppliers he thought we should try out."

"I'm sure he did. Who handles all that for Lombardo Simulations, anyway?"

"That's Nate's area. He uses an accounting firm that Caz recommended."

Zak snorted. "This is all beginning to feel a little incestuous. Like the tentacles of an octopus wrapping around everything."

"That was never my area of expertise," she explained, "so I was happy to leave it all to someone who knew what they were doing."

"I'll bet they did. Let me ask you this. Did you keep any records personally? I mean, not on the server but your own hard drive?"

She shook her head. "Not originally. I didn't see any need to. But after I saw that information at Nate's place, I immediately went back to my office and copied as much as I could. And I saved it on my personal laptop, rather than the Lombardo server. I also saved all the original files of the simulations we'd done since Nate came on board. And finally, I copied everything to a brand new cloud account that no one has the password for except me. I crunched the files and coded them, then changed my password for the cloud again, just in case." She played with the hem of her shorts. "I had a feeling it might be a good thing to do."

"Whoever Nate was meeting with that day probably threw a fit when he discovered Nate left the info up on his screen. They wanted to make sure you didn't start digging into the files of your own company too deeply. That explains the break-in at your house. They were looking for your laptop. The attempt to run you off the road was to at least incapacitate you and get your off their trail. You were sticking your nose in and making somebody very nervous."

"But who?" She spread out her hands. "Who would that be? Nate might have been a slimeball, but this was definitely not his style. So who is the evil presence?"

"Whoever's behind Nate's money," he told her. "And whoever framed you tonight. Okay. Where's your house key?"

She frowned. "My house key? Why?"

He held out his hand. "I want to check and see if anyone's been snooping around there again and if they left any kind of a trace. While I'm there, I might as well pick up some stuff for you."

"What for?"

"I plan to stash you in a safe house, and you'll need more than those shorts and T-shirt to carry you through."

"Do you think it looks suspicious for me to be ducking the police? They'll want to question Nate's partner, and I was at the party, after all."

"Under other circumstances, yes. But someone went to a lot of trouble to set you up for this. I'm sure the plan was to get rid of Nate, who must have outlived his usefulness, and set you up to be arrested. Much as I hate to admit it, they could have someone on the force in their pocket who can make you disappear or have an *accident*."

Her jaw dropped. "You're kidding."

He shook his head. "Not even a little. They could also arrange for you to *commit suicide*, distraught over killing your partner. They want you where they can get their hands on you and make you go away."

"So why not kill me when they killed Nate?"

The fear in Zoe's voice stabbed at Zak. But he needed to keep his emotions under control and not lose his head here. That would only bring trouble to the table. Business, he kept telling himself. Just business.

"Because someone has to take the fall and you're it." *And they almost got away with it.*

"So where can I go?"

"I'll figure it out. Meanwhile, give me your house key." He pulled a pad of paper from the coffee table drawer along with a pen and handed them to her. "Make a list for me. I'll sneak in while it's still dark, check everything, and get you some of your stuff."

"Can you get my laptop, too?"

"I could, but if you've got everything stored in the cloud, I'd rather get you a brand new one and you can download to it. Do you have your programs in the cloud, too?"

She nodded. "I wanted everything someplace besides the company system. I pulled as much as I could access, but I had to do it in increments." She frowned. "The house system is set up to track anyone who accesses files and what those files are. I figured out a way to get around that, but I had to be very careful and only do a little at a time. I looked at the file directory, and there are still a lot more to copy."

"Smart about the cloud, but I'm not surprised about the files. Too bad. I just know there's something in there that triggered Nate's murder."

She picked up her purse from the end table, pulled out a ring with one key on it, and handed it to him. "I still remember what you told me about keys."

*Don't keep your car and house keys on the same ring. If your car gets stolen and they have your address, they can get into your home.*

He blinked in surprise. "Good girl. Now. While I'm gone, write down every name you can remember from the list you saw on Nate's computer. Even if it's only a partial. And anything else on that screen that stuck in your mind."

"I didn't see it for all that long," she reminded him.

"Doesn't matter. It gives us a starting place. Just put down whatever you can." He studied her face, trying to keep his own emotionless. "You've got a sharp brain, Zoe. You'll probably remember more than you think you do."

Unlocking a panel in the wall, he carefully removed a small handgun. He checked that the magazine was loaded and there was a round already chambered, then he shoved the weapon into the small of his back.

"What are you doing?" Zoe asked, her heart rate accelerating. She'd had enough of guns tonight. "You think you need a gun to go to my house?"

"Just making sure I don't find any surprises when I get there. Someone killed Nate, and their plan to have you caught at the scene didn't work. They may decide it's better to just eliminate you."

"Zak, I—" She swallowed and tried again. "Listen, I—"

He turned to her, placing his hands on her shoulders. "It's okay. Don't sweat it. I didn't think this would be a cakewalk. And I know how to be careful."

"I know you do. I just…"

"I'll be as quick as I can," he told her. "And careful. While I'm gone, don't go near any of the windows and don't answer the door or the phone. Right now, this very minute, Zoe Lombardo has to disappear from sight. As soon as I get back, that's the first order of business."

## Chapter Four

Zak tried to focus on the situation at hand as he drove through the darkened streets to Zoe's house.

The itch on the back of his neck told him Dunning's murder was just a small piece of a big puzzle, and Zoe was being staked out as the sacrificial goat. Even as he tried to anticipate any problems that might be waiting, his brain was still processing the shock of hearing her voice tonight after all this time. He'd lost count of the number of times during the past two years he'd regretted the words he'd thrown at her. Wished he could take them back. Wished the whole thing had never happened.

But she'd been quickly wrapped up in her business and developing a relationship with Nate—although he'd never known exactly how intimate that was. He'd just waited too long to tell her what an ass he'd been. That he'd only had her best interests at heart. That he wasn't trying to run her life, only help her. Too bad his testosterone had gotten out of control and in the way of his brain. She'd just made him so fucking mad, pushing back every time he brought it up. He reminded himself not to point out she'd let her emotions override her smarts, since he'd done the same thing.

He took a quick moment to call Reno and let him know what he was doing. The agency had a firm rule and a good one. Never walk into danger without checking in. Someone had to know where you were at all times, just in case.

*Just in case is right.*

Zak parked one street over, behind another car pulled into the curb, one that looked as if it was parked for the night. He had a feeling whoever had orchestrated the death of Nate Dunning would be keeping an eye on Zoe's place. Unexpectedly, she'd slipped through their fingers, so it stood to reason they'd try to pick up her trail. She was a loose end they couldn't afford to leave dangling in the wind.

As he eased through darkened backyards, hugging shrubbery and trees, he wondered if his connection to Zoe would be on their radar or if the two years since the breakup would be enough to keep him off the list of people she might contact. Once he got back to his house and got her squared away, he'd have to do some research there and make sure no one decided to connect the two of them. Otherwise, they'd both have to hide until he could find some answers.

Zoe's neat backyard looked pristine in the moonlight. The patio was furnished with wrought iron table and chairs, a lounge chair, and a swing with an awning, all covered in bright cushions. Huge pots of flowers stood at each corner of the concrete rectangle.

Zak crouched low as he broke from the cover of two tall oaks and headed for the back steps.

As he approached the back porch, he took his time to examine the flowerbeds that bordered the house, checking for signs of recent visitors. He easily identified the indentations of ladies' sneakers, an indication Zoe had worked in her gardens not too long ago. But his senses cranked up when he saw many of them wiped out in places, as if someone else had stepped here and brushed away the trace.

He mounted the stairs, stepping carefully, checking for thin wires or anything else that might indicate a trap. Then, looking left and right and not seeing or hearing anything, he inserted the key in the lock and turned the knob. But instead of pushing the door, he kicked it open and jumped back. Just in case.

An explosion erupted inside the house.

Zak leaped down the steps and threw himself on the lawn, covering his head as pieces of wood, brick, and glass rained down around him. When he'd told Zoe he didn't want any surprises at her house, this wasn't exactly what he'd had in mind. He pulled the gun from the small of his back and rolled over, waiting to see who might appear.

Suddenly, lights popped on in the surrounding houses, and he heard people shouting. Brushing the debris from his body as best he could and gritting his teeth against the sting of cuts and bruises, he rolled over again and belly-crawled to the back end of the yard. He made it safely through the hedges and slipped out to the street where he'd parked. Before he'd gotten out of his car, he'd turned off the switch to the inside lights so there was only blackness when he quietly opened the door and inched inside. Nothing to give him away.

Looking through the window on the passenger's side, he could see flames shooting into the air as Zoe's house succumbed to the bomb that had been set. Reaching in the glove box for a rag he kept there, he wiped his face and arms, wincing as he saw the smears of blood on the cloth. His back felt as if he'd been stabbed multiple times, and he knew he'd have some bruising from his flying leap to the ground, but at least he was alive.

If nothing else, it was very clear that someone heavy was behind this. Someone who could kill a man and set a woman up to take the fall. Who could, in a short amount of time, rig a house to explode? If they couldn't have Zoe in jail with no logical defense for murder, then they'd simply kill her. And they obviously had the ability to move fast and do what needed to be done.

God knew what else they had up their sleeves.

The question now was whether or not these people, whoever they were, could connect the two of them and whether Zoe would be safe at his house after all.

Turning the corner, he punched speed dial on his phone for Reno.

"More problems," he said when his partner answered the phone He gave him a rundown on what had happened.

"Are you hurt?" was Reno's first question.

"Scrapes and bruises, that's all."

"I'll get one of the men over there," Reno told him. "Someone who can blend in and sniff out what's happening. I'll call you in a little while at your house. Just make sure Miss Lombardo's safe." He paused a moment. "You, too, Zak. These aren't amateurs."

"Don't worry. I will." He punched the End button.

*Zoe, Zoe, Zoe. What in the name of all that's holy have you gotten yourself into?*

\*\*\*\*

Zoe had been pacing from the moment Zak left, unable to sit in one place, her still-foggy mind working overtime to pull together the loose threads dangling in it. When she heard the garage door slide up, she rushed to the side door to open it. One look as Zak walked in from the garage and panic sluiced through her again. He was streaked with dirt and blood and grass stains, and his face and arms were peppered with tiny cuts.

"Ohmigod, what happened?" She stared at him. "You're bleeding. Look at you."

"Nothing a shower won't take care of." He tossed two plastic bags he was holding onto a chair and pulled his T-shirt off over his head as he made his way toward the stairs. "Good thing you didn't see me before I cleaned up a little."

"But what happened?" she asked again. "Did you have trouble at my house? That's it, isn't it?"

He turned, and she nearly bumped into him. Anger raged in his eyes, but she sensed it wasn't against her.

"Don't freak." His voice was low and soothing. "I'm fine. I'm just glad I was the one who went there, not you. And that my business makes me naturally suspicious."

"Tell me everything," she demanded.

As she listened to him describe in detail what had happened, the blood drained from her face and her heart stuttered erratically.

"My house?" She couldn't absorb what he was saying. "Someone blew up my house?"

He nodded. "I'd say it's pretty well destroyed. Whoever set the explosives did a good job. These people are playing very, very rough." He let out a long slow breath. "Even *this* house may not be safe enough for you if they get any idea you came to me."

"Zak—"

"It'll be okay. I'll make it okay. But before I do

anything else, I need to wash off this junk. Then we'll talk." He reached out to touch her, then drew his hand back. "Everything's gone. I am so sorry."

"Gone?" She took in a steadying breath. This was no time to fall apart any more than she already had. She swallowed and clenched her fists. "It's nothing that can't be replaced. Even the laptop, as you pointed out. At least you're alive. Go take your shower while I make some fresh coffee." She tried on a weak smile. "I think I still remember where things are."

"Coffee sounds terrific. I don't think we'll be getting sleep any time soon."

They were so close she could feel his breath, fanning her cheek. Without warning, his head lowered and his lips brushed against hers. She was totally unprepared for the spike of electricity that jolted her system.

From the look in his eyes, so was Zak. He stared at her, heat in his eyes, then backed away and walked upstairs to the master suite.

"See you in a few minutes," he called over his shoulder.

Zoe was only able to hang onto her control with superhuman effort. Her hands shook slightly as she filled the coffee reservoir with water, fiddled with filters and grounds, rinsed out their mugs from earlier, and set them back on the counter. Things she could do automatically, without thinking, because her mind was racing.

She hated the fact Zak had been injured because of her. The thought he might have been killed was like a ball of ice in her stomach. And what about that kiss? God! It singed her all the way down to her toes, enough so that she wanted to rip off both their clothes and press herself all over him.

She was still scrabbling to pull her thoughts together when Zak walked into the kitchen. His still-damp hair lay in familiar unruly waves, and the way the clean T-shirt and jeans outlined his lean body made her think of the kiss all over again. His face and arms were marked with tiny scratches that he'd applied antiseptic ointment to.

"Coffee's ready," she told him. "We need to sit down and figure out what to do now."

Zak opened his mouth to say something when a chirping sounded in his jeans pocket. He fished out his cell phone and hit Answer.

"Delaney." He listened intently, mouthing a *Thank you* as Zoe handed him a mug of coffee. "Uh-huh. Uh-huh. You're sure, right? Okay, thanks. Later." He snapped the phone shut. "That was Kenny."

*The lab tech.*

She wrapped her hands around her mug, wishing its heat could melt the ice forming in her body. "What did he say?"

Zak took her arm and led her back into the family room. The touch of his fingers set up that little tingle again, and heat began to invade her blood stream. She'd left the television on, the volume muted, but Zak ignored it, steering her to the couch and sitting down next to her.

"What he said must be pretty awful," she commented shakily.

"Someone laced your drink with a heavy dose of something called flunitrazepam, more commonly known as rohypnol."

"The date rape drug?" Anger made her hand shake and coffee spilled onto her knees. She dabbed at it with the bottom of the shirt she was wearing. "Damn! They really wanted me out of it, didn't they?"

Zak took her mug from her and set it on the coffee table, then closed both of his hands around hers. "Yes, and they used something known to be very effective. Besides that, one of the most popular properties of this drug—besides knocking out the person who it's given to—is that it causes partial amnesia. You can't remember things that happen while you're under the effect of it."

"Which is why I couldn't remember anything prior to waking up." Her mind was spinning.

Zak nodded. "The effects can last up to four hours. Unfortunately for whoever did this, I'm guessing you woke up long before you were supposed to."

"My god!" She felt totally violated at what had been done to her. If she'd been angry before, she was enraged now. "Who could want to do this to me? And why?"

Zak tightened his grip on her hands, the touch of them sending waves of long suppressed need through her body. "We're going to find out. Count on it. Listen, I got one good piece of news from Kenny."

She looked up, a smidgen of hope in her heart. "What?"

"No gunshot residue on your dress. And the amount on your hands was so minimal it could have been blowback from someone standing close to you when Nate was shot."

"So you believe me."

"Zoe, I believed you from the beginning."

Something eased inside her at his words. She'd had no right to expect anything from him, but Zak being Zak had stepped right up to the plate. The argument seemed even more idiotic looking back on it. If she didn't already have a headache, she might bang her dumb head against a wall.

"Did you write out that list for me?" he asked, interrupting her train of thought.

She picked up the pad of paper from the coffee table and handed it to him. "There isn't much, but maybe you can work your magic on it."

"I'll call the office and see who's doing the overnight shift." He winked, an obvious effort to relieve the strain. "One of the advantages of being part of a big agency. It never sleeps. I'll fax this over to them and get someone started on researching everything on the list. Give me a second here."

Zoe watched while he speed dialed a number on his cell and spoke in a low voice to whoever answered as he walked toward the den. She heard the sound of the fax machine, and in less than a minute, he was back.

"Okay," he told her. "They'll get started on it right away, see what they can find out about any of these companies or people. You realize these may all be fake names, right?"

"I know. But that in itself is something, right?"

"It's a place to start. Meanwhile, let's go back to the party at Dunning's. Have you been able to remember who you spoke to? Chatted with? Maybe what got you into the den?"

"I've been thinking about that. Somewhere in the back of my mind, I remember a piece of conversation with a man who'd been at other parties. I think…maybe…he wanted to chat with me in private. I don't know. It's just so fuzzy. And frustrating. It's like now I can almost catch it, but then it disappears."

She raked her fingers through her hair, pulling at it as if she could yank the lost memories out of her brain. But nothing came. She hated this, despised how frustrated it made her feel, how out of control. This was not her at all. She needed to get her shit together and figure out with Zak how to fight back. And even more than that was the anger slowly growing that people she'd trusted, people she'd met through Nate, would treat her with such callous disregard.

"Okay." He pulled her hands down from her head and moved them gently into her lap. "Let's try all this from a different angle. Forget about tonight for a minute. We'll have to hope your memory comes back more and more. But you've been to parties at Nate's house before, right? Who usually went? What kind of guest list did he have?"

Zoe bit her lip in frustration. "Nate had a lot of parties, and he invited the same basic people every time. Always a few new ones thrown into the mix, but then they'd become regulars."

"Do you think you can remember who any of them were? People you might chat with more than others? Anyone usually standing close to you? Whoever did it would have to be able to watch you without anyone thinking it curious. Someone who could get you out of the room without raising any eyebrows."

Zoe frowned. "Mostly it was Nate's business associates, his clients, their wives. Max. Caz. Lombardo Simulations clients. Uncle Ivan and some of his law partners. My cousin, Sergei."

"Yeah, Uncle Ivan." Zak made a face. "The man who got you into this mess in the first place. I'm not as enamored of him as you are. I'd love to know if he's got his fingers in this pie."

"I'm positive he doesn't. His partners would kill him. He has to work twice as hard to prove he's not involved in anything like this. Besides, like I told you, he looked out for Mama and me since my father died."

"All right, all right." Zak put up a hand. "I'm a lot more suspicious than you are. It's the nature of my business. So let's not argue about that right now. We need to take care of the problem of the moment. Which," he added, "I think goes beyond your partnership with Nate."

"What do you mean?"

"Something smells very bad. Something that goes beyond normal illegitimate activities. All my sense are tingling, and that's not good. Zoe, my gut tells me Nate's murder is connected in some way to the things you confronted him about regarding the company. The two things are so closely connected. And just from what you've told me, what I'm sensing is there's a good chance Nate was using your company to launder money."

"What?" Her throat tightened. "Launder money? For who? Why? God, Zak. Nate Dunning is…was a billionaire. He had legitimate enterprises."

Zak looked at her steadily. "Did he? Are you sure most of it wasn't from illegal activities and sources? Let me tell you, I know a lot more about those things than you do. That's why I wanted to know if you'd ever discussed this with his partner or his advisor."

She shook her head. "Whatever's going on, they

sure want to get rid of me."

He nodded. "You must have pulled the devil's horns when you started asking questions. They broke into your house before and then tried to kill you. Framing you for Nate's murder was supposed to get you out of the way, but you woke up too soon and ran away. This thing obviously goes beyond whatever Nate was using Lombardo Simulations for. Someone's playing rough here. They must be furious that you managed to slip away from Nate's before the cops arrived. Let's hope they think you got blown up with the house so we can keep you off their radar."

"Isn't blowing up my house a little extreme?"

He brushed a stray wisp of hair from her face, his touch so tender it made her heart ache. "Remember, you were supposed to be the one opening the door. I'd bet money the front door and the one from the garage into the house were set up the same way. I think they decided they'd be better off just getting rid of you."

She stared at him as the raw truth of what he was saying hit her. What was wrong with her? Here she'd been clinging to the remnants of that disastrous argument for two years, wasting all that time they could have been together, and for what? To show him she was independent? He already knew that.

All she'd accomplished was to cost them two years of their lives over a man who apparently had brought evil into her life. If she'd just listened to Zak, she'd have seen what a cesspool she was walking into, Nate Dunning might still be alive, and tonight would never have happened.

From the moment Zak picked her up in his car tonight, those old feelings were back. She'd told herself while she waited she had no feelings for him anymore except trust. That would always be there. But a minute with him, and she knew what a lie that was. One look at him, and suppressed emotion welled up inside her, gripping her with its force and dragging her back to their past. She'd promised herself to keep this businesslike, but she couldn't deny her feelings any longer.

She launched herself against him, forgetting everything except that he could have died at her place tonight. "You could have been killed tonight. Oh god, Zak."

She leaned into him, feeling his warmth. When his arms came around to hold her tightly against him, the heat of his body seeping into hers, a thought suddenly popped into her mind.

*Home. I've come home. This is where I belong.*

And just as happened earlier, her nipples hardened at once, aching for his mouth. Her sex throbbed, and moisture dampened her panties. She wanted his mouth on her, his hands all over her, his cock inside her. The familiar feel of his arms around her felt so good, and she didn't ever want to move.

But what if he didn't feel the same way and decided her feelings were too much of a complication? Still, she couldn't bring herself to move. She wanted him, pure and simple, and what did she do with that?

"Hey, hey, hey." He stroked her back the way he used to, soothing her. "It's all right. I'm not dead. I'm right here. Fine and dandy."

When she lifted her head to look up at him, his face was so close she could count the bristles on his cheek. He dipped his head a fraction of an inch, and the kiss that followed was so natural she didn't think twice about it. She just let herself fall into it and responded with everything she had.

His lips were warm and soft, lightly brushing hers at first, the tip of his tongue tracing the seam of her mouth before coaxing her to open for him. His tongue was like a flame, scorching the tender inner surface of her mouth, licking in a sensuous movement that woke up every dormant hormone in her body.

The surroundings faded away and nothing existed for her except this man, his very talented tongue, the exquisitely erotic kiss, and the way her body reacted to his. He buried his fingers in her hair, molding his hand to her head to hold her in place while he devoured her mouth. His arm around her pulled her tight to his body, crushing her breasts to his chest. She wanted to rip away the clothes that kept her from feeling his naked skin.

When they broke apart, they were both breathless, panting. She wasn't sure who was more surprised at the charge in the air between them. She shifted her body slightly away but not enough to break the contact.

*Let him move if he wants to. But please don't let him want to.*

It was obvious to her that what she felt for him never went away, no matter how she'd tried to bury it.

And what about him? What was this kiss about to him?

She waited for him to break the contact, but he stayed where he was, his body still touching hers. He moved his lips lightly over her cheek, peppering soft kisses along her jawline and then the column of her neck. When he placed his mouth over the hollow of her neck and licked the place where her pulse beat like a jungle drum, she grew weak, holding onto him to keep from falling.

Eventually, he lifted his head and looked at her for an endless moment. She couldn't breathe, waiting to hear what he had to say.

"Don't do this if you don't mean it, Zoe. It took me two years, and I couldn't manage to get over you. And I don't want this as gratitude for anything."

She wet her lips and had to swallow twice before she could speak.

"I never got over you, either. And I've punished myself ever since that night for being such a hotheaded, stupid idiot. There's nobody for me except you. There never was, and there never will be. And gratitude has nothing to do with it."

He locked his gaze with hers for so long she wondered if he was ever going to say anything.

"Okay," he said at last. "Good. Because my life hasn't been the same without you."

"Mine, either."

"We both let things get out of hand, but I'm never going down that path again. I won't try telling you what to do—"

She touched his mouth with her fingertips. "You can always give me good advice. And I'll be smart enough to listen to it."

He smiled, and despite the situation they were in, her world righted itself.

"Meanwhile," he told her, "we have a situation to deal with that is critical."

"Yeah. That someone definitely wants me dead."

"And that's not gonna happen."

His gaze strayed past her shoulder, something catching his eye, and he shifted enough to pick up the remote and turn the television volume back on.

"That reporter is back again doing his schtick in front of Nate's house. Let's hear what he has to say."

"We have just learned that a canvass of the neighborhood has turned up a vehicle registered to Zoraya Lombardo, CEO of Lombardo Simulations and one of Nate Dunning's business partners. Witnesses say she attended the party and apparently had a heated argument with the deceased during the evening. Her car was parked some distance away from the area the valet parking service was using."

An enlarged photo of herself, one she recognized from her brochures, flashed on the screen.

"Zak." For a moment, she couldn't breathe. "They're showing my picture."

"If anyone has seen this woman or has any knowledge of her whereabouts, please call the number at the bottom of your screen," the reporter finished.

"Lord, my mother will be going out of her mind with worry. I have to call her." She looked around wildly for a phone.

Zak's fingers circled her wrist. "You can't call your mother or anyone else. You'll lead the police straight to where you are. You can bet they've already got a tap on her phone and anyone else they think you might contact. They consider you a fugitive. Getting a warrant to tap phones is no problem in a situation like this."

"But—"

The chirping of Zak's cell startled them. He pulled it from his pocket, looked at the readout and pressed the button to answer. "Yeah? I'm watching it right now. Uh huh. Okay. Thanks for the heads up." He looked at Zoe. "That was Reno. He's been mining his own resources. The car being found has really kicked things into high gear. Is anything coming back to you yet that happened after someone handed you that glass of wine? Any little bits and pieces?"

Tears of anxiety, fear, and frustration threatened to spill from her eyes. She forced them back, grabbing his arm. "I swear to you. I still remember nothing. But I would have given my car to the valet service. It's what I always did." She frowned. "That means someone had to get my car from them and move it. Wouldn't that have raised anyone's suspicions?"

Zak shrugged. "Whoever it was could have used a million plausible excuses. This is a hired service, Zoe. Working for a billionaire. They would have no reason to question anything, nor would they want to."

She looked up at him. "And you? What do you say?"

"I say someone is hammering one more nail in your coffin." He muted the sound again and tossed the remote back onto the table. "Do you remember the name of the service Dunning used? Anything about it?"

"No. I really never paid any attention." She squeezed her eyes shut, trying to call up an image, then shook her head. "No. All I can remember is the uniforms they wore—black pants, white shirts and gray jackets. No company logo. But I'll keep trying," she told him with desperation. "Something has to come to me."

"Maybe. Let me call the office again and have someone start digging up that little piece of information." He made his call, then turned to her with a sigh. "In any event, we're in deep shit now. The cops will be looking for you and pulling out all the stops, so we're on a short leash with time here."

"I am just so damn sorry I got you involved in this. I just didn't know—"

"Hush." His voice was firm yet soothing. "It just means we have to regroup here a little." Zak pulled her gently against the hard wall of his chest. "We'll handle this, kitten. I promise you."

*Kitten.* No one had ever called her that besides Zak. For a moment, the tears she'd been holding back threatened. She swallowed them back and leaned into him, drawing on his strength.

"Not to worry, we'll figure this out." His voice was calm, comforting. "That's what I do, remember?" He tucked strands of hair behind her ears. "Let me talk to Reno again. It looks like we're going to have to move you out of here sooner than I'd hoped."

"Okay. I'll do whatever you say. Whatever you think is best." Because he knew what he was doing. Wasn't that why she'd called him?

"Time to get you someplace safe. I'd keep you here, but if they come looking for you, they'll know Guardian is involved and that would complicate things more. Right now, we aren't even on their radar with this. I promise you someone will always be with you. More than one person. I'm going to be very careful with your safety."

"I know." She sighed. "I have to get away from here. Away from you."

"That's right. Zoe, both the police and the bad guys will be doing an all-out manhunt for you. My name is bound to pop up sooner or later, and I'd rather it be later. Much later."

"Okay." She blew out a breath. "But where will I go? Do you have some place you can take me?"

"I do. I also picked up a few things to tide you over, since obviously, I couldn't get anything from your house. Hold on a sec." Zak jogged to the door that led from the house into the garage, the car door slammed, then he returned, holding two plastic bags. He handed them to her. "Temporary substitutes," he told her. "I made a speedy trip through an all-night Wal-Mart." His lips twitched in a grin. "I think I remembered the sizes."

She gawked at him. "You nearly got your head blown off, and you thought about buying me clothes?"

He sighed. "It's just a bag from Wal-Mart, Zoe not a wardrobe from Saks."

"Didn't anyone wonder why you looked the way you did?"

He laughed. "Have you ever seen the people who go to Wal-Mart at this hour of the morning? Now go on, wash your face while I make some calls and set things up."

"What about my mother?" she asked again. "Are you sure there isn't some way I can let her know I'm all right?"

Zak shook his head. "I'm truly sorry, but she's just going to have to worry until I can figure out how to get word to her."

"Thank you."

"Listen. Your mother is a strong woman." He leaned forward and brushed his lips against hers, a light touch like before. "Like you. She's not going to fall apart."

Zoe was touched at his thoughtfulness in such a dangerous situation. This was far more than she had a right to expect from him after the way things had ended between them. She clutched the bags to her chest, unable to find the right words to thank him, blinking back yet another flood of tears that threatened.

Damn tears. All these waterworks weren't her style and wouldn't do her any good. What she needed to do was hold onto her anger.

Again she realized what a stupid fool she'd been. Look what he'd done for her tonight, and all she'd done was wring her hands, cry all over him, and bemoan what happened to her. For someone so smart, she'd been really, really stupid.

But she wasn't going to be stupid now. She'd made a huge mistake going into business with Nate Dunning, but that was the last mistake she was going to make. She was a computer genius, for heaven's sake. A woman who headed her own corporation. Zak had always told her how smart she was. Now she needed to prove him right.

He lifted his hand and ran his knuckles lightly along her cheeks, giving her a tiny smile. "It's okay. Go on. Go clean up. Then we'll talk."

## Chapter Five

Zak knew he was being sucked right back into the emotional whirlpool that was Zoraya Lombardo, but he wasn't sure if that was a bad thing or a good one. Something still tied them together, and it didn't seem he could avoid it. He'd managed to submerge his real feelings for her for two years, but they were still there.

*Admit it, Delaney. You're still in love with her.*

If he'd had any question at all about that, tonight answered them.

But he'd have to find a way to push that aside for the moment. Stash his emotions, which was becoming increasingly harder to do. He couldn't afford to let emotions cloud or blur his thinking. There were things he needed to get started on before any more time passed. Like making sure the place he took Zoe was secure.

He dialed his partner once again and in a short conversation found out what he needed to know. He'd discovered soon after the merger that there seemed to be an endless list to Guardian's resources. Tonight just drove that home again.

"By the way," Reno said, "you were right about her house being wired."

"What did you find?" Zak asked. "And how did you find out without anyone getting suspicious."

Reno laughed. "I sent Keith. He's great at this. He

has a little dog he takes with him, and he walks up and down a street as if he lives there."

Zak found himself returning a chuckle. "You guys think of everything. So what did he say?"

"From what he overheard, the front, back, and side doors were all wired to blow as soon as anyone opened them. Good thing you're smart and kicked the door in first."

"Didn't blowing up her house defeat the purpose of setting her up as the killer? That doesn't make sense."

"Chuck said he overheard two cops speculating that she did this herself, to get rid of any incriminating evidence about so-called criminal activities."

"That's just fucking stupid. Do they think she's an idiot?"

"They think they can get away with anything. We're not dealing with nobodies here. To pull all of this off the way they want, they have to have some people in their pocket, including some cops."

"That just makes me sick," Zak told him. "Okay, we'd better set the next piece of the plan in motion."

"We're on it at this end," Reno assured him.

Zak had just disconnected the call when Zoe walked back into the room. Although her eyes were still swollen and she was paler than snow, her face was scrubbed clean, her hair pulled into a braid, and she'd put on a pair of the jeans and a new T-shirt he'd picked up at Wal-Mart. Despite everything, she looked so good he couldn't help smiling.

"Not bad." His gaze raked over her. "Not bad at all."

Her answering smile was more valiant than real. "I can't believe you took the time to pick out lacy, um, undies."

"I couldn't see you in basic white cotton," he joked, trying to lighten the atmosphere. He swallowed a grin at the red flush on her cheeks. Was she actually blushing?

"You did good on the sizes," she told him. "You were right. You did remember. Thank you. If you let me know how much I owe you—"

"Forget it. That's not even on the list of things we need to talk about." He waved a hand as if brushing it away. "Got a question for you. Can you get into the Lombardo Simulations computer system from remote locations?"

"Of course, but they'll know the minute I do."

"That doesn't matter now. The need for stealth in that area disappeared with Dunning's murder and the explosion at your house."

"Okay, then. I still have all the codes and passwords in a cloud file. All I need is a computer."

"Good. Come with me." He led her to his desk and sat her down at his laptop. "Do your thing."

"What am I looking for?"

"Anything that isn't a simulation. Financial information. Correspondence. Anything you can find."

"Okay. I'll see if it lets me in "

"If it does, once you get in there, start pulling all the files you can and saving them to the cloud, so you can access them from wherever we stash you. Copy them to my hard drive, too. It's big enough to hold a lot of data in case we are someplace with it where there's no Internet."

Zoe nodded and started clicking keys.

A glance at his watch told Zak it was just past five

in the morning. The people he needed to talk to were used to calls at ungodly hours. Sleeping until five would almost be a luxury for some of them. And he needed to do this before they were faced with full daylight. He took his cell into the kitchen where he had one of the security monitors set up and began speed-dialing the people who could get things moving. All the while he kept his eyes glued to the screen on the monitor. When he was in the den with Zoe, he'd looked at the monitor there and had seen some activity that made him uneasy.

"Yeah, we have to time this just right," he said into the phone. "An unmarked car has rolled past here three or four times since I got back from the disaster at Zoe's house. I caught it on the monitor, but I haven't said anything to her. It means we're about out of time to get this thing done. And we'll have to be very, very careful pulling this off."

"I hear you," Reno acknowledged, "and I've been working on it."

"Thanks. I know you'll make sure she's well taken care of."

"This is Job One at the moment," Reno told him, "because it's personal. You just get her ready. I'll take care of the rest."

How did he say this?" Reno, I don't know how to thank you—"

"It's what we do for each other," Reno interrupted. "I know you've heard the story of how Nick led a covert operation to México to rescue my daughter from a cartel leader. The baby was barely a year old at the time, and Sarah was in the hospital. So let's get this done."

He walked back into the den to find Zoe staring at the laptop, an angry look on her face.

"Damn it," she swore at the computer.

"Problem?" he asked.

He went to stand behind her, watching her fingers fly over the keyboard as she frowned at the Access Denied message that kept flashing.

"I'm in the system, but I can't get into any of the financial files or corporate documents the way I could before. It doesn't matter what I try. It's obvious someone's put their own back door into the system. Damn!" She spat the word. "They must have hotfooted it over to the offices the minute Nate was dead."

"Or before," Zak corrected, "because they knew what was going to happen. I'm sure they did this before the law could stick its nose in. That explosion at your house was probably as much to destroy evidence you might have at home as it was to get rid of you."

"But evidence of what?"

"Just what I said before. Money laundering. And that may not be the only thing Nate was into. There's no telling right now what all he was involved in. I have an itchy feeling he kept a lot of his records on the LI computer network because he was afraid someone would find them on his own servers."

"Let's hope the files are just blocked and not deleted."

"I'm gambling they're still there. I have a hunch he stashed information he didn't want on the Dunning International network. Whatever he was doing with your company that was illegal, those files will hold the records. He's not going to get rid of them. And I don't think he'd trust them to a flash drive that could get lost or stolen."

Zoe nibbled on her lower lip. "I'll have Internet wherever I'll be staying, right?"

Zak nodded. "Of course."

"Okay. Let me work on it there. You learn a lot of things writing code." She grinned. "One of them is how to crack someone else's code."

"Guardian actually has a couple of people who excel at that. I'm going to get them started on the Lombardo International system, to see what they can pull down. I'll also tell them to hack the Dunning International computers and see what we can get there. We'll be looking into Nate's finances and information on how he got started. You keep after the files you know should be there."

"Okay. I fiddled around with a program called Escape that I planned to turn into a game. I want to try using some of the code from that to get into the LI system and see if I can find what you want."

"That would be amazing."

"So if I find them and open them, what am I looking for?"

"The best place to start is with Nate himself. What was going on with his own business, who he hung out with, who's involved with his various operations. Stuff that you may not have any idea about but that he kept on your servers so they'd be away from prying eyes. Also, whatever backup documents he might have kept on your servers."

"I want to know what you find," she told him. "I want all the details on that scum."

Zak took a healthy swallow of his coffee. "I told you I was making some arrangements for your safety, and I have. I hope to keep the cops and the bad guys off our backs for a little bit and give us some breathing room."

"What happens with Lombardo Simulations now? What about the staff I had working there?"

Zak shook his head. "No one is going to be doing any work there for a while. Even while they're waiting for the warrants, the district attorney has the authority to shut the business down."

"Crap. This just keeps getting worse."

"I agree. But look at where we are. Nate's dead. Fingers are pointing at you. The district attorney will want to stick his nose into the business where you were partners. As soon as he can he'll have people going over everything at Lombardo with microscopic precision."

Zoe leaned back in her chair and rubbed her forehead.

*Why is this happening? This is a nightmare, and I'll wake up any minute.*

She'd be back in her house, which would still be whole instead of a pile of ashes. Getting ready to go to work in a still flourishing business. The dizziness that hit her now wasn't from any drug but from the reality of the situation. The realization that everything about her life had spiraled out of control.

*All because you were too hard-headed to listen to Zak two years ago. See what happens when you're an idiot?*

He cupped her chin and forced her to look at him straight again. "You still trust me, right?"

She nodded. "More than anyone in the world."

His face was close to hers again, close enough that

his warm breath fanned across her cheeks. Her heart leapt at the whispery touch, her pulse accelerated, and need curled low in her belly.

*Kiss me, Zak, and tell me everything will be all right.*

His eyes darkened and held that familiar flash of heat again. Then his phone made its chirping sound, and the moment disappeared like smoke. He hit the button to accept the call.

"Yeah? Okay. Good. We're on our way." He disconnected and looked at her. "Sit tight for a minute."

He left the room, and when he returned, he had an old duffel bag in his hands. "Not signature luggage," he joked, "but it'll serve the purpose."

Unzipping it, he stuffed into it everything he'd gotten for her at Wal-Mart.

"Get your purse," he told her, "and bring it here."

Zoe hurried into the family room where she'd left the purse on the table. Lifting it, she realized the gun was still inside. She handed it to Zak as if it would bite her.

"Good."

He took a padded envelope from a desk drawer and emptied everything from the purse into it including the gun. He took a moment to separate the battery from her cell phone and disable the GPS chip. Then he locked everything in a wall safe. The empty purse he dropped into the duffel with her other things.

"No phone?" Her phone was her lifeline.

"Don't worry, you'll get a new cell. I won't leave you without a way for me to keep in touch with you." He took her hand. "Let's go."

Then very quietly, he led her out the side door and

through the trees in his backyard. They sidestepped through his neighbor's yard in the rear, using trees and high shrubs to shield themselves from the rising gray of dawn. They made it to the street that ran behind his house where an SUV sat at the curb with its engine idling.

Zak opened the passenger door.

"Quick." He pointed to the driver. "This is Dean McMann. He knows the score. Do whatever he says."

The two men exchanged a nod, and Dean handed something to Zak. He closed the door and tapped it twice. Zoe watched through the passenger window as the SUV pulled away from the curb. Zak was already melting back into the trees.

Turning around, she curled in a corner of the big SUV, chilled despite the rising warmth of a Texas summer morning. As soon as they were a few blocks away from the pickup spot, Dean handed her a navy windbreaker and a Houston Astros ball cap and told her to put them on. In the back seat was the duffel Zak had lent her with everything she had to her name.

"Put this in your pocket," Dean said, lifting a cell phone from a cup holder in the console. "It's a throwaway with five hundred minutes on it. You won't need them all, but we like our clients to be prepared."

*Clients!*

Somehow, she hadn't thought of herself that way, but that was what she was, albeit a nonpaying one. It bothered her that Zak was spending Guardian resources on her like this, but she also knew if she offered him money, the argument they'd have wouldn't be worth it.

"I gave a clean one to Zak just now," Dean added, "with this number programmed in. He's the only one who has it so if it rings you'll know it's him."

Zoe stuffed the phone in her jeans. "Can I also call *him* on this one?"

"Sure, if you really need to. Or if something happens and you panic, just hit the number two twice. That will speed dial him."

"Thank you."

"No problem. Guardian keeps a supply of disposable phones just for situations like this."

Dean McMann, huge and stolid, sat comfortably behind the wheel as he drove, his face giving nothing away as they wound through one street after another, making so many turns that her head was dizzy.

"Where are we going?" she asked, breaking the silence, her curiosity pricking at her.

"Didn't Zak tell you?"

She shrugged. "Just said some place where he thought I'd be safe. At least for now."

"The place where you'll be staying isn't on anyone's radar. No worries on that score."

"Good. Thank you."

Dean followed two more streets until he hit the Frontage Road for IH 10, then took the first on-ramp for the interstate, heading toward downtown San Antonio.

"Where are we going?" she asked again, squashing the anxiety that suddenly crept up.

"Just a little detour, making sure we don't have unwanted company. Nothing to worry about, I promise."

\*\*\*\*

Zak had just poured himself a fresh mug of coffee when the doorbell rang. Taking one last quick look around to make sure there were no traces of Zoe left, he padded to the door barefooted, his T-shirt hanging loose over his jeans. He didn't have to do much to make himself appear rumpled at this point.

When he pulled open the door, the familiar figure of Detective Joe Morales of the SAPD stood there. He and Zak had come in contact a number of times and developed a good working relationship. Zak had found as long as he shot straight with the detective, he could expect the same in return.

Morales's mouth twisted in a rueful smile, and a uniformed cop stood uncomfortably behind him.

"Joe." Zak nodded. "It's always nice to see you, but to what do I owe the honor? And at this hour of the day? Someone in need of good security?"

"I wish." Morales fidgeted, looking over his shoulder at the cop with him, then back at Zak. "I need to take a look through your house and see if you have a guest. They probably sent me because we know each other. I brought a helper with me."

"And what guest would that be?"

"I think you know everyone's looking for Zoraya Lombardo."

Most of the force knew Zak and Guardian Security, and their reputation as straight shooters. Reno Sullivan and Nick Vanetta, the third partner, had made it a point to have strong relationships within the SAPD. This cop didn't appear any happier about the visit than Joe or Zak.

Zak raised an eyebrow. "I don't know why you'd look for her here. Your information must be a little out of date. We broke up two years ago."

"People stay in touch." Morales shifted

uncomfortably.

"So, is this an official visit?" Zak looked at the detective's obviously empty hands. "I don't see a search warrant. What does the SAPD think they'll find here, for god's sake? Is this a fishing expedition of some kind? I can't imagine what you'd be fishing for in my house."

"Come on, Zak." Morales huffed in frustration. "You can't tell me you haven't watched the morning news and seen what's going on. Nate Dunning was murdered in his home last night. As his partner, your girlfriend—excuse me, *former* girlfriend—is the prime suspect."

Zak didn't move from his deceptively casual pose in the doorway. "Being someone's business partner automatically makes them guilty of a crime? What evidence do you have that she's the one who killed him? Nate Dunning is a major international player. He's got to have a lot of enemies. Anyone could have killed him."

"We have information that she was at the party at his house last night and they had a loud argument," the detective snapped, his impatience with Zak's stonewalling very obvious. "She stayed behind after everyone left. And her car was parked away from the house, for a quick exit."

Zak lifted an eyebrow. "Did you get that from the anonymous source the news is quoting?"

"Oh, so you *did* see the news. Then don't play dumb with me, Zak. If she's not here, you have nothing to worry about. One quick peek, and we're out of your hair."

"I'm telling you, she's not here."

"Listen to me. Don't be an idiot. This woman is a fugitive. She's one step away from being arrested, so if she's here, just hand her over."

"Tell me again why you think she'd contact me after two years. Our breakup wasn't exactly amicable."

Morales studied his face. "Her damned house burned down last night. If you haven't seen her, I guess you wouldn't know about that, right?"

Zak forced a look of surprise on his face. "Her house? You're kidding. But doesn't that give you a clue that someone's after *her*?"

Morales shook his head. "The district attorney thinks she arranged it. To destroy anything in there she didn't want us to find."

Zak actually laughed. "Don't you think that's a little extreme? I mean, come on."

He sighed. "You don't need this kind of trouble. Be smart. I'd rather do this in a friendly manner."

Zak shook his head. "Do what? You think it's friendly for the cops to show up on my doorstep bright and early and accuse me of harboring a fugitive?"

"Again. Miss Lombardo seems to have vanished," Morales said in a slow, deliberate voice, "and my lieutenant thinks she might have landed here" His gaze raked over Zak with a professional's eye. "I've known you a long time, Zak. You go a long way for your clients, but you've never gone up against the cops before. Broken any laws."

*That you know of.*

"If you let us in, I'll explain," the detective said.

"But no search warrant, huh?" Zak stared at Morales. "I'm guessing it's because all you've got is that anonymous call. You don't have one hard piece of evidence against her. Judges are getting a little antsy about issuing warrants on supposition these days, right?"

"Let us take a look and see if she's here," Morales pleaded, "and we'll be on our way. Your cooperation will mean a lot." He tried to peer around Zak into the house. "Can we come in? Please?"

With an exaggerated sigh, Zak stood aside to let the two of them enter. "Since I'm such a nice guy, I'll forget about the piece of paper. Come on in and look around."

Morales started toward the kitchen, then stopped, frowning. "How come you're still home, anyway? Aren't you usually out at the crack of dawn doing your thing?"

Zak's jaw muscles tightened. "If you didn't expect to find me home, why are you here? Were you planning to break in with a crowbar or something?"

"Zak, Zak, Zak." The detective tried to make his tone placating. "I put away my rubber hoses and stuff a long time ago. I called your office, and your secretary said you were working at home this morning." He held Zak's gaze. "Any special reason why?"

"Yeah. I had a project to set up for a client, and I didn't want to get caught up in all the office crap. Is that why I'm on the hot spot? Because I didn't go to work today?"

Morales' face sobered. "You're on the hot spot because you used to be engaged to Zoraya Lombardo. You're a big security hotshot. This would be the logical place for her to come, despite the fact that the two of you broke up."

"She didn't do it, Joe."

Morales stared at him. "And you know this how?"

"Because I know the kind of person she is." He pinned Morales with his gaze. "This is all some big mistake."

"Mistake? So far she's not only our best suspect but our *only* one. Like I said before, my lieutenant thinks there's a good chance she called you for help. She'd need someplace to hide and someone who knows what they're doing. I'm here to check that out."

Zak snorted. "The last thing Zoe ever said to me was she never wanted to see my face or hear my voice again."

"Yeah, maybe." Morales scratched his neck. "But big trouble can make strange bedfellows."

"Well, you're welcome to look as much as you want." He made is tone as casual as possible. "I'll be in the den when you're finished."

The detective cocked an eyebrow. "You don't want to check out what we're doing?"

Zak shrugged. "What for? You won't find anything. Just don't make a mess, okay? My housekeeper doesn't come in until tomorrow."

It took every ounce of discipline Zak had to make himself sit at his computer and create busy work while Morales and the cop thumped their way through his house. It seemed to take them forever, but he sneaked a glance at his watch and realized only forty-five minutes had passed before the detective appeared in the doorway to the den.

"Just so you know," Morales said, "I told my lieutenant we wouldn't find anything, but he's covering all bases."

"Covering his ass is more like it," Zak retorted. "So

I hid the body pretty well? Is that what you're telling me?"

The detective leaned his shoulder against the door frame. "This is nothing to joke about. People at the party last night heard Ms. Lombardo in a loud, shall we say heated, conversation with Nate. I understand this isn't the first time it's happened. Word on the street is there was big trouble in paradise there, and she was mad as hell about something."

"Word on the street, huh?" Zak gritted his teeth to keep from spitting out what he really wanted to say. "Business partners argue all the time. That doesn't mean one murders the other."

Morales tilted his head. "Yeah, word on the street. Rumor has it Nate was about to pull the plug on Lombardo Simulations. Yank all his money out, for whatever reason. That couldn't have made her very happy."

"Again, there are ways to settle a business dispute besides a gun." Zak was having a hard time keeping his anger at bay.

"Well, a word to the wise," Morales told him. "If you hear from her at all, convince her to turn herself in. It will be better all around."

"Yeah? For who? Certainly not her." Zak stood up. "We done here?"

Eyes narrowed, Morales studied him, then he pushed away from the door jamb. "Don't get in the middle of this, Zak. I'm telling you this as a friend as well as a cop. You'll get burned."

"I'll be sure to keep that in mind. And here's a piece of advice for you. Despite our personal animosity, I'd stake my reputation on the fact that Zoe Lombardo didn't kill Nate Dunning or anyone else."

"You may have to. I'm sure I'll be back again."

Zak closed the door after the two men and reset the alarm, then stood in the front hall, hands jammed in his jeans pockets, trying to sort everything out in his mind. He didn't doubt Zoe and Dunning had argued, especially after the things she'd told him. But no way did he see her shooting him. If he'd threatened to pull his money, she might actually have been relieved to be rid of him under the circumstances. He'd talk to her more about that tonight. They still had so much ground to cover.

On the other hand, if the people behind Nate saw both him and Zoe as a potential danger, what better way to solve the problem than to kill one and build a tight frame around the other? The key element here was finding out where Nate's money came from and who was pulling his strings. He hoped Nina and her crew were making headway getting into Dunning's computer systems and that they'd managed to find something.

Right now he had an urge to talk to Zoe, to hear her voice.

\*\*\*\*

The streets weren't yet busy with the normal traffic of the day, so they sped through the lights without much delay. On Houston Street, they pulled into a multi-story parking garage, Dean took a ticket from the machine and drove up the ramps until they reached the floor just below the roof.

At the far end of a row of parked vehicles, they turned into an empty space next to a four-door pickup truck. As soon as Dean killed the engine, a man climbed out of the truck and walked over to them. He was of medium height, dark-skinned with thick, longish black hair held back with a leather thong.

He smiled and held out his hand to Zoe. "Keith Diaz. I work for Zak. I'll be taking over from here."

"I have no idea what's going on," she told him, letting him help her out of the SUV.

"Just following Zak's orders," he told her. "Don't worry. You're in good hands. Zak will kill us if anything happens to you." His gaze seemed to be looking everywhere at once before he turned to Dean. "I don't see anyone coming up here behind you. No tails anywhere along the way?"

"Nope. And if there was one, I would have found it. You're good to go."

"Okay, then. This way, Miss Lombardo." He tossed the duffel Dean handed him into the back seat of the truck cab, opened the passenger door, and pulled out a plaid, western-style shirt. "We need to make a quick change before we leave here."

She handed him the navy jacket and shrugged into the plaid shirt. The Astros ball cap was replaced with a straw cowboy hat, and Keith handed her a pair of wraparound sunglasses.

"Am I in a spy novel?" she asked, amazed that she could find humor in this. She reminded herself these people knew what they were doing.

Keith grinned. "Let's hope not. Okay, in you go."

"What about Dean?" she asked, buckling her seat belt.

"He'll go get a cup of coffee, hang out for a while then take a little tour of the countryside. If anyone has sniffed him out, they'll be in for a scenic tour."

They followed the interstate west before pulling off

into a neighborhood of small houses, neat apartment complexes, and strip centers in what Zoe would classify a lower middle-income area. Men were leaving their homes and climbing into pickups, heading out to work. Women stood on porches, seeing them off, then shooing children on their way to school. Like every other neighborhood, from the lowest level of income to the highest, the Lone Star was in evidence wherever she looked—in hammered iron stars affixed to porches, on chain link fences, in flags flying everywhere.

*Texas. There's no other place like it.*

Another couple of minutes, and they stopped in front of a well-kept house made of adobe and limestone. A chain link fence surrounded the property.

Keith pressed a button on a remote clipped to the sun visor, and the gate in the fence slid open. Another touch, and the garage door rolled up. They drove inside.

"What is this place?" Zoe asked, opening the door and climbing down from the cab.

"One of the houses Guardian keeps just for situations like this."

"*One* of the houses?" Just from casual information, she knew Guardian Security had taken a big leap in growth the past few years, but exactly how big was it? How far up the ladder had Zak moved when she wasn't looking? "How many does the company have?"

Keith chuckled. "I think you'll have to ask Zak that yourself. I'm just a hired hand."

She shook her head as if to rid it of cobwebs. "I must have missed a lot in the past two years. I thought I knew everything that goes on in this town."

"Guardian Security pretty much flies under the radar except for the kind of people who need our services," he told her. "A lot of what we do is a well-kept secret. That's what makes us good."

Zoe had to agree. What little she did know about the company had come from bits and pieces of conversation she'd overheard from Nate's clients. She'd made a deliberate effort to avoid seeking any information about Zak for the past two years, so all of this had happened without her realizing it. She'd called Zak because she trusted *him* and because he had resources she would need. But this! This was more than she could have hoped for. Now she had the safety of a huge organization wrapped around her.

Keith walked her through the house, showing her where the bedrooms and bathrooms were, how the appliances worked in the kitchen, where things like towels and soap were kept.

"Why don't you take the big bedroom? You'll be more comfortable in there," he told her. "I've got a couple of cartons of grub for you. Just staples. There are television sets in the living room and all the bedrooms, and Guardian pays for a full cable package."

"Just out of curiosity, how long am I supposed to be here?"

He shrugged. "As long as it takes for Zak to get you out of hot water, I guess. Let me get that food."

After he'd carried everything inside, he showed her how to set the alarm panel by the front door, giving her the code.

"This is always on," he told her. "It only gets turned off when Zak or one of us has to go in or out, and they'll call first." He grinned. "The code word is kitten."

*Kitten. She had to smile at that one.*

"Well. Thank you. I guess."

"My pleasure. Don't go outside or look out the windows. I'm going to turn on the security cameras and the monitor. That way I can see who drives up. Or around."

She raised an eyebrow. "You're staying?"

"For the moment. You don't think Zak would leave you alone, do you? I think he plans to be here later, and then he'll tell you what other arrangements he's made."

Zoe wandered through the rooms, trying to ignore Keith as he went about his business. The furniture was plain vanilla, nothing special to distinguish it, purchased for its functionality. All the colors were earth tones from the beige carpet to the chocolate bedspread in the room she chose. That was fine with her. She didn't need any fancy decorating, only safety.

There was a small backyard with high hedges lining the fence. Every window had blackout shades, even the living room. When she checked the cupboards, she found the food Keith had stocked for her was as basic as the furniture, but at least she wouldn't starve while she waited.

*Waited.*

Waited for what? Standing in the middle of the living room, in the empty house, she realized that, despite her bodyguard, she was completely alone. Except for Zak. Being with him had gotten her over the initial panic and helped her keep it together. Knowing he would get to the bottom of things eased her anxiety. After that the anger had taken over and was fueling her now.

She wished she could hear his voice. As if her thoughts had triggered it, the cell phone in her jeans pocket trilled, startling her, and she pulled it out and answered it.

"Zak?"

"It'd better be, since right now, I'm the only one with this number." His deep voice was like balm to her frazzled nerves. "Just checking to make sure Dean and Keith took good care of you, and you got settled in all right."

"Yes. Thank you. They're great." She swallowed. "The house is very nice."

His laugh drifted over the connection. "I guess nice is a good enough way to describe it."

"Have—Have the police been there yet? At your house?" She was almost afraid to ask the question.

"Just left."

"Did they—" She stopped and tried again. "Are you…"

*Are you in trouble? Are they hassling you?*

She couldn't seem to get the words out.

"I'm fine," he assured her. "They searched every corner, believe me, but they found nothing. I made sure to clean up every trace of you being here after you left with Dean."

"But they definitely want me, right?" Nausea clawed at her again. She wished Zak was here to wrap his arms around her and chase away the nightmare.

"The important thing is they don't have you. And they won't. Listen. I have a lot to do right now, but you're safe where you are, and Keith's with you. I'll check in with you during the day. You've got the security code, right?"

"Yes." A tiny chuckle escaped her lips. "Very cute."

"I wanted something you'd remember. Listen, I had Keith pick up a laptop on his way to the house. Set it up however you need to in order to get to work. Keith will give you the password to the Internet so you can access your cloud files."

"Good." She was silent a moment, chastising herself for what she wanted to ask him. "Will—will I see you soon?"

"Yes." His voice softened. "I'm bringing dinner tonight. And a laptop for you, so you can do some homework. Try not to freak out too much, okay?"

"I'm good," she lied. "Call when you can."

The moment she snapped the phone shut, she felt disconnected from more than the call. She was alone in a strange house, in the worst trouble of her life, and only sheer determination was keeping the panic at bay.

*I trust Zak. That's why I went to him in the first place.*

She kept repeating that to herself as she went to unpack the few things Zak had bought for her, wondering if she'd ever get her life back. Finally, she set up the laptop, used the password Keith had given her to log onto the Internet, and went to work on the Lombardo Simulations network. She might have brought this mess on herself, but she was damn well going to help clean it up. Starting right now.

## Chapter Six

At eight o'clock, when Zak was sure his favorite techie would be at the office, he called Guardian and asked for Nina Colbert. Nina had magic fingers and an incredible ability to break any firewall ever erected. He wanted to know what was on the Dunning International computers, and she was the person who could find out.

"So you're saying you want me to hack into the computers of one of the biggest international conglomerates?" she teased.

Zak chuckled. "Did I say the word hack?" Then he sobered. "Nina, this is more important than I can possibly tell you. Run it past Reno if you'd feel more comfortable—"

"Hey!" she interrupted. "I worked for you before you hooked up with Guardian. You want me to do this? I'm on it."

"I don't need to tell you I need this yesterday, right?"

"As if that's new." Now it was her turn to laugh. "Okay. I'll get the usual suspects to work with me."

After he hung up, he thought about showering and changing, but a phone call from his contact delayed that activity. The very brief conversation alerted Zak that the cops were reaching out to every possible place in their hunt for Zoe Lombardo.

"Forget about that so-called two year hiatus," his

contact said. "The cops aren't buying the idea that the two of you are colder than Alaska. Your name is on their list of possible contacts, so you can expect visitors again this morning."

"Surely they have other places to look," Zak said.

"Not a lot. They'll be after you any minute, looking for her, asking questions."

"With a search warrant?" Zak asked out of curiosity.

"You know they can't get their search warrants until she's officially charged," the man said, "but they want to take a look and maybe catch the two of you off guard."

"They certainly are in a rush," Zak commented.

"People like Nate Dunning," his contact reminded him, "don't get killed without a full court press being generated. They could even call in the Texas Rangers. They're supposed to be the murder experts."

*Thank god I moved Zoe before the sun was up.*

Deciding it would be better to stay home and wait for them rather than be confronted at his office, he called Carol Joslyn, his secretary, to tell her he'd be late.

"Is Reno in yet?" he asked.

"I'll check and see."

In a minute, the familiar gravelly voice came over the phone. "How are we doing? How are *you* doing?"

"I got a heads up that the cops are going to pay me another informal visit, hoping I'm hiding Zoe in the closet."

"You got everything taken care of, though, right?"

"Yes," Zak assured him. "Made the handoff as arranged, and she's safe and secure."

"Good. We're still trying to trace those names you gave us. I'm even working on it myself." Reno made a noise of disgust. "So far all we've found is that someone was very determined to wipe out all leads to whoever these people are."

"I called Nina and asked her to see if she could peek into Dunning International's computers, hoping we can find something there. I guess I should have checked with you on that first."

"What for? I'd be telling her the same thing in your position.

"Listen," Zak said. "I really appreciate Guardian standing behind me on this. And you spending your own time on it. I'll cover all the out of pocket expenses myself, and—"

"Stop." Reno cut him off in midsentence. "You'd do the same for Nick and me. We may have grown a lot here, but we're all still family. Guardian will absorb whatever costs there are. Zoe Lombardo's safety is the most important thing right now." He paused. "As well as yours."

"I hear you." Zak was aware he could also become a target if the killers thought he could lead them to wherever Zoe was or had information they wanted. "And Reno? Thanks."

After disconnecting the call, he opened his laptop in his den, booted it up again, and set some innocuous files on the desk next to it. Then he went through the house wiping down every surface Zoe could possibly have touched. Again. If traces of her perfume lingered in the house, well, he could just hint that he'd had a "friend" spending the night.

Seeing Zoe again had been such a shock, but it

hadn't taken long before he felt the old chemistry charging the air. He'd had a hard time not throwing her down on his bed and running his hand through the silk of her hair. He wanted to trace the familiar curves of her body with his fingers, feel and taste her essence again. Bury himself in her liquid heat.

That kiss they'd exchanged had carried an electrical charge he still felt. Holding her while she sobbed out her desperation had made him harder than a spike, a condition his cock didn't seem to want to relinquish. Even in the middle of danger, he wanted her naked in bed with him. But more than that, he wanted the emotion they'd shared.

Listening to Zoe when he'd called, Zak had sensed the fear in her voice, as well as the determination not to give into it. He'd always admired her grit. He hoped it would keep her from falling apart. Tonight, when they talked, he needed her to focus, because he had some specific questions for her to answer. He planned to rip apart her relationship with Nate Dunning and expose all the flaws. And he didn't want her to freak out on him.

He had just finished sanitizing the den when his business cell lying on the desk chirped at him.

"It's me," Nina said. "Call me back on a clean phone."

He pulled the one out of his pocket he'd used to call Zoe and dialed her number.

She picked up at once. "Zak?"

"What's up? I was just about to call you and get a progress report."

"You're in luck, then, because I actually have one for you. We're into Dunning International's mainframe. Don't ask, don't tell, right?" she added when he started to say something. "You said to do what we had to, so we did. Don't worry. We won't leave any cyber-fingerprints."

Nina, who looked like an air-headed angel with her slight frame, long blonde hair, and blue eyes, had run the Information Technology Department for Delaney Security that Zak believed was second to none. When he merged with Guardian, he'd brought the whole crew with him.

Her techies could do anything she asked of them. And most importantly, knowing the lapses in other corporate security programs, she'd built so many shields for Delany Security that not even the best hacker could get in.

Designing security systems for computers was one of the options Guardian Security offered, and with the addition of Nina, their IT department had mushroomed beyond anyone's expectations. Her expertise had landed them several fat contracts, both government and corporate, in an area that had begun strictly as an in-house department.

"Be very, very careful there," he warned. "And stay away from Lombardo Simulations for the moment. There's trouble there and Zoe's working on it. I will let you know if she needs help."

"The cops are gonna be royally ticked off if they can't get anything from the LS system," she said.

"Not any more than Zoe already is." He sighed wearily. "Okay. Put together what you've got. How's Jay doing with the list of names I sent him? Any luck with anything there? Or locating the name of the valet parking company? And has he had a chance to run profiles on Dunning's business associates? The ones he has the most contact with?"

Jay Browning was another computer expert, only of a different kind. If you wanted to know anything about anyone's business operaticn, their associates and competitors, Jay could find out without making a ripple on the surface of the business world or in cyberspace.

Zak had meant what he'd told Zoe about the possibility of money laundering. It was the first thing that popped into Zak's brain when she told him what she and Nate had been arguing about recently. That made it even more imperative to find out about Dunning's business contacts and to take a hard look at the companies that made up Dunning International.

He hoped that between Nina and Jay they'd find the answer. Then he'd know which way to jump. The last thing he wanted was for the police to get a hint of it first and convince themselves that Zoe was a willing partner and she'd killed Nate over division of the spoils.

"He's on it," Nina assured him. "And Reno called down to say he was working on things from his end. I think he and Jay are coordinating on this. So far no news there, though."

"Okay. So what did you get from Dunning International?"

"More than I bargained for," she answered. "I'm putting everything together to email to you."

"No, don't do that. Take a laptop out of stock, format it, and encrypt it with my personal code, then copy whatever you got from DI to the hard drive. I want to go over it with Zoe tonight."

"Tonight, huh?"

He caught the teasing note in her voice.

"Business, Nina. Zoe and I were finished a couple

103

of years ago on a personal level." *Liar!*

"Whatever you say. Okay, I'll take care of it."

"Thanks. I'll call you later and swing by to pick it up. Right now, I've got some people to see myself."

He opened his safe and removed the gun he'd taken from Zoe. Then he sat at his kitchen counter drinking another in the endless cups of coffee and examined the gun thoroughly. It was a South American-manufactured Taurus, a handgun with which he was very familiar. Comparatively inexpensive. Lightweight. Small. Specially designed grips. Easy to carry, easy to use. It nestled snugly in his hand and could easily be carried in a woman's purse without being noticed.

And so common it would be almost impossible to pin down.

Of course, the serial number had been filed off. No big surprise.

But he'd learned in the course of his business that different types of people had a tendency to favor certain kinds of weapons, even those with common use like the Taurus. Digging up that information could be difficult, but he knew just the person who could help him out.

Pulling the clean phone from his pocket, he dialed a number he knew from memory.

"What?" The voice that answered sounded like steel rolling over concrete.

"I see you're still your usual charming self," Zak said.

"Charm is my middle name," Rick Boston said. "By the way, I hear your former lover is on the hot seat with the cops. They looking at you yet?"

"Looked and left. Listen. I need to pick your brain."

"I think it's already been picked too much." He punctuated his tired joke with a hoarse laugh. "What do you need?"

"Not over the phone," Zak told him. "We need to meet somewhere."

"You know the rules. No place too public.

"Okay." Zak shifted the phone to his other ear. "Name the place."

"Remember the dive where we used to meet for breakfast?"

"Yeah, how could I forget? I was always afraid the guy would poison us."

Boston laughed again. "You just have no taste for common food, my friend. All right. See you in an hour. Appropriate dress. Oh, and don't bring any company."

In other words, blend in with the clientele and lose any tails.

"See you then."

Zak made one more call before he headed for the shower.

Forty-five minutes, later he parked in his usual spot at the building where Guardian Security had its headquarters and rode the elevator up to his office.

"I'll be locked up in here for a while, and I'm hanging out a Do Not Disturb sign," he told his secretary. "No calls. No visitors."

"You have messages," she told him, handing him a pile of pink slips.

He shuffled through them, glancing at each one, took two off the top and gave her back the rest. "I'll handle these. Call everyone else; see if you can help them. If not, tell them they'll hear from me by this afternoon."

"No problem." Carol had been with him since he started Delaney Security and it was just the two of them. She was used to him by this time and seldom asked questions. He was daily more and more grateful for her.

Inside his office, he shed his jacket and shirt, pulled on a western shirt, and took a straw Stetson from the clothes he kept at work for occasions like this one. His shoes were replaced with a pair of well-worn boots.

Finally, he pulled a set of keys from a drawer in his desk. They were duplicates of sets his partners had.

Using the back entrance to his office, he took the stairs down to the garage rather than the elevator. He scanned the parking area where Guardian kept its company vehicles. Nothing was out at the moment, so he made his choice and moments later drove out of the underground garage in an anonymous-looking gray truck.

He took the Interstate to downtown San Antonio and spent a few minutes cruising the busy streets, carefully watching in both his rearview and side mirrors. He punched the button to turn on the radio and found a station with the local news. The big story, of course, was Nate Dunning's murder and the fact that his partner in Lombardo Simulations, CEO Zoraya Lombardo, was being sought as the prime suspect. Along with that was the story of the destruction of Zoe's house.

"Police are speculating that Miss Lombardo arranged for the explosion that caused the fire," the reporter added. "They believe it was set to destroy any evidence she had at home regarding her activities with Dunning, anything that could provide a motive for the murder."

Zak turned off the radio in disgust. That theory was farfetched even for the police, but he could imagine they were getting pressure on this case from everywhere. And the press would be in a feeding frenzy. They liked nothing better than a murder that involved a leader in the international business community, billions of dollars, and a suspect that was both beautiful and smart.

Damn it to hell, anyway. He had to get her out of this.

Back on the Interstate, he exited and re-entered a couple of times, once even changing direction. By the time he reached his meeting place, he was positive no one had followed him.

The restaurant, a combination diner and bar open twenty-four hours, was located on the east side of San Antonio, not far from where the annual rodeo was held. Because of its proximity, it was a regular hangout for riders, livestock haulers, and general hangers on. In his well-worn clothes, Zak fit right in with the crowd. No one would spot him here; he was sure.

Rick Boston sat in the same booth in the back corner where they'd met many times. Very few people knew this was only one of many such places Boston owned. It provided him locations to conduct his business, whatever that business happened to be at the moment, without exposing himself to curious eyes.

As Zak slid onto the seat, a heavy-set unsmiling waitress appeared next to them. Dressed in jeans and a denim shirt about two sizes too small for her, she slapped a mug on the table in front of him, filled it from the pot in her hand, and walked away.

"You have her well trained," Zak told Boston.

"My sister," he said. "She runs the place for me. No one trains her, not even her husband, the good-for-nothing. What can I do for you, my friend?"

Zak stirred sugar he didn't want into his coffee, organizing his thoughts.

"Like I said on the phone, I know your old girlfriend's in trouble," Boston told him. "So if this is about her, let's have it."

Zak sighed and dropped the spoon on the table. "You know more about guns than anyone else I know."

"Guns? This is about guns?" Boston looked at him, curiosity lighting his eyes. "You want to buy guns from *me?* Why? You're legit. You can even order them online if you want."

"No, no, no." Zak shook his head. "I'm not in the market. Except for some information."

Boston held up a hand. "I can't talk about my customers."

"I know. I'm not asking for names, just generalities. I need to know who favors a small Taurus these days. Forty caliber." He described gun Zoe had taken from the murder scene.

Boston ran his fingertip around the edge of his mug. "Big business in Taurus these days. Good for concealed carry." Texas law had long allowed those who qualified to carry a concealed handgun, and a significant number of the population took advantage of it. "The Taurus models are actually knockoffs of Smith & Wesson, but they're a lot cheaper and easily obtainable out of the country. Because they're made in South America."

"Out of the country? But then they'd have to find a

way to get them in. I thought, since 911, the government was tightening border controls."

Boston's laugh was humorless. "The people who buy these in quantity don't have to worry about that. They have ways the government hasn't even thought of yet. Besides people would hide under their beds if they knew how porous our borders really are." His stare was piercing. "What is it exactly you want to know, Zak?"

"I want to know who buys this gun in quantities. Whose signature it is. You know enough about who buys what. If you don't know about it, it isn't happening. Come on, Rick. Just give me a direction to follow."

Rick Boston was silent for a moment, sipping at his coffee. Zak could almost see his brain clicking through a checklist.

"Try the Russians," he said at last.

"The Russians?" Zak tried to swallow his surprise.

There were a lot of lethal people running around Texas these days, especially San Antonio, not the least of which were the powerful drug cartels. But Russians? This was the first time he'd heard they might have a significant presence in this city.

Dalton nodded. "This seems to be the gun they favor right now. Cheap. Easy to carry, easy to use. And there are so many of them in distribution they can actually be anonymous. Just file off the serial numbers and dispose of them when you're done."

"Let me get this straight." Zak kept his voice calm. "You're talking about the Russian mob, the *mafiyah*, right? Here in San Antonio?"

"Who else?"

Zak frowned. "I haven't heard even a sniff of them

operating in Texas, let alone in this city. Aren't they worried about the drug cartels defending their turf?"

"That's not my problem." Boston spread his hands. "You asked me a question. That's my answer. But you might want to remember this. The Russian *mafiyah* makes the drug cartels look like a Sunday School class."

A sick feeling crept from Zak's stomach to his throat. He hadn't had dealings with the Russian mob personally, but their brutality and disregard for life was legendary. How the hell had they gotten a foothold here? And without the rumor mill going wild?

His thoughts went back to the Demoffs, Zoe's relatives on her mother's side. But her uncle Ivan had been a part of the high profile legal community for too long. The firm where he was a partner had an impeccable reputation. If the man was entrenched with the Russian mob, Zak was sure he would have smelled it out by this time. And there would have been more visible activity involving Ivan. The Russians weren't shy about making themselves known, convinced they could intimidate anyone who got in their way. Or kill them. More than that, his partners would have gotten rid of him, unwilling to have their skirts soiled by him.

In addition, Ivan was the one who had made the match between Zoe and Nate. He couldn't see the man putting his own niece smack in the middle of danger. Boston's answers were generating even more questions.

He took a swallow of his coffee, not cooling and bitter. "Okay," he said, setting down the mug. "One more thing."

"No." Boston shook his head. "That's as much as I can give you."

"Listen, I didn't come all the way for a five minute conversation."

"That's four minutes more than I give most people." Rick's smile had no humor in it. "You're smart. You know what to do. Just take it from here."

Great. Just what he needed to be doing. Poking around in the business of the Russian *mafiyah*. Somehow he had trouble seeing Nate Dunning involved with a bunch of criminals without souls, no matter how well they dressed. From everything he'd found out about the man, he'd have been scared shitless. Although maybe that was what happened. Maybe he didn't mind a little run of the mill corporate trickery or siphoning money to the usual numbered offshore accounts. So what did he stumble over that precipitated everything?

He drained his mug and stood up. "All right. Thanks. At least for this much." When he pulled out money to leave on the table, Boston gripped his forearm.

"Don't insult me by trying to pay for a lousy cup of coffee in my place. And let me give you a strong word of advice, my friend. If the *mafiyah* are the ones after Miss Lombardo, getting her out of town won't be the answer. Another planet might help. And if you try to bring down their operation, buy plenty of bullet proof clothes."

"Thanks for the warning. And the information."

Driving back to his office once again, via a winding, circuitous route, gave Zak plenty of time to mull over what Boston had said. And to acknowledge the possibility that what the man said was true.

*How the hell has Zoe gotten herself into this mess, anyway?*

## Chapter Seven

"You've got visitors," Carol told him when he buzzed her that he was back.

"I do? I wasn't expecting anyone that I know of."

"That's right, Mr. Delaney." Her formal tone told him the person was within earshot of her desk. "I know your schedule is tight, but Mr. Demoff and his son say it's urgent that they see you."

Well, well, well. He was getting a chance to see for himself Demoff's reaction to this situation. But why did he have his son with him? Sergei had a well-earned reputation for being uncontrollable. As good as Ivan's reputation was in the community, Sergei's was that bad. He had a temper and an ego, both key ingredients for trouble. When he'd researched Ivan two years ago, he'd found nothing but good press on him. Sergei, on the other hand, was the typical arrogant rich kid who, at thirty, still couldn't manage to stay out of trouble. Zak wondered how Ivan handled that with his partners.

Just what he needed to make his day even worse. A Russian hothead.

"All right, Carol. I have to make a quick call. I'll let you know when I'm ready. Probably no more than five minutes."

He took a moment to change out of the clothes he was wearing and back into the slacks and shirt he'd worn to work. Exchanging boots for loafers and stashing the Stetson, he picked up the phone and pressed the extension for Reno's office.

"He's got someone waiting to see him," Amy, Reno's secretary told him. "But if it's urgent he can take your call."

"Urgent in capital letters."

"Okay, hold on."

"Another crisis?" Reno asked when he came on the phone? "I had no idea what interesting women you had in your life."

"I could do with one a little more ordinary right now. Listen. What do you know about the Russian mob? Or who can you get hold of that can fill you in?"

"The *mafiyah?*"

Zak could hear the note of surprise in his partner's voice.

"Here in San Antonio, if you can believe that. And a very reliable source has convinced me that's what's happening."

"What the hell has Zoe Lombardo gotten herself involved in?"

"That's what I'm trying to find out," Zak told him. "Can you help?"

"Yeah, actually I can," Reno told him. "I've got someone waiting for me that will take about half an hour. Then I'll get on it. But it could be tomorrow or so before I have any answers."

"I'll take anything," Zak said. "And thanks."

Hanging up the phone, he buzzed Carol and told her he was ready. He was sitting in his chair behind his desk when a light tap sounded on his office door. It swung open, and Carol ushered two men inside.

"I'll bring a coffee tray," she told Zak as she closed

the door.

Ivan Demoff was tall, well over six feet, almost as tall as Zak, with broad shoulders and a muscular frame. He wore his thick, silver hair short, framing a typical Slavik face of high cheekbones and broad forehead. Piercing blue eyes stared out from beneath heavy brows. He'd met Ivan several times when he and Zoe were together. The man had always been polite but reserved and had a definite air of power about him. The media continued to paint him as a mover and shaker in the community.

Zak's contact with Sergei had been infrequent and usually unpleasant. A younger version of his father, Sergei always looked at him as if he'd take great pleasure in slitting his throat. But then, Zak had figured out a long time ago that was Sergei's usual expression—a penchant for violence that barely concealed a lack of the same intelligence his father had. He wondered what it took for Ivan to keep his son on a leash.

Zak shook hands with both men and waved them to the chairs in front of his desk.

"Thank you for seeing us," Ivan began.

"We want to know where Zoraya is," Sergei interrupted before he was even settled in his seat, his voice rough and edgy. "We *demand* to know."

Ivan glared at his son. "We agreed I would do the talking, Sergei. It's very possible Mr. Delaney may not even know where your cousin is. If he does, he may not feel it is safe to tell us. Remember, our first priority is to make sure Zoraya is safe."

"Bull," the younger man spat. "He has her somewhere. You know it and I know it. Otherwise we'd be able to find her. Or she'd have come to us, her family."

"Sit down." Ivan spit out the words in a voice as cold as ice. "If you cannot conduct yourself in a professional manner, then you cannot be included in this meeting."

The door opened, providing what Zak thought was a welcome interruption, and Carol entered carrying a tray with filled coffee cups and a small plate of pastries. Zak swallowed a smile. He could be entertaining a murderer, but his secretary would stick to protocol at all costs. She'd done the same thing when it was just the two of them, determined to set a certain tone for clients. She set the tray on the small table between the two client chairs, handed one filled cup to Zak, and left as quietly as she'd walked in.

"Please help yourself," he told the two men. With all the coffee he'd already had this morning, his own drink was more a prop than anything else.

"We didn't come here for social niceties," Sergei objected rudely.

"Once more," Ivan said, "and you will be done here. Your behavior is beneath us. Take your coffee and let me do the talking." He looked at Zak. "I apologize for my son. He is something of a hothead, but he means well."

Zak doubted that.

As soon as they had settled back in their seats, Ivan turned his hawk-like face back to Zak. "Again I apologize for his manner. He is just concerned, as we all are, for Zoraya. This is a terrible situation."

Zak swiveled his gaze from one to the other, carefully keeping his face impassive. "I would love to help you gentlemen, and I agree Zoe is in an impossible situation. I worry for her safety. However, I don't know what makes you think I have any idea where she is. We broke up two years ago. And I'm sure you're aware the circumstances were less than pleasant."

"I am," Demoff nodded. "I am sorry it happened. But she is in terrible trouble and her resources right now are limited. They've frozen her bank accounts so she has no funds. She hasn't come to her mother, Sergei, or me, so who then?" He spread his hands, palms up. "There is no place else for her to go."

"How do you know about her bank accounts?" Zak asked, carefully keeping his face blank.

Ivan made a deprecating sound. "Please. I am her uncle and an attorney. It wasn't so hard to find that out. If she had available funds, she could at least hide herself someplace. But all she has is whatever cash was on her personally. Since she did not come to us, you are the next logical person, despite your...falling out. She is innocent. We must help her prove that."

"She is a foolish female," Sergei broke in, a scowl creasing his forehead. "She was mad at Nate. They argued frequently."

Zak lifted an eyebrow. "So her solution to the problem was to shoot him?"

"Everyone knows women react emotionally. Poof! She gets rid of him."

"Sergei, shut up." Ivan's voice was so cold even Zak felt chilled. "Please show proper respect. Zoraya did *not* kill Dunning, and I don't want to hear this foolishness from you anymore."

Zak wondered, with the obvious affection Ivan had for his niece, if there wasn't some jealousy in there on

116

Sergei's part.

Ivan turned back to Zak. "Zoraya may have been hot-tempered—a result of both her Italian and Russian heritage—but her weapon was her brain, not a gun. She is no killer. That I believe. But she is in terrible trouble and she needs her family. I can help her with this."

Zak met Ivan's knife-like gaze and held it for a heartbeat before speaking again. "You're the one who introduced her to Dunning. Didn't you have any reservations about that? Worry about who his other associates might be?"

"Nate was a client for many years," Ivan explained. "A good one. My partners and I traveled in the same social circles as his family. His father has an impeccable reputation. I know there has been some…gossip about Caz Morgan, but the man is a financial genius. Many of us are clients of his investment firm. Under his guidance, Nate amassed great wealth. I handled the legal affairs for Dunning International, and nothing ever seemed amiss. Everyone I came into contact with was as professional as Nate. There was never a sniff of anything that would result in this." He stared back at Zak. "Do you think I would deliberately put my niece in a dangerous situation?"

Sergei growled something at his father in Russian. Ivan made a slashing motion with his hand and answered him in a voice colder than ice. Zak watched the two of them much as he would observe two snarling animals, and wondered what Sergei's role in all of this was.

"Let me assure you," he told them. "I am as concerned about Zoe as you are. I only wish she had come to me so I could protect her and help her find out who did this, who set her up."

"Her mother is very worried about her," Ivan told him again. "Distraught. A friend is with her right now, but I fear for her health if Zoraya is not found soon." His tone changed to a pleading one. "I am asking you, Zachariah, man to man, if you know where Zoraya is. If you have hidden her somewhere, convince her she should be with her family."

"I told you I don't know where she is," he repeated. "So I guess it's up to you to make sure Zoe's mother is cared for and reassured."

"I could do that much better if I had answers for her." Ivan studied his face with his glacier-blue eyes. "You swear to me you don't know where she is? If you *are* hiding her, you could be putting her in terrible danger."

"I'd say she's already in more danger than she needs to be. If Zoe wanted to go to you, she would already have called." He leaned forward. "If you know anything about Nate Dunning's business that can provide answers here, my advice to you would be to tell the police right away."

"We have already spoken with the police."

Again Sergei barked something in Russian. Again his father snapped at him, rose from his chair, and indicated Sergei should do the same.

"I'm sure you realize we are bound by the rules of client confidentiality," Ivan said to Zak. "However, I would not put that before Zoraya's safety. I hope you mean it when you say you don't know where she is." There was a hint of underlying menace in his tone. "I would hate to think Sergei is right and you are lying to us about something so important. She belongs to *us*,

Mr. Delaney, not you. We need to find her."

Zak couldn't doubt the sincerity of the man's tone. It was Sergei who roused his suspicions. He rose from his desk chair, indicating the meeting was over, and shook Ivan's hand. "If I have occasion to see her, I'll be sure to tell her to get in touch with you."

"Please. I hope you mean that." He reached his hand across the desk.

*In a pig's eye.*

Sergei did not offer to shake hands. Niceties weren't part of his personality. "I still think you are a liar, Zak Delaney. I hope you do not cost Zoraya her life."

He turned a cold glare to Sergei. "That's the very last thing I would want to happen. Keep that in mind."

Again Ivan muttered to Sergei in Russian, then turned back to Zak.

"You know where to find me. Please call me at once if she gets in touch with you. As I say, her mother is sick with worry, as are we all."

"I'll keep that in mind," Zak told him.

He watched the two men leave, Sergei still muttering in Russian in a low voice.

*Well, weren't we just a couple of junkyard dogs in a pissing contest.*

He picked up his desk phone and pressed three numbers. Jay Browning picked up at once.

"I'm working as fast as I can, Zak," he said without even a hello. "Reno handed what he had learned, which wasn't much, off to me because he had a client meeting, and I've had three people working on it. But I can tell you this much. None of the companies on the list you gave me exist. And I've tried every combination of letters and every possible source I could find to see what I could come up with. The actual owners are buried so deep I'm having to write a program just to unpeel the layers."

"Damn." Zak rolled a pen between his fingers. "I think I expected that."

"Also, *nada* so far on the valet parking."

"Are you telling me none of the valet parking services in this entire area worked Nate Dunning's parties?" Zak dropped the pen and sat up in his chair.

"That's exactly what I'm saying. It's gotta be another privately owned enterprise like the ones on this list, with no public face."

"Makes sense," Zak muttered, "considering who they probably work for."

"You want me to ask Keith to help? He's got the street creds to ask questions."

"No, I have Keith on something else. Larry Blake's just back from his job in Mexico for Continental. Let me put him on it."

"Okay. Tell him if he can just get me a name, I can do the rest."

"Fine. Listen. I need you to get your team to keep working on that list. I have a special project. I want everything you can find about Ivan Demoff, his family, his friends. Especially the son. Everything including what grades he got in school and who he ate lunch with. And I want it—"

"I know, I know," Jay broke in. "Yesterday. I'm on it."

"I'm leaving here at four. Whatever you've got by then, load onto the laptop Nina's getting ready for me and have someone bring it to my office."

"I'll do it myself."

****

Zoe leaned back in the desk chair and rotated her head to relieve the strain on her neck. She'd lost count of the number of different combinations she'd used to retrieve the files from the server, but everything seemed to lead to a dead end. She'd been so sure the program she was writing for Escape would do the trick for her. The non-simulation files were there, she could just feel it, but every time she pulled up the file directory and clicked on one, she got the same response—access denied.

She'd told Zak she'd have thought they'd just delete the files. He pointed out to her that they needed the information to track what might be millions of dollars in activities. They just had to prevent her from seeing them. Being shut out of her own computers had made her angry and also frightened her. She'd designed the security for her computer system herself, so whoever hacked it had talents she hadn't seen yet.

Finally, she decided to take a break and get a cup of coffee.

*As if I haven't had enough today for a permanent caffeine addiction.*

Despite the fact she hadn't slept for hours, unless she counted her drugged nap, she wasn't sleepy and couldn't seem to settle down. Zak was right. This was no longer merely a business problem with Nate. This whole thing was being carefully orchestrated by someone, and she'd only missed being caught in the trap by a stroke of luck. Someone with a lot of power was pulling the strings, someone out to destroy her. But was she a primary target or just collateral damage as they got rid of Nate?

For a moment, she was back in Nate's den with a dead body and a gun, and panic threatened to break free. Then she deliberately pushed it back. Very little shook her. She'd built a successful business on grit and determination, then had the guts to take it one step beyond that. But had her desire for that growth been a velvet trap? She was suddenly a target for people who could frame her for murder, blow up her house, and wipe out her computer system from a distance.

And being locked up like this wasn't doing her any good. The only result was to give her too much time to think. Keith was solicitous to a fault, trying to entice her to take a break from the laptop. Watch some television with him. He also showed her the reading material kept in the house. He tried coaxing her to eat a little something after they got to the house, then tempting her with a sandwich at lunch.

"If you get sick and die on me, there goes my pension," he joked.

To satisfy him, she'd gagged down as much as she could.

But she felt trapped, both by her own ambitions and the walls of this house, which were closing in on her. What if she'd paid more attention to Zak two years ago? What if she hadn't taken Uncle Ivan's and Sergei's recommendations that Nate Dunning was her answer?

What if, what if, what if?

She wanted to pull her hair out by the roots.

Zak was the best at what he did. She knew it and she trusted him to take care of her, or she never would have called him. And he would get to the bottom of this. Especially now that he had all the resources of Guardian Security at his disposal. But she was frustrated that, even with her computer skills, she couldn't crack these files. It was driving her nuts. She'd have to talk to Zak about it tonight.

And then there was her mother, with whom she was extremely close. Even though Zoe had her own place and had been busier than ever with Lombardo Simulations, she had made it a practice to call her mother once a day and lunch with her once a week. They had the type of relationships her friends often envied. Mama would be in hysterics by now, worried out of her mind.

Uncle Ivan would do his best to keep her calm, but the news was full of the murder and her picture was on every newscast. How much could her mother take? She had to do something to ease her mind. Since her father died, her mother was more important to her than ever.

Zoe nibbled on a fingernail. Zak had said not to use the cell phone to call anyone but him. She wasn't stupid. She knew the danger in sending out that signal. But how much could one phone call hurt, especially if she kept it short? It would make both of them feel better, and at least she could then concentrate on her own troubles. Not worry about her mother.

Of course with Keith watching her like a hawk, checking on her every few minutes, making the call was almost impossible.

Her cell rang, the sound piercing the silence and startling her.

"You okay?" was the first thing he asked.

"Just dandy." She tried to keep her voice even.

"I know that's not the case," he told her, his voice

soft. "But you're safe and that's number one on my priorities list. How's the computer work coming?"

"Don't ask. I'd love to know who they paid to create this cyberwall. I might want to hire him."

"Take a break," he told her. "Nina managed to get into part of it, and I'm bringing what she got with me."

"Damn." She shook her head, even though he couldn't see her. "I wanted to do it myself. I have the skills, Zak."

"I know you do, but Nina could out hack anyone. I'm on my way with Chinese food and another laptop, with additional homework for you."

"Okay. Good. Thank you."

So his cyber person could do things she couldn't. So what? Maybe she could pick up where that person had left off.

A glance at her watch told it her it was just after five. Maybe she could sneak in a quick call to her mother before Zak got there.

She jumped at the light tap on the door.

"Yes?"

The door opened a crack, and Keith stuck his head in. "Just making sure you're okay, Miss Lombardo."

If he didn't leave her alone, she was going to scream. Then a crazy idea popped into her brain. "I'm fine, Keith. In fact, I think I'm going to take a long shower. See if it relaxes me before Zak gets here."

"Holler if you need anything," he teased, but his voice was respectful. Whatever Zak had told his men, they treated her like visiting royalty.

"I'll let you know as soon as I'm done."

What she was about to do was risky as well as probably idiotic. Oh, wait, no probably about it. But if she was smart enough to keep things brief, no one would ever have to know she'd violated Zak's instructions. The sound of the shower would cover her conversation. When the water was running strong and hard, she dialed her mother's number.

"Zoraya?" Her mother's voice sounded shaky. "Is that really you?"

"It's me, Mama. I just wanted to let you know I'm all right. So you don't worry."

"Not worry? My sweet thing, the police have been here so many times. They say you killed Nate." Her voice hitched on a sob.

"You know me. I didn't kill anyone. Someone else is doing this." Zoe tightened her grip on the phone. "I can't talk long. I just wanted you to hear my voice. Okay?"

"Please come home," her mother begged and lowered her voice. "Uncle Ivan can help you with this, with the police who won't leave us alone. He knows everyone."

Weakness grabbed Zoe, and she sat down quickly on the closed toilet seat. The police! Were they there now? In her mother's house?

*Oh God! What have I done?*

What if they tapped the phone? What if *the others* were tracking her? Oh dear sweet lord. What had she done? For a smart person, she hadn't given this the kind of thought she should, simply acted on emotional impulse. After all the trouble he'd gone to, Zak was going to kill her if anything happened because of this call.

"I have to go, Mama. Right now. Just don't worry."

She disconnected and leaned her forehead on her

closed fingers. Inside, every bone and muscle felt as if they were shaking. She'd barely been on the phone for a minute. Surely that wasn't enough time for anyone to trace the call, was it?

*Idiot, idiot, idiot.*

She couldn't repeat the word often enough. Stupid after all. Dumb.

Oh, lord. She'd done it now.

Putting herself and Zak at risk.

Maybe it would be all right. Maybe the call had been short enough not to bring trouble. She hoped. Maybe she wouldn't have to let Zak know she'd completely ignored his instructions.

Zak.

His image blazed across her mind.

It hadn't taken long for the old chemistry to ignite. There was simply no way to ignore what was going on between them, no matter what she told herself. Those kisses still branded her lips, and the warmth of his body as he'd soothed her through her meltdown had awakened urges she hadn't felt since...well, since she'd walked out on him.

And what a dumb thing that had been. Talk about being an idiot. If he found out about her latest stupidity and decided to wash his hands of her, she wouldn't blame him one bit. But she didn't know if she could survive a broken heart twice.

Dragging in a breath, she set the phone on the vanity, releasing it as if it were a hot flame. Pulling off her bra and panties, she stepped into the shower and just stood there, letting the water run down on her until it finally turned cold. She wanted to wrap herself in the towel and hide in the closet until it all went away.

\*\*\*\*

"How's everything?" Zak carried the paper sacks, along with the laptop, into the kitchen and put them on the counter. "How's Zoe holding up?"

He'd called Keith with the code and rolled smoothly through the open gate and into the garage. He had the familiar itch on the back of his neck that he hoped would go away as soon as he laid eyes on Zoe. The session with the Demoffs had ratcheted up his anxiety factor, and the information Jay had given him didn't help ease it.

"Fine," Keith told him. "At least, considering the circumstances. Maybe you can get her to eat something. I'm afraid she's going to starve herself to death before this is over."

Zak nodded to the paper sacks. "I brought her favorite. Chinese food. That ought to tempt her appetite." He pointed to the laptop. "And a little more homework to exercise her brain."

"Good. Listen, Zak."

"Yeah?" Zak was busy unpacking the food and lining the white cartons up on the counter.

"Did you happen to see a black panel van outside when you got here?"

Zak's hand stilled in mid-motion. "No. Why? Has one been hanging around?"

Keith shrugged. "I'm not sure hanging around describes it. When I did my perimeter check just before you got here, I saw one parked two doors down. But by the time I finished walking around, it was gone. Do we have one on our list?"

When a house was used for high profile safety, Guardian Security went to great lengths to know every inch and speck of the area. That included satellite photos of the street as well as the ones on either side, and notations on which vehicles were seen regularly. Even visitors to homes were logged and checked out.

"Not that I know of, but I'll call Nina. She's still at the office and can pull up the information. Did you get a license number?"

"No. Sorry." Keith dropped his eyes. "It was only here for seconds. I caught it as I turned the corner to the backyard, but when I hustled out front, it had taken off. I think I dropped the ball."

"It could have been nothing," Zak told him. "Don't beat yourself up about it. But let's keep an eye out. Maybe head outside again but stay out of sight. Let me know if it shows up again."

"Nobody knows we're here, right?" Keith asked. "I was very careful when I drove Miss Lombardo here."

"Nobody knows. We're probably jumping at shadows, but being cautious is our motto. I'm going to check on Zoe, then dish up the food. Why don't you go ahead and fix yourself a plate so you can eat at the monitor?"

"Nah. I'll get something later." He headed for the small den where a computer received the feeds from six security cameras mounted on the perimeter of the property.

Zak tapped lightly on the door of Zoe's room and opened it, poking his head inside. She was sitting in the middle of the bed, arms wrapped around herself, looking so distressed his heart cracked open. In a flash, he had closed the door, moved across the room, and scooped her up in his arms. When he sat down on the edge of the bed, he was cradling her against his body.

She pressed herself against him, fine tremors running through her body, her forehead pressing against the hollow of his throat. She smelled of soap and flowers and a scent that was distinctly Zoe. He felt his erection thickening and pressing against her bottom and wondered why she didn't say something about it. But he just kept holding her, smoothing his hand up and down her back while his mouth pressed kisses against the silk of her hair.

"You're okay, kitten. Everything will be okay. I promise."

"Oh, Zak." She pressed harder against him. "Just hold me tight. Please."

His soft chuckle teased the fine strands of her hair. "That's easy. I love holding you."

"I'm so sorry, Zak." With her face still buried against his chest, he could barely hear her words. "I know you keep trying to change the subject when I bring it up, but please let me get this out."

"Get what out?" He cupped her chin with his free hand and tilted her face up to him.

"About walking out—no, storming out—the way I did two years ago." She drew in a shuddering breath. "I know you said we'd talk about it later, but I want to get it said now. I made a huge mistake. Enormous. I deserve to be in this mess."

The muscles in his face tightened. "That's bull, and I don't want to hear you say that again. Ever."

She burrowed against his chest. "I wish we could go back to that night and start all over again."

"We can't do that, but when we get this all cleared up, we can take a look forward." He was reluctant to commit to more than that, no matter how badly he might want to. Right now, Zoe was running on fear and desperation. What if her feelings changed considerably when her life settled down again? The last thing he wanted to do was take advantage of her vulnerability. And was he really ready to risk his heart again? She might just be caught up in the heat of the moment, clinging to him as her anchor.

"I won't feel any different," she insisted, as if reading his mind. "I need you in my life. I want you."

The Chinese food was in the kitchen and the laptop was waiting, along with Keith, but suddenly, Zak just didn't give a damn. He took her mouth in a kiss both hungry and marauding, licking the soft inner flesh and sucking her tongue into his mouth. When he scraped it lightly with his teeth, she shuddered and moaned.

Easing up the fabric of the sweater, he raised it until her bra was exposed and he could pinch her nipples through the fabric. She moaned into his mouth and pushed her breasts into his touch. He pinched harder, then moved to the other taut bud, giving it the same treatment.

She dropped one arm from around his neck, slid it in between them, and found his cock through the fabric of his slacks. When she squeezed, he gasped and bit down lightly on her tongue. The feel of her fingers around his shaft was like magic, just as it had always been. She squeezed again, and he moaned. With one swift movement, he tugged her sweater over her head, tossed it to the side, then unclasped her bra and dropped it with the sweater.

Naked. He wanted her naked. Wanted to lick and kiss every inch of her.

He bent and took one nipple in his mouth, teeth

scraping the pebbled flesh before he soothed it with his tongue. Cupping one breast, he squeezed the warm flesh, his teeth and tongue still teasing that hard nipple. By the time he worked his magic on both breasts, he was sure her panties were soaked because her familiar scent carried up to him.

"More," she murmured against his lips when he pressed his mouth to hers. "More now. Take off your shirt. I want to feel your chest against my nipples. Do it, Zak."

"More. Yes!" Impatient, he yanked his shirt off without unbuttoning it and dropped it on the growing pile of clothing. Then he proceeded to trail kisses along the column of her neck, from shoulder to shoulder and down the valley between her breasts. When he placed his open mouth over the hollow of her throat where her pulse was thundering and sucked hard, there was nothing soft about the moan that she gave.

His hunger spiked again, and he unfastened the button and zipper on her jeans and just stripped them down her legs, along with the little bikini panties he'd bought for her. He ran his fingers between her thighs, sliding them through her slit. Damn, he loved the feel of her slippery flesh and the heat of it. Pinching her clit, he drew a cry of need from her that echoed his own feelings.

*Slow. Take it slow. Don't rush this.*

But it had been so long since they'd been together, since he'd been able to touch her like this, that his control was all but shredded. Lifting her by the waist, he placed her on the bed, knelt before her with her legs on his shoulders, and licked the full length of her slit.

"Ohhhhh." The cry slid from her mouth on a puff

of air, the sound making him even hotter.

He did it again, then spread her lush, pink lips and plunged his tongue inside her.

*Jesus!*

She tasted even better than he remembered if that was possible. He slipped his tongue in and out, a rhythm both new and familiar, her little cries forcing his need even higher. When she moved her hips back and forth, riding his tongue, he pinched her swollen clit, tugged on it a little, and in a flash, she exploded. Her inner walls grabbed his tongue, and her hips matched the rhythm of his thrusts. Her cries grew louder and the thrust of her hips jerkier and more forceful. He drove his tongue deep inside her, gave her clit one final pinch, and drove her over the edge.

She rode his tongue, thrusting herself at him while her liquid filled her mouth. He had barely let her recover when he stripped off his jeans, rolled on a condom, and took his place between her legs again. With his hands beneath the cheeks of her ass to lift and hold her, he drove into her with one hard thrust.

*Jesus!*

He had to close his eyes and reach for control or he would embarrass himself. She was so hot and wet and tight. And buried in her, he felt as if he'd come home after a long unhappy journey. He tried to pace himself to give her time to recover, but it appeared she was ready before he expected.

"Do it, Zak," she cried. "Fuck me. You know how."

And he did, hard and fast and deep. Again and again and again, until she wrapped her legs around his, locking her ankles at the small of his back to pull him even deeper inside her. The soft skin of her breasts against his chest was an aphrodisiac, her cries driving him higher, the walls of her cunt gripping him like a wet vise.

And then they exploded. together. He took her mouth in a hot kiss to capture her cries as he rode them both to completion.

He had no idea how long it was before he lifted his head and looked into her eyes, desperate to read what was in there. The love he used to see, the incredible need and desire, were back again, and relief swept over him. It wasn't until this moment that he understood how much he wanted this. He opened his mouth to say something, but she touched them with the tips of her fingers, smiled, and shook her head.

"You don't need to say a word," she told him. "I feel it, too."

"It never went away. It was just hiding. We're never going to lose it again."

"No, we're not." Then her lips curved in the smile that filled his heart. "We're damn sure not."

"We should move," she said at last. "Where's Keith? Did we entertain him through the closed door?"

"I sent him outside to keep an eye out for a black van that's come by a couple of times."

And just like that the fear was back.

"Zak, I—"

He shook his head. "Don't say anything, but we need to get dressed. I'll see what the situation is and then we can eat."

"Did you find out anything about those companies I wrote down?" she asked anxiously when she was all put back together. "I didn't remember much. And some of the names were only partials. Like I told you, I only got a very quick look."

"I've had people researching them. Even Reno took a crack at some of them." He shook his head. "So far all of them are fakes. Big surprise, right? But my super-techie wrote a program to see if that would help us. We're running it on one of the computers to see what we come up with."

"That doesn't sound very optimistic," she told him.

"Let's just wait and see what shows up. Nina has worked miracles before. Meanwhile, how about we get something to eat? I brought your favorite. Chinese food."

"But—"

"Then I have some homework for you. Maybe you'll spot something that will help us with our search. Okay, kitten?"

"No." The small grin she gave him made his heart turn over. "But I can be bought with sweet and sour shrimp and sesame chicken."

"Then come on." He took her hand. "Let's feed the inner man. Or woman, as it were."

Zoe was surprised that she was actually hungry, but the tempting aroma of the food was too seductive to resist. Zak insisted on making small talk while they ate, putting aside the situation they were in for just an hour. She tried to ignore his frequent check-ins via the handheld radio with Keith, who was keeping an eye on things from the den.

He had not seen the black van while he was outside, but as Zak pointed out, that didn't mean anything. It could show up at any time or it could already have gotten what it was there for. She was at least grateful that Keith acted as if nothing out of the ordinary had happened. She wondered if he had to practice the poker face he wore.

"He'll watch the security monitor and keep checking the perimeter," Zak told her after the last all clear. "Dean will be here about midnight so Keith can get some rest."

"Don't you have to take a turn?"

He smiled. "I'm the boss."

When they had put away the leftovers and cleaned up the kitchen, Zak took the laptop off the counter, set it up in front of her, and booted it up.

"What's this for?" she asked.

"Stuff. Nina downloaded everything they were able to pull off your main frame before they got shut out. I want to see what you recognize and what you could possibly resurrect. And there's also information on there they dug up about Caz Morgan and Max Detwiler." He pulled up a chair next to her. "So let's get started."

Three hours later, Zoe had a raging headache, Zak's frustration was palpable, and they weren't much further along than when they started.

"Okay." Zak poured them each a cold drink. "I think it won't take much to summarize here." He held up his hand and ticked off the items on his fingers one by one. "First. Caz and Nate met when Nate was just out of college, back here in San Antonio, and trying to hustle his way into the oil lease business. Caz had connections, Nate had the right personality, and they were off to the races."

"Second." He touched the next finger. "Caz was the one who found Max and his money when they needed an infusion of capital to swing a major real estate deal. We still don't know where Max's cash came from." He made a sound of disgust. "I think I need to take lessons from these people on how to bury information."

"And third," Zoe picked up the thread, "there's definitely something wrong with these simulations. There're changes in here I didn't make, but I can't tell you what since I don't have even one complete file."

Zak flipped a chair around and straddled it. "Tell me what the new simulations were about and how they could be adapted for commercial use."

"Okay. It's really not complicated. We—I designed simulations for corporate clients to use to practice security techniques. We tailored them to specific clients as the requests came in. We also did some hostage rescue operations sims for a huge mercenary company and even for a couple for airlines to teach their employees how to behave in a high-jacking situation. Then we'd wipe any reference to the company and anything that could indicate who the original design was for, make some modifications, and voila! A video game." She frowned again.

"What's wrong?"

"Like I said before, there are some strange adjustments here that I can't figure out." She stared at the screen, rubbing her forehead.

Zak pulled the laptop around, shut down the programs, and closed the computer. "Enough for tonight. Let's get some sleep and start fresh in the morning."

She rubbed her eyes. "I guess you're right."

When she stood up, she and Zak were so close

there wasn't room for a sheet of paper between them. Heat flashed in his eyes, and his rock-hard erection pressed against the softness of her tummy, making her breasts ache and every pulse in her body throb. She had missed this so much. More than she wanted to admit. And that hot interlude when he got here didn't go far at all to make up for lost time.

Then his head came down and his mouth was ravenous against hers, taking and giving at the same time. When her lips parted slightly, his tongue swept in, bringing liquid fire with it.

She melted, her bones fluid, her muscles limp. She clung to him, locking her arms around his neck as much to keep herself upright as to hold him tightly to her.

When he lifted his head, his breathing was uneven, but no more so than hers.

"This is impossible." He blew out a breath of frustration. "I can't believe myself. Your ass is on the line, I don't even know who's after you, and all I want to do is make love to you."

"Sounds good to me," she breathed, the combination of danger and the chemistry between them a powerful aphrodisiac.

"I can't believe I want you again so fast."

She ticked up one corner of her mouth in a half smile. "You used to want me all the time."

"Apparently, old habits never die." He sighed. "Kitten." The word was like a prayer on his lips.

One hand slid up along her rib cage and cupped her breast, his thumb chafing the nipple. Zoe heard a low moan and realized it was hers.

"We either need to stop now," he told her, "or take this into the bedroom."

"I vote the bedroom." Her voice was no steadier than his.

"Good. We have a lot of lost time to make up for."

The moment the bedroom door closed he pulled her into his arms again, showering kisses on her forehead, her cheeks, her chin, before slipping his tongue inside her mouth again. She twisted hers with his, tasting the flavor of him. When he gently bit down on hers, spikes of electricity shot through her and the pulse between her legs beat harder and faster.

She wanted him, wanted the familiar feel of his body on her, in her, driving her to an almost unreachable plane of ecstasy that she'd never been able to forget. The hot electricity was still there. What happened earlier was the appetizer. She wanted the full meal.

He walked her backward to the bed, stopping when the backs of her knees hit the mattress. When his hands released her face and he lifted his head, she reached to yank her T-shirt over her head, but his fingers encircled her wrists.

"No. Let me do it."

Slowly, he drew the soft fabric up and over her head, his eyes eating her alive as they focused on her breasts nestled in their lace cups. His hands slid up to cup her breasts, his thumbs grazing her nipples. They hardened, and she knew he could see their firm, dark tips through the sheer material. When he bent his head and ran his tongue across the top edge of her bra, a wave of weakness swept over her and she had to clutch his forearms to keep from falling.

"Your skin tastes as good as it always did," he murmured, drawing circles with the tip of his tongue.

"That taste has haunted me all this time."

Zoe drew in a deep breath, moved her hands to his waist, and tugged his shirt free of his jeans. His back was warm against her hands, taut muscles playing beneath the smooth skin. The simple contact sent heat blazing through her and ratcheted up her heartbeat. She and Zak had always had the most incredible chemistry. Now it seemed, if anything, it was stronger than ever.

Zak moved away just a fraction and slowly removed the rest of her clothes, kissing every area of her skin as he uncovered it, as if he hadn't just seen every inch of her mere hours ago. The fire and heat of his tongue were like a flame tracing paths everywhere, melting her. Grabbing the covers on the bed with one hand, he flung them back and placed her gently on the cool sheets.

He took the gun from the small of his back where he carried it, placed it on the nightstand, and began to undress. She watched as he removed his clothes, eyes capturing the familiar shape of his body, the defined muscles, the soft dusting of hair on his chest, the magnificence of his cock as it rose out from his body, ready and wanting her. How had she lived without this for so long? How had she been so stupid and hard-headed as to throw this all away?

His eyes glittered as they raked over her body, as if they were reacquainting themselves with every inch. His gaze never broke as he bent and lifted his jeans, fishing in a pocket for a small foil packet.

Zoe's eyes widened. "You planned—"

"I hoped," he interrupted. His mouth tilted in a lopsided grin. "I didn't know how long my willpower would last, and I always like to be prepared."

When his body came down on top of hers, she felt the same thing she'd sensed when she'd cried on his lap.

*Home. I'm home.*

Then all thought left her brain as his mouth began to move over her again. He placed a sucking kiss at the hollow of her throat, licking the pulse that pounded there. Lips like rough silk brushed at the swell of her breasts, closed firmly around each aching nipple, traveled a path along her tummy and lower.

His warm breath was a match to her skin, blowing across the thatch of her pubic curls. His mouth traveled lower and lower, his hands pushing her thighs wider to give him greater access. The touch of his tongue licking its way up the inside of her thighs made her inner muscles quiver and her pulse beat erratically.

Zoe hitched her hips at him, urging him to move to her center, to pay attention to her demanding sex. And then he was there, his educated tongue tasting her liquid and flicking at the throbbing, furled nub. She grabbed his head with both hands, pressing him against her, afraid he'd stop too soon.

The coil of need that had been wound tightly inside her for so long began to unwind with amazing speed, the onset of orgasm rushing through her.

When his tongue slipped inside her and his thumbs pressed on her swollen bud, the climax exploded with such force it shook her from head to toe. If Zak hadn't been holding her, she was sure it would have tossed her off the bed.

Every muscle in her body clamped and convulsed, again and again, until she couldn't breathe. But when it was over and she lay panting, his glittering gaze looking up at her from between her thighs, she knew it hadn't been enough.

"Zak…" She moaned.

"I know." His voice was hoarse and thick with desire.

Sliding up her body, he kissed her, hard, her juices still fresh on his lips. He groaned into the wet cavern of her mouth as his tongue did magical things to hers and his big hands gripped her.

Zoe couldn't get enough of touching him, her hands racing everywhere over his heated skin. The familiar shape of his shoulder, the lean muscles of his back, the taut lines of his buttocks—everything coming back to her like a well-remembered map. She wanted him inside her. Now. Right now.

When he settled himself in the cradle of her thighs, she welcomed him with a sigh. At last he slid inside her, his thick cock filling every inch of her. He eased it out slowly, dragging it against her inner flesh, then thrusting forward again. With each movement of his hips, each drive of his hard shaft into her hot, grasping sex, the need grew stronger. Wrapping her legs around him, she locked their bodies together so they moved in concert.

"Look at me," he demanded, his voice rough and low.

She opened her eyes and found him looking into hers with so much emotion her heart cracked. Her body strained to reach that elusive peak as he pounded into her again and again.

"Now," he ordered. "Come now, Zoe."

And just like that she exploded, her body shuddering with his, heart slamming against her ribs, her lungs starving for air. And then it eased and they relaxed into each other, still locked together. She knew, at least for the moment, nothing else mattered.

This was so right. It was definitely so right. If she could just convince Zak.

## Chapter Eight

The cell phone in the man's pocket rang, and he punched Talk.

"Is it done?" he asked.

"It will be in a minute," came back the answer. "We scoped the place out pretty good. Everyone's inside, no outside guards. A perimeter check every thirty minutes, which gives us a good window."

"How will you do it? I don't want you caught under any circumstances."

"Same old same old. We won't even have to get out of the van."

"Fine. Good. Call me when it's done. And there better not be any mistakes this time." He punched the End button, trying to ignore the bad sensations teasing at his body.

\*\*\*\*

A knock on the door woke them. Zak glanced at the clock on the nightstand, the red numbers reading three o'clock. Zoe's warm body was nestled against his, her rounded ass fitting nicely against his thighs. With an effort, he rolled away to face Dean in the doorway. At the sight of the gun in the man's hand, he was instantly alert.

"What?" he asked.

"Sorry to bother you like this, boss, but that van Keith told you about is back. It's parked two houses down, but no one's gotten out of it. I don't like the smell of it."

In an instant, Zak pulled on his jeans and shirt.

"What's going on?" Zoe sleepily rolled over. Spotting Dean she came instantly awake, sat up, and tugged the covers up to her shoulders. "Dean? What happened?"

Zak took a second to kiss her forehead before he picked up his gun from the nightstand.

"Get dressed," he told her. "Throw everything you can in the duffel bag, including the laptops, and wait here for me."

"What's—"

He touched a finger to her lips. "No questions. Just do as I ask, okay?"

She swallowed hard and nodded.

Zak turned to Dean. "Let's go."

Keith was watching the monitor carefully, his own gun out. A muscle twitched in his cheek. "Still no movement," he said. "Something funky is going on."

"It can't be about us," Dean said. "No one knows we're here. Or anything about this house."

"We'll know in a minute if someone's found us or not."

Three pairs of eyes were focused on the screen. As they watched, the side panel of the truck slid partially open and the vehicle began to roll along the curb. They could just make out the outline of something protruding from the space.

"Jesus," Zak breathed. "We need to get the hell out of here."

"What if they've got the back covered?" Keith asked.

"They don't," Dean assured him. "I scanned the area with the infrared. Nothing except bodies in the houses, and the count matches what we expect. If we're going, we need to do it right now. I have secondary transport waiting for us. Let's move, people, before we're history."

Zak raced for the bedroom where Zoe had just finished zipping the duffel closed. When she looked up, her eyes were wild with panic, but she was holding herself together.

"I'm ready," she told him.

"Let's go."

Scooping up his cell phone, he grabbed the duffel with one hand, her arm with the other, and raced through the house with her. Dean and Keith were waiting by the back door, holding it open. All four of them dashed through into the backyard just as a loud *thunk* echoed in the night air followed by the sound of breaking glass and an explosion.

"Grenades," Keith hollered, looking over his shoulder. "Rocket fired."

For the second time in as many nights, Zak found himself the target of flaming debris and flying objects. But this time, he couldn't worry about protecting himself because he had Zoe to think of. His fingers tightening around her wrist like a manacle, he dragged her through the yard, following Dean's racing figure.

Shots echoed behind them, and he knew it was Keith, laying down covering fire to forestall anyone who might leap out of the van and come after them. At the far corner of the yard, Dean pushed the shrubbery aside until he found a keypad, tapped it, and an invisible gate hidden by the bushes slid open.

Dean was through it before it stopped moving, Zak behind him towing Zoe with him. A dusty SUV was parked in a vacant lot between two houses, nose to the street. Dean lifted his hand, pointed a remote at the vehicle, and the locks snapped open. Zak shoved Zoe into the front seat and told her to keep down, then jumped into the back. In seconds, Keith was beside him, slamming the door shut. In less than ten more seconds, Dean had them rolling.

"Damn, damn, damn," Zak swore, yanking out his gun.

"Van's coming around the corner," Keith reported, shifting to his knees to steady his aim on the back of the seat.

Zak leaned over the back of the seat as Dean slid down the rear window. Two guns bucked as they aimed for the tires on the pursuing vehicle.

"Got 'em," Keith said with satisfaction as the van began to slew sideways, the right front tire punctured.

Zak shot twice more, getting the other tire, and one of the rear ones as the van continued to slide sideways.

"Push it," he yelled at Dean. "I don't want to give them a chance to call in reinforcements. Besides…" He looked around as lights popped on in houses around them. "The cops will be here before long, and we definitely don't need a conversation with them."

They all breathed a little easier when at last they hit the Interstate. There wasn't much traffic to get lost in at that hour, but Dean pulled off and on enough times to assure them they didn't have a tail.

"Those guys meant serious business," Keith said, putting a fresh clip in his gun. "Your average crook doesn't carry grenade launchers around with them."

Dean caught Zak's eye in the rearview mirror. "Why do you suppose they waited until now to attack?"

"I'd say they wanted to be sure everyone on the street was in bed, all the lights out, so they didn't risk being noticed."

"But we could have moved Miss Lombardo before they got back."

"You can bet they were someplace keeping an eye on the house," Zak told him. "They aren't the kind of people to leave anything to chance."

"Seeing you arrive was a bonus for them," Keith pointed out.

Zak speed dialed a number on his cell. "Reno?"

"It's got to be urgent for you to call me at three in the morning." Reno Sullivan's voice was edged with traces of sleep.

"Yeah, sorry to wake you again. I'll try not to make a habit of it, but we've had an...incident tonight." He summed up what had happened as briefly as possible. "I need a crew out there. Cops are probably all over the place by now, and the fire department, so you'll have to lie low until they finish."

"I'll get a crew on it," Reno promised. "We just need to manipulate around the crime scene tape."

"Yeah," Zak agreed. "I know. But you know we always manage to figure a way around it. Maybe the team you send can find any fragments of the grenades and see where they can lead. Also, someone needs to review the security tapes. I want to know if there's a visible license plate for the black van. Call me in an hour and let me know where things stand."

He hung up and raked his fingers through his hair. What an incredible mess. How had he slipped up? What had they done wrong?

"I'm assuming the cameras fed to the hard drive on that computer in the den?" Zoe asked him. "Wouldn't that all be destroyed in the fire?

"Probably, but we're set up so everything from the computer also feeds to the office. Someone monitors all that stuff twenty-four/seven."

"I'm impressed," she told him in a voice still shaky. "Big time stuff, Zak."

"Just part of the service, ma'am." He was doing his best to lighten the mood, without much success.

"They'll have trouble doing anything with police all over the place," Keith pointed out.

"Whoever Reno sends will figure it out. They always do. But what I want to know," he went on, "is how the hell these people found us. We covered all our tracks. We're the only ones who knew Zoe was here, and we sure didn't tell anyone. Hardly anyone even knows about this house."

"Someone at the office?" Keith asked.

"No. Not even Carol. *Especially* not Carol. Not that I wouldn't swear by everyone at Guardian anyway, but no. No chance for a leak there. And I know there wasn't a tail when you drove here this morning, Keith. I made sure I wasn't followed tonight, too."

"So did I," Dean added.

"Then how—"

"Zak?" Zoe's voice was so low he almost didn't hear it.

"Yeah, kitten? You okay?" He reached over the back of the seat and squeezed her shoulder. It seemed such an insignificant gesture to him. What he really wanted to do was yank her into the back seat and crush her in his arms. "I thought for sure I had you stashed someplace invisible. Sorry about this."

Zoe wet her lips and tried to swallow the sudden nausea rolling up from her stomach. She could hardly get the words out, knowing in advance what Zak's reaction would be.

*Idiot, idiot, idiot.*

*Well, go on. Just blurt it out and get it over with.*

"I…I think it was me."

"What was you? What are you talking about?"

She'd have given anything not to have to confess her incredible stupidity, but she knew she was the problem. Zak was truly going to kill her. "I think they found us through me."

"That's crazy. You've been with one of us every single minute."

*Just get it out fast. Spit it out.* "I—I called my mother."

The SUV lurched as Dean's foot slipped on the accelerator, then steadied again.

"Boss," Keith protested. "She never got away from me. I swear it." Then he smacked his forehead. "Of course. The damn shower. Great place to hide. Boss, I am so damn sorry."

When Zak spoke, she heard controlled fury in his tone. "Your mother? You called your mother? Please don't tell me you used the cell I gave you."

She nodded silently. He had every right to be mad. She'd be mad, too. Maybe insane with someone who was supposed to be so smart and did something so completely stupid.

Zak rubbed his hand over his face, anger radiating like flames in his body. He wished he wasn't sitting in the back behind Zoe where he couldn't see her face. "Pull off this next exit and find a place to stop for a second."

Silently, Dean did what he was told, and in seconds, Keith was in the front passenger seat and Zoe was in the back.

Zak gripped her arms tightly. "Did I tell you not to use that phone to call anyone except me?" He shook her slightly. "Did I?"

One dip of her head was all she could manage. The rage flowed from him in palpable waves. She wanted to sink through the floorboard and disappear. It wasn't as if she was unaware of the danger or the apparent intelligence of the people weaving a diabolical frame around her.

"And it didn't occur to you that both the police and the killers might have a tap on your mother's phone?" He lifted his hands from her, as if fearing what he might do and rubbed his face, his eyes avoiding hers.

Zoe's stomach twisted into a cold knot. "I got off very quickly."

All the warmth and connection from earlier in the night had disappeared. She felt as chilled as if she'd been trapped in a block of ice. She'd done an incredibly stupid thing, put not only herself, but Zak and his men as well, in jeopardy and violated his trust by doing so. There was nothing he could say that she wasn't already saying to herself.

Nobody said a word in the long silence that followed. The elephant in the room filled up the vehicle until Zoe could hardly breathe.

Finally, Zak shifted, grabbed her shoulders again and forced her to look at him. "I gave you that cell because it was clean. Unregistered. A throwaway. No one could trace the ownership and the number doesn't show up anywhere. I thought I made myself clear on that point." His hand tightened on her chin. "The only way someone could locate it would be if you called a phone they already had a trace on. Did you understand that?"

"Yes." She wanted to cry, but she refused to give in to the weakness. "I said I'm sorry. I know that isn't nearly enough, and I know I put us all in danger—"

"Yourself, Zoe," he ground out. "Forget about us. You put yourself in danger. What you did completely negates all the effort we went to in stashing you away someplace safe."

"Zak, I—"

"Cell phones can be triangulated," he went on as if she hadn't spoken. "Especially if you have one point of origin. And if people are ready and have very good equipment—which, by the way, I'm sure everyone after you does—it can take them less than a minute to get a specific address. We're just lucky the cops hadn't yet gotten a warrant to tap your mother's phone or we'd have had them on our doorstep, too." He shook his head. "Although, at this point, you might be safer with them after all."

"Zak, no," she cried. "You don't mean that. Anyway, I know all about triangulation, but I—I didn't realize they could locate the source that quickly."

She tried to look away, but he refused to let her.

"So what exactly were you thinking?" he demanded.

"I wasn't," she admitted. "I knew when I did it, I was being stupid. But Zak, my mother is so upset. She's so worried. I had to let her know I was okay."

"Listen to me. This may sound harsh, but forget your mother. She has Ivan and the rest of the Demoffs to take care of her. She'll be ten times safer than you are. You can *not* afford to worry about anyone but yourself. Do. You. Understand?"

She wrenched her head away. "Yes."

She used her own anger to cover her shame at her stupidity and the awful realization of what had happened because of it. For a smart person, she was really dumb. Zak was right. Given a choice, her mother would have preferred not to hear from her rather than have her do what she did.

"Yes, I understand. It was dumb and idiotic, and I'm a lot smarter than that. I let my emotions and my concern for my mother get the best of me. It won't happen again." She turned back to look him in the eye. "For any reason."

*And I hope you got the meaning behind that message, Zachariah Delaney. Tonight should never have happened. That's clear now.*

"Damn straight it won't." He leaned forward and tapped Dean on the shoulder. "We have work to do, but first I need to stash Zoe someplace where she'll really be out of danger. Call Marty. Tell him to get himself together ASAP, then head for the airport." He leaned back in his seat.

Zoe knew she should keep her mouth shut, but since she'd never been able to do so before, she didn't think she'd be starting any time soon.

"Where are we going?" she asked. Where could they take her now? She didn't think Guardian Security would be anxious to put another of their safe houses at risk.

Zak gave her a piercing look. "Someplace where all you'll have to worry about are cowboys and Indians."

****

They drove down a narrow road to a private airfield surrounded by a high fence. Zoe was convinced that, if someone didn't know where they were going, the facility would be impossible to find.

"Why all the secrecy?" she asked as she climbed out of the SUV. "And a location so far out of the way?"

"We need the privacy and security." His words were short, clipped. It was obvious he was still angry with her. "A lot of our clients need to come and go without eyes on them. Also, I need the same situation for some of my teams I send out on special assignments."

Yes, being part of Guardian Security had taken Zak a long way from where he'd been. Maybe even beyond what Zak expected, although his own company had been nothing to sneeze at.

A sleek black helicopter that bore the legend Guardian Security was waiting on the tarmac at the front of a private hangar. Zoe had never flown in one, and she wasn't sure she wanted to this time, especially taking off while it was still dark. However, it didn't seem she had a choice. Zak literally dragged her across the pad and handed her into the helicopter, throwing the duffel in behind her.

A broad-shouldered man in the pilot's seat with headphones on nodded at Zak. "We're cleared to go."

"Good. Give me a minute." Zak stood by the SUV talking briefly with Dean and Keith, then he climbed into the copilot's seat and shut the door. The whine of the rotors starting cut through the air, and in seconds, they began slipping off to the west, the ground falling away below them. Zoe took one look through the window at the SUV and saw it pulling away, then tried to get comfortable in her seat.

Zak turned around and shouted, "Where's the cell phone? The one you called your mother on?"

"In the duffel." She pointed behind her.

"Can you reach it?"

She nodded.

"Get it and give it to me."

She maneuvered enough to reach the bag and fish out the phone. When she handed it to Zak, he took it apart, cracked the window in his door just enough and pushed the pieces through. Well, no one would be able to trace it now, she thought, still feeling sick at what she'd done.

Trying to distract herself, she stared out the small window beside her at the lights of San Antonio getting smaller and smaller. Soon there were sparse stretches of black nothingness broken just briefly by small clusters of lights or sometimes a lone spotlight. She knew from the direction in which they'd taken off and the stretches of emptiness that they were flying over the Hill Country, a landscape of pastures, miniature mountains, and thousands of acres of hay.

She'd traveled through it plenty of times taking the famous Texas Wine Trail tour, wandering through the antique shops in the little towns, and driving past thriving cattle, sheep, and goat ranches. Each time she'd enjoyed herself, discovering new places. She didn't think she'd be doing much sightseeing now.

She'd be lucky if Zak didn't chain her up in a closet.

Nausea at what she'd done rose in her throat. The situation at Nate's and the explosion at her house should have been enough warning for her that she was way out of her league. By waking up too soon in Nate's house, she had become a liability to whoever killed Nate. They would do whatever they needed to get rid of her and leave no trace. To the police, she would be another fugitive on the run. They might shoot first and ask questions later.

Zak was right. Uncle Ivan would take care of Mama. She had to take care of herself and, at the same time, not endanger the people kind enough to help her with that.

When they got to wherever they were going, she'd knuckle down with the laptop. See if she could figure out what was going on with the simulations and go through the information on Caz and Max again. She wasn't brainless. Computer software—writing it and exploring it—was her area of expertise. Somehow, she'd find answers for Zak. Maybe she could find a way to redeem herself.

The helicopter dropped, and Zoe's stomach dipped with it. The gray light of dawn was finally spreading over the landscape, and she squinted to see what was below. They appeared to be arriving at a ranch with a low single-story house, a cluster of buildings to the left, and pasture stretching off to the horizon and the distant hills.

They landed in a clearing next to the house, and Zak was out the moment the skids touched land. A man in jeans and a denim shirt came running toward the helicopter, spoke to Zak, then reached to help Zoe step out. Bending low to avoid the rotor wash, Zak leaned in to take the duffel bag, slammed the door, and the helicopter took off.

A light breeze tickled Zoe's face, and from the barns, she could hear the faint neighing of horses and stamping of hooves. She didn't see any cattle, but they could be in a distant pasture. She wondered exactly how big an operation the ranch was and who it belonged to. Was she putting yet another person in danger?

"Let's go." Zak's voice was flat. Uninflected.

He had come up beside her, his footfalls covered by the sound of the helicopter. His fingers felt like bands of steel as he wrapped them around her upper arm and pulled her toward the house. The other man jogged ahead of them, opening the side door to let them in.

Zak led her into a small den and pointed to a chair. "Sit." He turned to the man with them. "Frank, this doesn't fall under your job description, but do you think you could put on a pot of coffee? We're sort of sleep deprived, and we still have a lot to do."

"No problem. Just give me a sec."

When the man had left the room, Zoe looked at Zak, her fists clenched. "I know you are hugely ticked off at me and with good reason, but will you at least tell me where we are?"

Zak was at the desk, booting up a computer, and answered without looking at her. "My ranch."

She was sure her jaw had dropped so much it would hit the floor. "*Your* ranch? Since when do you have a ranch?"

"Since last year," he told her, his fingers busy on the keyboard. "Can you just sit there quietly for a minute, please?"

Oh, yeah. He was well and truly pissed at her. She thought of a hundred smart answers and wisely swallowed them.

When the printer began spitting out paper, he turned to her, legs stretched out, fingers laced together over his belt buckle. "I bought the ranch last year so I'd have some place to get away from things. It had a small, thriving cattle operation, and I've expanded it some."

Zoe frowned. "Even I know ranches are expensive."

Zak gave a short laugh. "You bet. To buy and to operate. But this one was running in the black and, thanks to good people, continues to do so."

"So you bought this after the merger with Guardian?"

He nodded. "That deal has been very lucrative for everyone concerned. With the expanded staff and resources, we've been able to bid on some fat security contracts. We were lucky enough to get them. Then our Information Technology department, under the guidance of Nina the Wonderful, developed some incredible security software and we snagged some contracts for that."

"So the merger was a good thing?"

He snorted. "That's a mild way of putting it. But it's a two-edged sword. It gave me the money to buy the ranch but keeps me so busy I don't get out here nearly as much as I planned. Fortunately for you, however, it's a good place to stash you."

Zoe worked hard to keep her voice even as she attempted to apologize yet one more time. "Zak, I want to tell you again how very sorry I am for what I did. I knew it was dumb when I did it, but I guess I didn't realize just *how* dumb." She fisted her hands on her knees. "I'm not stupid. I don't know how many ways I can say this. I was concerned about my mother, and I thought I got off the phone in plenty of time."

Before Zak could say anything, Frank—whoever he was—walked in carrying a tray with two filled coffee mugs, sugar, and milk.

"I wasn't sure how you took it," he told Zoe, setting the tray on the edge of the desk closest to her.

From somewhere, she dredged up a smile. "Just black is fine, thanks."

He nodded and left the room.

"Frank's my foreman," Zak explained. "We don't have a very big operation here, and he runs it practically with his eyes closed. But he'll have them open and on you while you're here."

Zoe clenched her fists, keeping her voice as even as possible. She didn't know how long she could deal with his attitude, no matter how justified it was. It was killing her to have this lying between them. She wanted to throw herself in his arms and beg his forgiveness. But she'd been doing that in different ways since they fled the safe house and it didn't seem to cut any ice with him.

She decided to give it one more shot.

*What the hell.*

"You can't imagine how humiliated I am that I did what I did," she began. "I dragged you into this and then put everyone at risk over a stupid telephone call. I don't know what else to say."

Zak leaned forward, and when he spoke, his voice

was a little softer. "I know that. And I know how important reassuring your mother was. I think you've apologized enough for that, okay? But I'm not sure you understand that these aren't ordinary people who are after you. That's the problem. They're pretty scary, and they'll stop at nothing to get you out of the way now."

"But who are they?" she cried. "Do you know?"

"I'm checking it out, but a source of mine is pretty sure we're dealing with the Russian mob. The *mafiyah*."

Zoe stared at him. "You're kidding, right? The *mafiyah?* This is a joke."

"No joke. And your cousin Sergei might be smack in the middle of it."

"What? No. No, no, no." She shook her head. They'd been over this before, and she still didn't believe it. "The Russian mob? And you think my family is involved? That's impossible. Just because we are Russian doesn't make us crooks."

"Your uncle got you into this," he reminded her.

"That is just too farfetched. My uncle would never risk his reputation or those of his partners and associates by being involved in criminal activity. I'm his niece, for god's sake."

Zak leaned forward and took one of her hands. She cringed at the impersonality of the touch. "Zoe, people get into trouble, and they do strange things. They bend to pressure. Someone wanted access to Lombardo Simulations, and Nate Dunning was the key. For you, a simple business deal. For them, entry into a high tech company writing sophisticated programs."

She raked her hair back, tucking it behind her ears. "This is just too unbelievable. The Russian mob? I thought that was only something made up on television and in the movies. Certainly there's never been a hint of it around our family."

"Shocked me, too. I haven't heard a whisper of them operating in this area, and we hear just about everything." Zak handed her a mug. "Watch this. It's hot."

She took it with both hands, cradling it in her palms to keep from dropping it. When she sipped at it, the warmth spread through her body, steadying her flip-flopping nerves. Finally, she raised her eyes, forcing herself to meet Zak's gaze. "Have you linked them to Nate in any way?"

"Working on it," he told her. "Reno Sullivan has connections that I don't. He's digging into it for me. I hope he has some information for me today."

"I have to do something to help. I know I have to stay here," she said quickly when he opened his mouth. "But let me get back to work on the laptop. Both laptops."

"It's shut down, right?"

She nodded.

"Okay. I want you to stay out of the LI servers and work strictly from the cloud."

"Why? I know there's more I never got a chance to download."

"Because we don't know who is monitoring the system," he explained. "We don't want them to have an electronic trace back to you and your laptop. Get out now."

Her stomach knotted at his words. She'd thought by going through her own firewall she was safe, but what if whoever had monkeyed with the files had done the same with the firewall? It was obviously someone with advanced computer skills.

"Okay," she told him. "I'll take apart every file I have backed up. I know if I keep at it long enough, I can figure out what they did and why."

He nodded. "We need that. I'm sure the answer is in there somewhere, and it's a lot more than money laundering. But first, I want you to give me everything you know about Morgan and Detwiler from the moment you met them. When, how, where. Any involvement they had in your dealings with Nate." He pulled the papers from the printer tray. "Jay Browning, who's been at this all night, sent this to me."

"What did he find out?"

"We already knew Caz has a very successful investment firm. Your uncle is one of his clients, along with a real catalog of the area's top players. But if he is, in fact, in bed with or part of the Russian mob, he would always be scouting for new opportunities. Your company has something they want. They targeted Nate as the person to open the door for them."

"But what could they want?"

"The drug cartels pretty much own this city, and Jay thinks the Russians wanted in on the action. Not just drugs but the gun business, that is very lucrative for them."

"But the cartels don't just roll over for someone," Zoe pointed out. "And they have plenty of control. Neither the local police nor the DEA have been able to shake them loose. Even I know that."

"Okay." Zak glanced at the papers again. "They needed a start. Something. And as I said before, LS had something they wanted."

"But how did they zero in on Nate?" Zoe was having trouble processing all of this. Nate, a part of the Russian mob? "From everything I know, he was the only son of a very wealthy family, living the fast life, and trying to make his own fortune."

"Nate was rich and good looking, had an inflated idea of his capabilities, and he wanted to play with the big fish. From all appearances, Caz made him richer. According to this, Caz brought in Max Detwiler, who we also think is *mafiyah*. He financed a company with Nate as the nominal head and the game was on." He shrugged. "Maybe they thought there would be chemistry between the two of you, other than business, and they'd have a solid situation to do what they want."

"But we still don't know what they want." Zoe took another sip of her coffee. "Do you think Nate knew what he was getting into?"

Zak shook his head. "Not in the beginning. By the time he realized who he was in bed with, he was not only in too deep but he was too hooked on the lifestyle."

"But why me?" she asked. "We still have no idea what he wanted with Lombardo Simulations. Surely there are other technology companies they could have bought into."

Zak laid the papers on the desk, picked up his coffee, and took a swallow. She could tell he was choosing his words very carefully. "They needed someone who was eager to grow and needed a lot of financing to do it. Nate came to you highly recommended and he had a reputation, so you didn't look as closely as other people might have.

Zoe set her mug back on the desk. "You mean, I

was greedy and hungry and had stars in my eyes." She twisted her lips in a grimace. "And excited that a man of Nate Dunning's wealth and stature would be at all interested in me. That's what you really mean to say, right? I was ripe for the plucking?"

"Don't beat yourself up too much," he told her. "You aren't the first one or the only one. There are others just like you—smart, inventive, looking to the future—that became the building blocks of Dunning International. People who were sucked in the same way."

"What if I hadn't stumbled onto those reports?" she asked. "How long would this have gone on?"

"As long as they needed you. That's what you need to keep in mind."

Chills invaded her body again. "And then, when they'd gotten what they wanted, I'd have been history."

"I can't say you're wrong. On the other hand, if they thought you had no clue about anything, Nate could have offered to let you buy him out. Say he wanted to move onto some other acquisition."

"But I started asking questions before they were ready to pull out."

"And somehow that made Nate a liability, too. We need to find out why. And also what it is about LS that made it a target. Each of the companies Dunning International owns gave them a foothold in something. What did you offer them?"

She brushed her hair away from her face. "There are dozens of companies doing what I do."

"Ah, but you must have some particular creative touch that they needed. Don't worry, we'll find out what it is." He stroked her arm with his free hand. "Jay

Browning, who is unequalled in ferreting out information in cyberspace, is working on finding out what happened with the other companies Dunning bought and the people who owned them. Many of the businesses are still operating, and I want to know who's at the head."

"I can promise you Uncle Ivan had nothing to do with this. I've known him all my life. His reputation in the city—the *state*—is one of the shining stars in our family tree."

Zak nodded. "And so far I've found nothing to indicate any difference." He sat back. "So, here's the plan. The first thing on the list for you is some rest. By the time you get up, Serita, my housekeeper, will be here. She'll fix you breakfast. Eat it. Then get back to work on the computer."

"What will you be doing?"

"I'm going back to my office to pull together everything my staff has gotten so far, meet with Reno, and see what he's come up with. Then I'll start rousting out my contacts and seeing what I can find out about the Russians in the San Antonio area."

Zoe knuckled her eyes, trying to wipe away the gritty feel. "This all still feels so very unreal."

"Oh, honey, it's real. Believe me. You got sucked into something you didn't even see coming." He held up a hand when she opened her mouth, and something flashed in his eyes that hadn't been there a minute ago. "And we're done apologizing, okay? Forget yesterday and everything before it. Let's get past this and see what's going on with you and me."

Her heart stuttered. "You mean there still might be a chance for…us?"

The look he gave her was totally unreadable. Then he let out a long breath. "No matter how angry I get with you, Zoe, I can't seem to get you out of my system."

"Maybe I don't want you to."

Again he looked long and hard at her. "Right now, we're in a dangerous, high tension situation," he said at last. "We'll see what happens when this is all over and life becomes somewhat normal again. Just...no more phone calls and no more high profile deals, okay?"

She swallowed. She wanted something more definite, but at the moment, she'd take what she could get. "That is a solid promise."

"Also, my team may have traced the grenade fragments to the manufacturer by now. And finally..." He gave a half-smile. "I'm going to see if I can track illegal gun sales."

"When do you plan to get some sleep?"

"When I can fit it into my schedule. Come on. I'll show you where you'll sleep."

*Which obviously isn't going to be with him.*

Zoe followed Zak out of the room.

# Chapter Nine

After catching barely three hours of sleep, Zak had called for Marty to pick him up in the helicopter. A thermos of Frank's coffee that he drank on the flight to his office managed to wake up most of his brain cells. He'd just have to keep feeding his system more caffeine until he was running on all cylinders.

Jay and Nina were waiting for him in Carol's office when he arrived. Neither of them looked like they'd had any more sleep than he had, but they were gamely ready to give their reports and see where they needed to go next.

Keith was also with them. Zak lifted an eyebrow at that.

"Yes, I got some of the information you asked for," he told his boss. "You wanted to know if the Russians have been cutting in on cartel territory, what the cartels are doing about it. And if they aren't doing anything, why not?"

"Who's running the stuff these days, anyway?" Zak asked. Last year, his other partner, Nick Vanetta, had been instrumental in helping the feds bring down the secretive and sinister Osuna cartel. But he knew the void wouldn't be empty for long. Too many gangs in Mexico were getting into the business and expanding their operations.

Keith yawned, then covered his mouth

apologetically. "Sorry. I plan to crash for a couple of hours when we're done here."

Zak nodded. "I'm surprised you're still able to stay awake."

"Actually, two smaller operations are trying to get a foothold and expand. There's been a lot of bloody competition, and the feds, at the moment, are letting them slug it out, hoping they'll all kill each other."

"I hear you."

"Anyway, after Dean and I dropped you at the hangar, I spent some time in a couple of places where I could pick up on what's going on."

"All right. Let's go into my office, and everyone can tell me what you've got. Maybe I can rustle up some coffee."

"Already done, boss." Carol emerged from the little kitchen at the side of her office carrying a tray with filled mugs and a carafe. "Also, Mr. Sullivan said to call him as soon as you got here."

Zak looked at his watch. "Do you know what time it is? You know I don't expect you to show up this early."

She set the tray on his desk and shrugged. "We've got an emergency here. That means no clocks. Apparently, Mr. Sullivan isn't sleeping, either, so it sure wouldn't look good for us to lay around." She winked at him. "Just yell when you want more."

"Remind me to give you a raise," he told her.

"If you'll excuse me? I have a ton of calls for you I need to deal with." She looked at all of them, then back at Zak. "I hate to rain on your parade when I just gave you good news, but some of those calls are from Detective Morales. He wants to see you immediately."

"Yeah, I'll bet." Zak picked up a mug and sat down behind his desk. "Call him and tell him you expect me in an hour. That'll give us time to see where we are."

"Got it." She closed the door behind her.

Zak looked at each of his employees in turn. Despite everyone's fatigue, the air was charged with energy. "So tell me, where *are* we? Exactly?"

"Me, first," Keith said. "I can lay down some of the foundation."

Zak nodded at him to continue, leaned back in his chair and took a swallow of hot liquid.

"I'll give you the condensed version." Keith shoved his hands in his pockets and began to pace. He'd once told Zak he always thought better when he was moving. "Word on the street is the cartel is very unhappy about the Russians, but so far, they aren't doing anything about them. First of all, the drugs the Russians import come from the poppy fields of Afghanistan, not Mexico or South America, so they aren't cutting into the basic cartel product. Secondly, they're more into wholesaling than street dealing, so they actually sell in bulk to the cartels."

"Which increases their raw supply," Zak commented.

"But they're missing one thing here."

"The cartels haven't yet realized the Russians are slowly inserting themselves into their business," Jay told them. "Moving into the void left when the Osunas were arrested. Encroaching on their territory."

"Right," Keith agreed. "So we don't have the beginnings of a war. Yet."

"Then what *are* they into besides drugs?" Nina wanted to know.

Keith stopped pacing in front of the desk, held up one hand, and began counting off on his fingers. "Prostitution. Smuggling girls into and out of the country for the white slave trade The old protection racket. Buying and selling arms. Stuff like that."

"But San Antonio's not exactly the hub of the world," she protested. "I should imagine they'd be pretty isolated here."

"Not at all," Keith said. "We're only ninety miles from the Gulf and we have an international airport that's getting more and more traffic every day. Easy in and out. And possibly a less conspicuous place for them to smuggle their compatriots into this country rather than New York where everyone's on high alert."

Jay pulled a single sheet of paper from his jeans pocket and unfolded it.

"That's all you've got?" Zak couldn't hide his skepticism.

"No, but I didn't think you wanted an encyclopedia up here. What I have is a good summary of their so-called legit businesses—night clubs, high-end restaurants, linen services, finance companies, small private banks—"

"And from what I've heard," Zak interrupted, "the people who borrow from them never get out from under."

"That's right," Jay agreed. "They lend to people and businesses who can't get financing any place else, and the interest rate is so high it never gets paid off."

"Then, if I'm figuring this right, every so-called legitimate enterprise became a subsidiary of Dunning International," Zak finished off. "Right?"

"Right," Jay agreed.

Zak idly fiddled with a pen. "Did your research happen to show you how many of the original owners of companies that became part of DI are still running those companies?"

Jay got a funny look on his face. "How did you know about that?"

"About what?" Zak dropped the pen and narrowed his eyes at Jay. "Am I right about most of them being gone?"

Jay nodded. "Nate Dunning—or whoever was pulling his strings—has replaced almost all of the original owners with people he's chosen."

"I asked because I have a sick feeling that's what they planned to do with Zoe. But what do they want with Lombardo Simulations in the first place? That's the biggie here. They don't buy companies just to increase them as legitimate operations. I'll bet if we looked hard enough, every component of DI has something else going on that's being covered up."

"There are a lot of things you can do with simulations that don't bear scrutiny," Nina told him. "Things the government wouldn't be too happy about. You said Zoe confronted Nate on financial statements that made no sense, right? Suppliers and customers she'd never even heard of. And Nate tried to blow it off."

"That's right. She said—"

A knock at the door was followed by Carol's immediate entrance. "Sorry," she breathed, closing the door behind her. "Zak, you need to turn on the television set to Channel Five. And the lobby guard just called. Detective Morales is on his way up."

Zak picked up the television remote from his desk

and punched the On button, then quickly flipped to Channel Five. The screen was filled with the image of a burning building, one that Zak was very familiar with. A sick feeling traveled over him.

"It seems we have yet another chapter in the current saga of San Antonio businesswoman Zoraya Lombardo," the reporter at the site was saying. "Those of you who have been following the story for the last forty-eight hours will remember she's the young woman accused of killing billionaire Nate Dunning, CEO of Dunning International."

The man looked over his shoulder, then turned to face the camera again. "Slightly more than an hour ago, the fire department answered an alarm to this location, the home of Lombardo Simulations, the company the suspect owns. I've been told part of the building was used for the technology division, the other for warehousing merchandise for shipment. Lombardo was at the forefront of high-end computer games, with customers all over the world."

The disconnected voice of the studio anchor came over the air. "Ross, does anyone know what caused the fire? The building seems to be built of pretty solid adobe."

"The arson inspector can't do a complete investigation until the fire chief gives the okay, but those on the scene are saying the building was wired with explosives. Probably on a timed charge."

"Have the police commented on this?" the anchor asked.

"In a manner of speaking. This is the second fire associated with Zoraya Lombardo in twenty-four hours. The last one destroyed her home. Police think she's doing her best to destroy evidence of whatever she and Dunning were doing before she finds a way to disappear completely."

"Shit!" Zak smacked the flat of his hand on his desk.

"You know they did it to get rid of the computers and any hard copies of whatever they were doing," Jay told him.

"Yeah, it figures. They got into the computer system and wiped out the files, but they needed to destroy the hard drives, just in case. And there were cartons of CDs in the warehouse area. They couldn't just drive up and get them without arousing suspicion. Not with Zoe's name all over the news."

Zak picked up his phone and buzzed Reno's office. "Did you see the news?"

"Unfortunately," his partner said. "Things don't look too good for our client, do they?"

"Listen, Reno, she's not—"

"You don't have to say it," Reno interrupted. "If she was really guilty, I know you wouldn't be ass-deep in this."

"Who can we get to in the fire department," he asked. "Quietly."

"It would have to be very quietly," Reno told him. "But I've got some contacts I can reach out to. Not a problem."

"I'd appreciate it. I'd really like to know what they find out about the explosives used to torch the Lombardo building. Like if they were the same kind used at Zoe's house."

"I'll see what I can dig up."

"Thanks." He paused a moment. "For everything."

"I told you before, no problem. That's what we do for each other."

"One more thing," Zak said. "Joe Morales is on his way up to see me. I tried to hold him off, but he's like a bulldog."

"Joe's good people," Reno pointed out. "He's just doing his job. If you need help, have Carol come and get me."

"Thanks again."

His Intercom sounded, and he hit the button for it.

Carol's voice floated into the room. "Detective Morales is here, and he says if I don't open the door in five seconds, he's going through it." Her laugh was forced and polite. "Right, Detective?"

"Give him his five seconds and send him in." He looked at the three people in front of him. "Keep digging on the Russians. Call me when you get something. I don't care how small it is. I have to know who's pulling the strings. Use the back door out of here. Move now. I don't need Morales to see you and ask more questions than he already has."

The door to the rear hallway had barely closed before Joe Morales bulled his way in and planted himself in front of Zak's desk. "I'm through screwing around, Delaney." Anger blazed in his eyes and every line in his face was deepened. "I want the truth from you. Right now."

"Nice to see you, too, Detective." Zak gestured at one of the chairs. "Won't you have a seat?"

"No, thanks. I'm just fine."

Zak gritted his teeth. "I said sit down. If you want answers from me, you won't get them looming over my desk."

Morales cursed under his breath but backed up and dropped into a chair. "All right. I'm sitting. I want to know where Zoraya Lombardo is, and I want to know right now."

****

Zoe's plan had been to crash as long as possible and wake up rested before getting back to work. As long as possible turned out to be less than four hours. Anxiety and the urgency of the situation had intruded on her, making her restless.

The room Zak had put her in was decorated in soft blues and cream, with a large window overlooking the barns and the corral. This morning there were horses loping in the sunshine, and a dog, a blue heeler, watching them from just outside the fence. Beyond that, she saw five ranch hands saddled and riding out of the barn, heading toward the north end of the property. This was what people imagined when they thought of Texas. Any other time, she would have enjoyed the pastoral nature of the scene.

She showered in the adjoining bathroom, put on fresh jeans and a T-shirt, then pulled her hair back into a neat pony tail. The fragrant aroma of cinnamon drew her to the kitchen.

A woman in jeans and a peasant blouse lifted a tray of sweet rolls from the oven. She was definitely middle-aged, her dark hair streaked with gray and pulled up in a clip. Close to five-foot-eight, slender but muscular, she moved with a lithe, easy grace.

She turned her head at the sound of Zoe's footsteps and a warm smile lit up her face.

"Good morning." Her voice had a musical quality to it. "You must be Miss Lombardo. I am Serita."

Somehow, Zoe had imagined Zak's housekeeper would be a woman in her sixties, short and round, with a big smile and a steady stream of conversation. The age was about the only thing she'd gotten right.

"You're awake," the woman went on. "I thought you would be sleeping much later. *Señor* Delaney left me a note not to wake you and to feed you well when you arose."

"Call me Zoe, please. And I don't think sleep is much of an option right now. But those rolls would tempt the devil."

"Sit." Serita waved a hand at the table. "*Señor* Delaney said you have much work today, but you must stoke the furnace first."

The cinnamon rolls literally melted in her mouth, and the coffee had a slight hint of spice to it that Zoe couldn't identify but which tasted delicious. When she'd eaten and drunk her fill, she had to admit she felt measurably better. Her brain even seemed to be working again.

"*Señor* Delaney said you would be working in the den." Serita cleared the empty dishes from the table. "I'll being you a carafe and a mug and let you know when lunch is ready. You can take a break or eat at the desk. *Señor* Delaney does that a lot when he's on a deadline for something."

"Thank you. You're very, very kind."

"*De nada. Señor* Delaney is a prince to work for."

A prince, Zoe thought as she headed for the den. Once he'd been *her* prince, and she'd thrown him away. Now, she'd not only angered him but she was sure she'd disappointed him, too. She'd come to him begging for his help, and at the first opportunity, she'd done the very thing she shouldn't do. She could only pray there were no more repercussions from her stupidity.

Her assignment now, according to Zak, was to take apart the simulations. He had his people working on attempting to open and retrieve files and information, but she was the sim expert. He was convinced they were doing something with them, and he wanted her to find out what.

Booting up the laptop, she opened one simulation after another and immediately hit a wall. Her frustration level grew as she was able to take each one only so far, then was locked out. When she had a problem checking the first simulation file, she thought she might have entered the information incorrectly in her haste to check it. But after fifteen minutes, nothing was as she'd thought. She wasn't just locked out of opening the other files. They had done something to the simulation files. Cracked her password and changed the coding.

What was going on here? She'd password protected them, changing that password frequently, as she did the password for the cloud. But damn! She hadn't thought to recheck all the files before she stored them the last time. They had reworked her programs? What the hell?

Rage swept through her, so hot and vicious that if Nate Dunning was alive and standing before her she really *would* kill him. She took a deep breath, let it out, pushed away from the desk, and began pacing. Zak was right. As usual. She'd been nothing but a means to an end for these people, whoever they were.

Somehow, she'd have to fix this problem with the codes if she hoped to eventually get back in business again. She seemed to be piling problems on top of problems.

Finally, she closed down everything she was using and went back to a DOS screen—Disk Operating System—the place she always started with when she wrote her programs. If she couldn't crack the rest of the sims open to find out what had been done with them, she'd start all over again, rewriting the code, and analyze each step as she went along.

By the time early afternoon rolled around, she had finished recreating one sim and was pulling up the codes on one of the ones Nina copied to the laptop Zak had brought to see where changes had been made. Again, she got only so far, but this time, something caught her eye, so she began to rewrite others from memory.

Taking a break from the intense dynamics of programming, she opened a word processing program and began to write down everything she could recall about how she'd met Caz Morgan and Max Detwiler. Any time they'd been together with her and Nate. And strangers who made her particularly uncomfortable. She actually remembered more than she thought she would. Then she went back to the programming.

Serita brought her lunch on a tray, which she ate without even paying attention to what it was. Then she went back to the simulations. By late afternoon, she had a glimmer of what had happened, but her eyes were blurring and her hands ached. She stood up from the desk and stretched.

She hadn't heard from Zak all day. Would he ever speak to her again except as necessary? Despite the fact that just last night he'd said they could look at the future when this was over, would the thing between them that had begun to bloom again be over, too? She tried to swallow the sob that lodged in her throat. Just when she'd realized she'd never stopped loving him, it seemed she'd managed to screw up things between them in royal style once again.

Serita knocked and came in to retrieve the tray and bring her a glass of iced tea.

"Has Zak… Has Mr. Delaney called the ranch today?"

Serita nodded. "Just now. He said to let you know the pilot will be bringing him for dinner and asked me to prepare something. He usually likes my enchiladas with rice and beans and Mexican slaw. Would that do for you?"

"At this particular moment, I'm grateful he didn't ask you to feed me hemlock."

Serita looked shocked. "Oh, *Señor* Delaney would never do such a thing."

Zoe smiled weakly. "Just a little gallows humor. Anything will be fine. Please fix whatever you know he likes."

"I told him you'd been in here all day working. He suggested you take a break and go outside for a while. There's a swing on the back porch if you want to sit. Or two of the hands are working new cutting horses in the corral. You might enjoy watching that."

"Thank you." Zoe picked up the glass and took a long swallow. The cool liquid felt good on her throat. "Maybe I'll do that."

\*\*\*\*

"Where is she?" Morales repeated, his tone a blend of anger, frustration, and discomfort. It was obvious from the stiffness of his posture he didn't want to be there. "No more fancy dancing, Zak. I want Zoraya Lombardo. You've got five minutes to produce her."

"That would be rather impossible." Voice calm and even. "Even if I knew where she was, five minutes wouldn't be nearly enough time. I can assure you she isn't in this building. Ask any of the guards or other employees."

Morales made a rude noise. "Listen, give me some credit for brains here. I know you wouldn't be stupid enough to bring her here."

*If that's what he thinks, maybe that's what I should have done.*

"Then exactly where do you think I have her, Joe?"

The man shrugged. "Hard to say. But Guardian Security keeps enough places where you stash clients that we could be looking until next year and never find her."

"Then perhaps you ought to get started." Zak's words were edged with sarcasm.

"Don't make me do things the hard way. Please. The woman is in more trouble than you want to deal with." He sighed and spread his hands out in an almost pleading gesture. "You've got a fat company and a top reputation. Don't throw them all away for some harebrained female."

"Harebrained."

"She'd have to be to shoot a man like Nate Dunning and think she could get away with it. Not to mention burning down her house and company"

Zak mentally gritted his teeth. He was tired and holding onto his patience with a thin thread.

"Just out of curiosity, what proof do you have that

she actually killed Dunning?"

"Enough." Morales shifted uncomfortably in his chair. "Anyway, I don't have to tell you anything."

"You do if you want me to produce her."

"Ha." Morales lunged out of the chair he'd dropped into. "I knew it. You *do* know where she is."

Zak held up his hands. "I didn't say that. I just said no one—not me or anyone else—is going to hand her over unless you have concrete proof that she's guilty. Everyone's trying to close the lid on this as soon as possible, and she's an easy mark."

"Listen, Delaney." Joe's face was turning red. "You may be a big hotshot, but you're out of your league here. Lombardo's guilty, and I'm going to get her, with or without your help."

"Just out of curiosity," Zak said, meeting Morales's glare head on, "if she's so guilty, who blew up her building this morning? And her house the other day?"

"One thing has nothing to do with the other."

"Oh, I think it definitely does," Zak argued. "A smart cop would think maybe someone was trying to get rid of *her*, too."

"A smart cop? Are you trying to tell me I'm stupid?"

Running on very little sleep, Zak had to struggle to hold onto his patience, but antagonizing Morales wouldn't help the situation. "Not at all. I'm just saying, wouldn't you wonder if she's a target, too?"

"For your information, the brass are convinced she did it to cover her tracks and disappear." He sat down again. "Zak, this is a real hot mess. You can't imagine the pressure we're getting to close this case. Be a good guy and help us out here."

"By turning over an innocent woman so you can crucify her?"

"And by the way, speaking of explosions," Joe demanded, "what were your men doing sniffing around the house that burned down on Estrella Street early this morning?"

"Probably looking into something for a client. We do have real clients, you know."

Morales looked apoplectic, his face redder than a ripe tomato.

"You have a good relationship with the SAPD," he reminded Zak. "Don't screw it up over this. There's too much high-level testosterone floating around here. Wherever Zoraya Lombardo is, get her and bring her down to headquarters. That's the best advice I can give you."

*When pigs fly.*

"I'll take it under consideration."

Zak stared at the door after Morales left, knowing he was on a short leash, aware that he would have to be the one to solve this thing because the cops thought they already had the right person identified.

He closed his eyes, and images of Zoe in bed with him danced across his brain. It hadn't been like it was before. No, indeed. It had been much, much better. As if in the intervening months they'd learned to value each other more. To understand what it took to make a relationship work.

Then she'd gone and pulled that stupid stunt with the cell phone, endangering everyone and everything. Was he mistaken? Was she just as impetuous and bullheaded as the night they'd had their famous blowup? He was so angry with her for doing that he couldn't think straight. A dangerous situation to be in with everything that was on the line.

He'd told her when this was over they'd see how things stood between them, but his practical brain told him he already knew. Being with her would be like holding a live grenade, always waiting for it to explode. And the thought made him very sad.

He'd get her off the hook and make sure she was in a position to start over again with her company, if that was what she wanted. And when he walked away this time, it would have to be for good. He couldn't handle the pain of another breakup. The problem was, what did he do with his heart, which over and above everything, was completely owned by her?

Then he thought about what Nick Vanetta had done last year, helping his friend Quinn, whose now wife Kate had been in big trouble. A woman who had also done some stupid things. But Quinn had never wavered in his feelings for her.

Zak also realized he'd been right in thinking Zoe was disposable to the Russians from the beginning. They'd kept her around as long as they needed her, and she was about to be toast. When Nate Dunning also became disposable, for whatever reason, they figured to kill two birds with one stone.

Zak thought about what his life would be like again without Zoe in it. It wasn't a good feeling. She'd apologized ten times over for what she'd done and certainly understood the insanity of it. He could even understand how overriding her concern for her mother was. Maybe he shouldn't be quite so hasty to toss her out of his life. They'd both made mistakes. Who was he to be so judgmental about a woman he had to admit he was hopelessly in love with?

He was still staring into space when Carol buzzed him to say Buddy Delahaye needed to see him. Buddy had led the team that checked out the fires and the explosion at the safe house.

"Okay." Zak shook himself out of his mental meanderings. "Send him in."

Buddy Delahaye was a laconic man who seldom showed emotion about anything. It was what allowed him to do the job he did. But Zak could see the controlled excitement on his face and in his eyes.

"Find something?" he asked.

Buddy nodded. "I was checking in the lab," he began before he even sat down, "and thought I'd bring this stuff up to you myself."

Guardian Security had a forensics lab that was the envy of many police departments.

"What have you got?" Zak sat down behind his desk again.

Buddy dropped two sheets of a lab report on the surface in front of him. "We almost got caught sneaking around the house on Estrella."

"I know," Zak interrupted him. "I had a visit from Joe Morales this morning who wanted to know what business we had there. I put him off with double talk."

"Did he say anything about the Lombardo fire? I took two of the guys, and we put on San Antonio Fire Department turnout gear. It was such chaos and confusion there, no one paid much attention to us."

"Do I want to know where you got the gear?" Zak asked.

One corner of Buddy's mouth hitched. "You know what they say. Don't ask, don't tell."

"I thought so. Did you at least get anything?"

Buddy nodded. "After we finished at the simulations place we went by Zoe's house and took some samples there. The lab pinpointed everything pretty fast."

Zak picked up the report and looked at it. "Russian-made grenades from a Russian-made missile launcher. Russian-made explosives." He lowered the paper. "They can tell that just from the small fragments you got?"

Keith grinned. "With everything in that lab downstairs, they could identify things from a piece no bigger than a toothpick. Get the chemical components, zip it through the data bases, and there it is."

"I guess we don't have to wonder anymore if the Russians are really involved in this." Zak's neck was itching again, and he wished he could pin down the source. He had a feeling it was right in front of his eyes if only he could see it. "What I need to know now is exactly what triggered the whole thing. There's something about the information Zoe stumbled over that holds the secret, and we can't seem to catch a break finding out what it is."

"I'd say we could try and track down who bought this stuff, but honestly, Zak." Buddy pointed at the report. "I think that's a lost cause. Russians don't exactly go into the local weapons store and buy this stuff on a credit card."

"Okay. Go find an empty room and catch some sleep. I've got people digging into Morgan's and Detwiler's lives again to see if we can get a handle on anything. So far it's a lost cause." He exhaled a long breath. "And I have the feeling we're running out of time."

Buddy had barely left before Carol buzzed to tell him Ivan Demoff was back, and this time he had Zoe's mother with him. In a day that turned out to be both interminably long and far too short, it was a tossup whether the low point was his confrontation with Joe Morales or his meeting with Demoff and Zoe's mother. The half hour he spent with them tested every ounce of Zak's patience.

Irina Lombardo was small and petite, like Zoe, and Zak could see right away she was as much a fireball.

"I want to know where my daughter is," she demanded. Her careful makeup couldn't hide the ravages of fear and concern on her face made her look even older than she was.

"Give the man a chance to at least say hello," Demoff told her in a steady voice. He looked at Zak. "I'm sorry, but she insisted I bring her here."

"No problem." Zak drew in a calming breath. It wouldn't do to piss off Zoe's mother. "Have a seat, "Mrs. Lombardo. Please."

"I'll sit when I know where my daughter is and that she's safe."

"We are all terribly concerned," Demoff said, "as I'm sure has been evident. I'm sure you're aware of my position in this city. If Zoraya could be convinced to turn herself in to me, I can make sure she doesn't spend one minute in jail and I will personally hire the best defense attorney for her."

"You might think you're in a position to make promises, but with all the attention on this case and the pressure, I doubt you could deliver." He indicated the client chairs. "Sit, please. Both of you."

Irina sat gingerly, refused the coffee Carol brought in, and clasped her hands tightly in her lap. "Ivan says you know where she is but won't tell him." She leaned forward. "We're *family*, Zak. You know that. You and my Zoraya were together for two years. Please, have her come home."

Zak looked at Ivan, standing like a tall block of granite behind his sister's chair. "You think this is a nice thing to do? Drag your sister down here to plead your case for you when she's already upset enough? Would Zoe be happy with that?"

"Zoe would be happy if you let her come home," Ivan said, his tone of voice carefully uninflected.

"I'm begging you," Irina said, dabbing at the tears that leaked from her eyes. "I need to have my daughter where I'm sure she's safe."

Zak stood up and came around his desk, crouched in front of Irina, and took her hands in his. "If Zoe thought she'd be safe at home, she'd be there. But I'm certain both the police and the people who actually killed Nate Dunning are watching your house. If she came home, she'd be right in the line of fire."

"So you *do* know where she is," Demoff exploded. "I thought so from the beginning. And you're keeping her from us. I tell you, I can pull strings for her."

Zak shook his head. "I'm just giving you a scenario, but it's common sense. Zoe is a very bright woman. She can take care of herself. She also knows her presence in your house could bring danger to you."

Irina lifted her tear-stained face and looked at him. "I—I never thought of that. Of any of those things." She stuffed her handkerchief back into her purse and stood up. "Zak is right, Ivan. It would be unsafe for

Zoraya to be with us." She turned to Zak. "Are you at least trying to find out the truth so she can come out of wherever she's hiding?"

He stood also. "Of course. Right now, it's my top priority. I promise you, I'll clear her name."

Irina turned to her brother. "Come, Ivan. Let us go home. It was a mistake to let me talk you into this."

Demoff was anything but happy about the turn of events. Zak thought the man might have a stroke on the spot, but he simply nodded and guided his sister from the office.

By now, Zak's head was pounding. He swallowed three aspirin with the dregs of his coffee and asked Carol to get him a sandwich from the deli on the ground floor. Finally, he called the ranch, not trusting himself to speak to Zoe, just getting a report from Serita and telling her he'd be there for dinner.

Seeing Zoe tonight would be a real test for him. Dining with her in the intimacy of the place where he could be just...Zak. Sleeping under the same roof. And managing to keep his distance.

But he was convinced, at this point, she held the secret to everything somewhere in her head. He needed to help her find it, get this done without putting her in danger again, and walk away. Just...walk away.

But would that be possible?

## Chapter Ten

Zoe propped one foot on the bottom rail of the fence around the corral, braced her elbow on the top rail, and sucked the last of the iced tea from her glass. In the lingering heat and sunshine of the day, two of the ranch hands were working a pair of cutting horses, teaching them to "cut" calves from a herd. She was fascinated by the way the horses responded to almost invisible signals.

It was such a nice change from the tension of the past two days when all she'd been able to think about was staying alive and finding out who had done this to her. She could almost, standing there in the middle of the Hill Country, pretend that none of it had happened. That tomorrow she'd go to her office and nothing would have changed.

The night she met Nate Dunning had changed her life in more ways than one. Her first impression of him, when she'd met him and Uncle Ivan at the restaurant for dinner, was of enormous power and electricity. His thick, dark hair had just enough of an artfully rumpled look to take the edge off the too-smooth appearance. His eyes were such a vivid blue they reminded her of a cerulean sea. And he had, of all things, a dimple that winked whenever he flashed his trademark smile.

In his expensively cut suit that fit his tall, muscular body like a caress, he looked like every woman's dream.

During dinner, he'd deferred to her when ordering the wine, rather than showboating his knowledge. He kept the conversation low key, telling her about himself as if he was a neighbor meeting her for the first time, downplaying the meteoric success of Dunning International, and instead, questioning her at length about Lombardo Simulations.

She floated home on a cloud, wrapped in a sense of euphoria that lasted through the signing of the contracts, the first infusion of capital, the boost in sales of the newly-designed games. Even Max and Caz had been deferential, lauding her business success in a male-dominated field.

The parties had taken her into a world she hadn't previously known. International businessmen mixed with minor royalty against a glittering background of high-dollar mansions and women with enough jewels to support a small country. It was a world she never in her dreams thought to become a part of, and she was swept along in the glamour of it all.

What an idiot she had been, falling for the line they handed her. No wonder Nate asked so many questions. He was looking to make sure she could provide him with what he wanted. Whatever that was, which she still hadn't discovered, although by now she had an inkling. If he just wanted to sell a lot of computer games overseas, even unique ones like she designed, he could have bought them from her and handled everything himself.

If only she had listened to Zak instead of letting her temper get the best of her. Her resentment at what she saw as interference and even, possibly, jealousy. God, she'd been so blonde.

Deliberately, she pushed the thoughts from her mind and focused again on the horses and their trainers.

"Beautiful thing to watch, isn't it?"

She hadn't heard Frank come up to the corral until he was suddenly beside her.

"Yes," she agreed. "The communication between horse and rider is like poetry."

Frank adjusted the brim of his hat. "These men have been doing this for a long time. They're two of the best."

"Zak said he bought the ranch a year ago. Did he hire you then?"

Frank chuckled. "Actually, I've been here at Arrowhead Ranch for almost thirty years. Started out as a wrangler. The man who inherited the ranch from his father decided last year he wanted to get out of ranching. Zak was here for a barbecue, the subject came up, and I think he bought it on an impulse."

"That's quite an impulsive action," Zoe pointed out.

"Yeah, but he's smart for an absentee owner. He made it worth my while to stay here and keep the hands we had. I run the ranch, and he gets to put up his feet when he comes out here. His contribution is handling the finances."

Zoe gazed past the corral to the open pastures. "He said you run a cattle operation here, but I don't see any of them."

He pushed his hat back on his head. "We're not a big operation. Zak wants to keep it that way, which is good. We've got about a thousand head of cattle we just moved up in the hills to the summer pastures. We move them around so no area gets overgrazed. The horses are all workers."

Zoe blinked. "A thousand head? That seems like a lot to me."

"Just enough to keep us in beans and show a profit," Frank joked. He turned his head and studied her. "I'm glad to finally meet the woman who's had Zak Delaney tied in knots."

Zoe was stunned. "You're kidding, right?"

"No, ma'am. Serita and me kept asking him why he didn't bring any women to the ranch, was he ashamed of us or something. Then he had a little too much bourbon one night and blurted out the woman he wanted had blown him off. That must have been some fight the two of you had."

"He was as much at fault as I was," Zoe told him defensively. "Did he tell you that?"

"He did. But it's burned at him ever since."

"Does... Does he ever bring a woman here at all?" God, she hated herself for asking the question. For even caring.

"Not a one. This is the place where he hides from the world. I think he's always hoped you and he would get back together again."

Before she could form a remark to his statement, they heard a droning sound coming from the east, a black speck appeared in the sky and in what seemed like seconds the black Guardian Security helicopter was overhead, the *whap, whap, whap* of the rotors cutting the air. It set down in the same space they'd landed last night, the side door popped open, and Zak leaped to the ground. He waved at the pilot, who lifted off immediately.

Then Zak was striding toward the corral where Zoe and Frank stood, and all she could think of was how very weary he looked. Was that worry lining his face? Was his concern for her merely that of one person for another or was this thing growing again between them real? Was she the only one who had hopes of them getting back together?

She closed her eyes and imagined the two of them—she and Zak—living on this ranch, enjoying the life, raising a family here. Zak had his obligations with Guardian, but she could actually work from anywhere. Be flexible according to his schedule.

That is, if he wanted it. And according to what Frank had just said, that was highly possible. She just had to figure out how to make it work. Get him to fully trust her again, to trust the fact that she loved him.

Oh, how she wanted to erase all the doubts and reservations she was sure he still wrestled with. This back and forth, high and low, was making her an emotional wreck.

Serita's dinner was delicious, but Zoe knew she didn't do it justice. She was too busy trying to analyze Zak's attitude, keep a low profile, and figure out how to get back in his good graces.

Frank ate with them, which eased the tension. He and Zak discussed breeding records, feed formulas, and the projected condition of the winter pastures. She wasn't sure how much longer she could keep herself from peppering Zak with questions. But eventually the meal ended and reality couldn't be ignored.

"Excellent meal, Serita," Zak complimented her. "But you didn't have to stay and serve it. Frank and I could have handled it."

"And I'm perfectly capable of serving food and clearing a table," Zoe put in acerbically.

Zak turned his gaze to her, his eyes carefully masked. "Yes, I believe you are." He rose from the table. "Serita, go home. We'll finish up here. I think I could use a glass of wine. Zoe, how about you?"

"Yes, thank you. I'd love one."

"I'll help Serita finish up so she can get out of here fast," Frank said. "Y'all go on and take care of business."

Zoe followed Zak into the den where he pulled a bottle of a Texas merlot from a cabinet and poured the ruby liquid into two goblets.

"Sit," he told her, indicating the big recliner. He took the chair behind the desk. "I have some things to report to you. Then I'd like to hear about what, if anything, you figured out today."

Giving her no indication if the news was good, bad, or useless, he pulled out the lower drawer of the desk and propped his foot on it. Although he'd changed clothes since yesterday, he was still dressed in ranch wear—a chambray shirt, twill pants, and the same boots.

Zoe thought how natural he looked, in the clothing and in these surroundings, and remembered suddenly he'd grown up on a ranch. One his parents had sold a number of years ago when they decided to move to Arizona.

She curled up in the chair, tucking her legs beneath her, and sipped at the rich liquid, never taking her eyes from Zak. Did he feel the sexual tension lying so thick in the room, or was she the only one who sensed it? And was that old familiar look in his eyes again signaling a possible change in his attitude, or was it just wishful thinking on her part?

The silence was almost palpable when he finally broke it. "Okay. Here's what we found out today."

He gave her a rundown on what they'd learned about the explosives, the grenades, and the gestation of Dunning International. He kept his sentences short and clipped, making sure she understood the significance of each fact.

Zoe rubbed her forehead. "It's just so hard to accept the fact that Russians are behind all of this. Right here in San Antonio. It's bad enough that we've always had the drug cartels here, but this..." She waved her hand in the air. "This is like something out of a movie."

Zak took a swallow of his wine and set the glass down. Dropping his foot from its propped position, he leaned forward toward Zoe. "There's one more thing I have to tell you. It won't make you very happy, but just remember, things are only things. They can be replaced."

Her heart tripped over itself as anxiety gripped her. She clutched her wine goblet. "What are you talking about? What else happened?"

"Someone set a sophisticated charge today and blew Lombardo Simulations into a pile of rubble."

"What?" Her head spun, her vision blurring, and a loud buzzing hummed in her ears. Her company? Someone had blown up her company? "But... But why? I don't understand?"

"I'm sure it was to destroy whatever was in the warehouse section. The district attorney was begging for warrants, and before the end of the day, someone would have been there looking around. Confiscating everything."

"Looking for what?" She was bewildered.

"Evidence of illegal activities. Anything suspicious at all. And the bad guys couldn't take that chance."

"They'd gotten into my computer system and wiped out all the files and programs," she reminded him.

"Yes, but they couldn't afford to have the police confiscate whatever merchandise was back there. And maybe they didn't want to take any chances that the cops could still retrieve something from the hard drives."

"But what could they find?" she asked again. "There was nothing in the warehouse except cartons of computer games waiting to be shipped."

"Are you sure?" She felt his eyes boring through her. "What about the simulations you write that are the basis of the games?"

Zoe shook her head. "We don't keep those on CDs. As soon as the program is finished, I run it for the client, then give it to him on a flash drive. He—or she—takes it back and runs it with whoever needs to see it and test it. When they're satisfied, I rewrite the program so it's just a simple game, encrypt the original, and save it to the cloud. I used to use thumb drives, but they are too easy to steal. I use two different cloud accounts."

"And you have them password protected."

"Of course." Zoe blinked. "Do you think I'm crazy? I can't have that stuff falling into the wrong hands. My clients would destroy me."

"What about hard copies that you might work from

or use in any way? Notes that you make."

"Yes. I use notebooks so I can always go back to the original source of my coding."

"Where are they?"

"In a safe at my house." She clapped her hand over her mouth, jerking and almost spilling her wine. "Oh my god, Zak. My house. The night that Nate was killed, all I could think of was getting away somewhere, hiding, finding someone to help me. You. Even when you told me about the bomb or whatever at the house, I was so glad you weren't hurt I didn't think about anything else."

Zak fished a cell phone out of his pocket. "Don't panic yet. Where's the safe?"

"In my den. Which probably doesn't exist anymore. There's a panel in the built-in bookshelves. If you press it in a certain place, it slides open, and there's the safe."

"If we're lucky, everything in the room was blown to smithereens. I'd rather have those notebooks destroyed than in the wrong hands." He started to press numbers, stopped, and smacked his forehead. "How dumb am I? I didn't even think of this before. I thought the bomb was just rigged as a trap for you."

"What are you talking about?"

"I don't want to freak you out any more than you already are, but there's another possibility here. That explosion could have been set to destroy the safe and its contents."

Zoe sucked in her breath. "They already tried to find them. They broke in looking for them. For anything I might have taken home."

"Exactly." He picked up a pen and began toying

with it. Zoe had her nervous habits, he had his. "They would have had to disable your security system, but for people like this, that wouldn't be a big problem. But they couldn't find what they were looking for, so they decided to destroy both you and the evidence. Boom! Everything gone."

"Oh, god. Who wants me dead so badly?" Serita's delicious dinner threatened to rise back up in her throat. She swallowed hard. Lifting her glass to her lips, she had to use two hands because she was shaking so badly.

"That's what we're trying to find out." He pressed a speed-dial number, then held up one finger while he waited for the call to be answered. "Buddy? I know, I know. I did say you could have the night to yourself, but I really need you to get your team and do something for me right away." He explained about the safe, where it was located, and what to look for. "There shouldn't be anyone around there now. The police and fire department have already tramped over the scene. But be careful. I don't know who might still be watching the place. Call me when it's done."

He snapped the phone shut and placed it on the desk.

"Did you notice anyone when you were there?" Zoe asked. "Someone strange? Anything at all?"

"No, and I was pretty careful about approaching the house. When the house blew, I had two objectives. Number one, not to get blown up with it. Secondly, to get the hell out of there before the police showed up and I had to explain myself. I didn't exactly want to answer questions about you, remember?"

Swallowing the last of her wine in one gulp, she set the glass on the table next to the chair and twisted her fingers together, an old nervous habit she'd found herself doing more and more lately. "Yes, yes, yes. Of course I remember."

She had visions of what would have happened with those notebooks in the hands of the Russians. A good programmer could decipher her notes and recreate her codes. Maybe they'd try to sell them or steal the programs. Or...

"Zoe? Zoraya, listen to me." Zak's voice barely penetrated her fog.

"Oh god." It was all she could say as the full impact of the incident hit her.

Strong fingers circled her wrists and forced her to be still. A hand cupped her chin, tilting her face up. Zak's whiskey-colored eyes had darkened to a rich chocolate. His face was taut with strain.

"Hear what I'm saying. I have people on their way to check what's left of your house right now," he told her. "I think it's highly unlikely that anyone has those notebooks. If the police had them, Detective Joe Morales wouldn't be letting me out of his sight until he found you. If the Russians had them, there'd be other activity suddenly popping up, and Keith has his ear to the ground listening hard. He's good working the streets. So is Jay Browning, who researches those things for me."

"But what if someone managed to get them? Went back after the police left and searched in the rubble?" Another desperate thought flashed across her mind. "What if they already stole them, and the explosion was actually set to cover it up?"

"No, I think I was right the first time."

"Zak, I have to let my clients know. I have to—"

"Do nothing until we hear back from Keith." His voice was firm. "I mean it, Zoe. And you certainly can't go calling your clients. The cops are just waiting for you to make another phone call. To anyone they can tie to you. Believe me."

"You're right, you're right. Of course I can't call anyone." She couldn't stop shaking.

Zak lifted her from the chair, sat down, and settled her on his lap, holding her against his chest. Zoe inhaled his scent, wishing she could stay like this forever.

Zak gritted his teeth and willed his body to behave itself. While danger still nipped at their heels, they couldn't begin to sort out their relationship. And he wanted to be absolutely sure of his own feelings before tackling the situation between them. Last night, he hadn't been able to resist the intimacy with her. The chemistry was still there, only stronger. But worst of all, he was still in love with her.

Did she feel the same way? Was it just the situation that intensified the chemistry, or was the feeling still there for real? He told himself to have control, be the one with discipline, yet here he was, cradling her against his body, feeling himself sinking right back into their incredible connection again.

When he found himself pressing his lips to the silk of her hair and tightening his hold on her, he mentally shook himself. Sighing, he stood up and set her back down in the chair. "Let me get you some more wine. Then you can tell me what, if anything, you figured out this afternoon on your laptop."

When he handed her the filled goblet, he was happy to see she was more in control of herself. The wine should put a little color back in her face. She took two swallows, then let out a long, slow breath.

"Listen." She was steadier now. This was no time to fall apart. "There's something funny with the sims. I said that before. Remember?"

He nodded. "Did you figure out what it was?"

"Not exactly. What I did was rewrite a couple of the simpler programs from memory and then try to compare the codes line by line for variations."

"And?"

"I found the place where the strings of code change, but I can't figure out what they were changed to. Nothing pops up. Someone's definitely been monkeying with my programs. And not to convert them to games, either."

She uncurled herself from the chair and went to stand by the small window that looked out over the barns. The sun had set and the pale crescent of moon was working its way up in the sky. The moonlight played on her hair and made her skin so translucent. He had to stop himself from ripping her clothes off and dragging her to bed. That wasn't going to fix anything except his raging hard-on and the ache in his balls.

"I did a lot of thinking today, too," she told him. "Writing down everything I could think of that had to do with Nate and Caz and Max." She turned to look at Zak, back behind the desk, looking at her with watchful eyes. "I analyzed it the way I do a program before I start writing it. Too bad I didn't have sense enough to do that two years ago."

"And what startling realization did you come to?" Had she actually come face to face with the truth of the situation? She'd already told him he was right, she should have listened to him. But did she really mean it, or had she just been playing him to get him to help her?

*Stop it! Decide if you want to prove a point or get through this and see if you and she have a future together.*

She looked at a spot on the wall as she told him what she'd written down that afternoon, the memories she'd pulled out of her mind. Her impressions in the beginning of the men involved and how they actually appeared to her now, with everything stripped away.

"They were just so smooth," she told him, rubbing her arms. "I was so flattered that a man like Nate Dunning wanted to invest in my business that I didn't stop to ask myself why. And Caz and Max, well, they just couldn't praise me enough, these two movers and shakers in the state." She gave a bitter laugh. "When Nate pretended to have second thoughts—and I know now it was all a sham, to throw me off my guard—Caz played his role of advisor to the hilt. Told him what a great investment it would be. How much money could be made in technology. With Max chiming in on the chorus."

Her body language told him clearly how difficult it was for her to tell him this, to admit she was taken in.

"I kept telling myself how lucky I was that Uncle Ivan and Sergei had steered them to me. Now I wonder if they were part of the setup, too." She pressed her fingers to her temples. "I didn't want to believe my family would do this to me. I *still* don't want to believe it. If it's true, I want to see proof."

"Let's hope we find some before things get any worse."

He waited, but all she said was, "I was stupid and

naïve, and now I'm paying for it."

She walked back to where her wine glass was and picked it up. Her hands were steadier as she lifted the goblet to her lips. Zak wanted nothing more than to take the goblet out of her hands and press his mouth to hers, to taste her flavor, comfort her, tell her no matter what, he'd take care of her.

*Careful, careful.*

While he was still debating the wisdom of that action, his cell phone chirped. He grabbed it almost desperately and flipped it open. "Yeah?"

"It's Buddy. The guys and I are here. Well, actually driving away."

"Did you find anything?"

"Yes and no."

"Damn it. Which is it, Buddy?" Zak tried to hold in his impatience. "Yes or no?"

"The study was blown all to hell, and there wasn't much left of the wall in the study. We found what was left of the safe under a pile of debris."

"And? Was it open? Did it look like anyone had been at it?" Zak had to bite back his impatience.

"Boss, I'm telling you, no one could find anything there. We only got lucky because we knew exactly what to look for. The explosion blasted everything to hell, including the safe."

Zak let out the breath he didn't even know he'd been holding. "Anyone see you?"

"You're kidding, right?"

"Okay. Thanks. Go back home and get some rest."

Zak put the phone back on the desk and looked up at Zoe, who had come to stand directly in front of him. The look in her eyes was equal parts of anxiety and fear.

"Did they find it?" she demanded, her voice not quite steady. "Had someone already gotten there first?"

"You can relax. At least on that point. Those must have been some huge charges they set. And I'm guessing as soon as the one went off, it set off the others. The explosion blew apart the wall in the den and the safe with it. Your notebooks are burnt trash. Maybe you won't have them but neither will anyone else."

She dropped like a lead weight into the big chair. Relief washed over her face. "At least I don't have to worry about them being in the wrong hands."

"You know, I've been doing a little rethinking since the other night."

She sat up straight, her body taut as a clothesline. "You don't want to help me anymore? I mean, I certainly couldn't blame you. It's a big mess and more than you thought, and—"

He held up a hand. "Stop. Don't put words in my mouth. I'm not saying that at all."

The tension in her body eased visibly. "Then what?"

"I was so sure money laundering was behind all this. I still think it's part of the picture, but now I'm convinced there's something more insidious going on."

A tiny vertical line appeared between her eyebrows as she pinched them together. "But what? If Nate wanted to pirate the games, he wouldn't even need to run it through our company. He could just have copies made somewhere and sell them himself."

"No." Zak shook his head and took a swallow of wine. "That's where the money laundering part comes in. He needs to show legitimate sources of income. But there's more here, and I need more information to move forward."

She rubbed her temples again, and her shoulders drooped with fatigue.

Zak finished his wine and stood up, taking her hand and tugging her from the chair. "I think we've all had enough for today. Right now, what we need is some rest."

Zoe curled her fingers into his palm. Zak gave her hand a reassuring squeeze, then released it as casually as he could. He saw the hurt look on her face and again had to fight the temptation to yank her into his arms and wrap her up close to him.

*Get through this first. Just get this all behind you. Then make sure you know how you feel.*

But he knew. He didn't need to wait. Except for their lives to stabilize again. Swallowing a sigh, he ushered her out of the den and down the hallway.

At the doorway to her room, he stopped. "Everything okay? The accommodations good?"

"Fine. Thank you." Her voice sounded as tired as she looked.

"If you need anything, just yell. Serita comes in early in the morning, and she can get whatever you want."

"I have everything. No problem." She was twisting her fingers again. "What happens tomorrow, Zak? I can't just stay hiding out on the ranch forever, although it's certainly a great place to do that. One of these days I have to get on with my life." She shrugged. "Such as it is."

"Tomorrow I go back to square one. Go over all the information we've gathered. Dig into the activities of Lombardo Simulations. Talk to some people." He scratched his head. "I know I'm missing something, but I can't quite land on it. Anyway, go back to what you were doing today, and I'll call you around noon. Okay?"

"Yes. Fine. Well, goodnight, then."

Zoe watched him walk away and disappear into his room, swallowing her disappointment that he hadn't asked her to come with him. Two nights ago she'd been sure she and Zak were getting back on track, recapturing what they'd had, only this time even better. Then she'd made that stupid phone call, and everything had changed.

She wanted to bang her head against the wall. One more time she hadn't listened, hadn't done what she should have. She hadn't even imagined what the consequences would be. The safe house had been blown up, people had nearly been killed, the target on her back got bigger, and everything had changed between her and Zak.

And of course, he'd been right about her mother. Uncle Ivan had things well in hand. Whether or not he was a part of what was going on, he still made sure his sister was taken care of.

Well, she'd apologized and apologized, to the point where it was becoming old. It was up to Zak if *he* wanted to trust *her* again on a personal level.

Tears burned behind her eyelids.

And that was another thing. She wasn't a crier, but she'd done more crying over the last three days than she had in the past three years. Throwing herself face down on the bed, she let them flow, wishing they could wash away the pain in her heart.

## Chapter Eleven

Zak was up early in the morning. Serita had not yet arrived, and he didn't feel like making coffee himself, so he did without. Carol would have it waiting at the office anyway. On his way out of the house, he paused at Zoe's door, thought about knocking, told himself it was early and to leave well enough alone, and headed outside. While he waited for the helicopter, he made some calls to the office to set up a meeting. On the ride into the city, he ran everything through his head, trying to make sense of things and figure out what had set this whole series of circumstances in action.

At the office, the situation wasn't much better. The first thing he saw on his desk was a copy of the newspaper with Zoe's picture prominently displayed above the fold. The major headline read "Have you Seen This Woman?"

Beneath that was a message telling people to call police immediately if they spotted her and the number of a tip line that had been set up.

"Great." Zak dropped the paper back onto his desk. "Just friggin' great."

Carol was right behind him with coffee and a pastry. "I don't know if you took time for anything before you left the ranch, but you'll need all your energy today."

The back of his neck started itching like crazy.

This didn't sound good. "What's happening besides this disaster in the newspaper?"

She gave him a look that he could only call pitying. "Ivan Demoff left several messages before I even got here. He's on his way and says he absolutely must see you. He insists he has the clout to help find Zoe and make things go away for her before she gets killed. He'll wait as long as he has to."

"Good luck to that," Zak muttered.

"Detective Morales called and says he's also on his way over." She gave a soft laugh. "Shall I put them in a client room together?"

"Oh, yeah. That'll be just great. Put Ivan in one of the small client rooms and see that he has plenty of food and drink. Tell him I'll get to him as soon as I can. Morales won't wait, and I don't want the two of them to catch sight of each other."

Guardian Security clients were often paranoid about their privacy, not wanting to run into others when they came to meet with one of the partners. To accommodate them, Reno and Nick had designed and furnished half a dozen rooms with comfortable chairs and couches, television sets, even a computer if they needed one. The object was to put them at ease as much as possible and keep them that way while they were waiting.

Today, Zak was afraid comfort wasn't a word that would apply to either of the men about to show up. And just when he least needed them around.

"I'll take care of it," Carol assured him.

"Thanks. I need to meet with some of the staff first, though, so you'll have to guard the door until we're done."

"I can do that," she assured him, "but you'd better make it snappy."

"What else?"

"A gentleman from Homeland Security wants to see you. This morning, if possible, and even if it isn't possible. What shall I tell him?"

"Homeland Security? What in hell for?"

Carol held up her hands in a gesture of helplessness. "He didn't say anything except that it has to do with Miss Lombardo."

"Oh, isn't that just great." He thumped his fist on the desk. "What could she possibly have done that they'd want to know about her?"

"I don't know, but if I were you, I'd find out in a hurry."

"All right, all right. Schedule him for after lunch, if you can make that work. Use your famous charm on him. Hold everyone else off. I need to have that meeting."

As soon as the door closed, Zak dialed the extensions for Keith, Dean, Nina, and Jay, told them he was in and to drop whatever they were doing and get themselves up to his office right now. In less than ten minutes, everyone was assembled, all showing signs of the stress they were under as the case on Zoe lurched forward.

"We should have had this meeting yesterday," Zak began, "but I foolishly kept hoping the police would find another suspect and get off of Zoe. Since that doesn't seem to be happening, we have some time to make up for. How are we doing with the things I called in about?"

"I'll go first," Jay said before anyone else could

jump in. He opened the folder he was carrying. "I sent all this to your terminal, but I brought hard copy for everyone." He handed out sheets of paper.

"What have we got?" Zak asked.

"The guest list for not just the party the night Nate was killed, but for the last five."

"And where exactly did you get these?" Zak wanted to know.

"Larry Blake came through for us. It took him a little while. People aren't very chatty about the Russians."

Zak's smile had no humor in it. "I'm sure not. So what did he get for you?"

"The name of the valet service. I thought at first Dunning International might actually own its own service, but I couldn't find one so I had to wait for Larry. This one's owned by a Russian immigrant—"

"Hold it," Zak interrupted. "Did you say Russian immigrant?"

"Uh huh. And they were only too happy to give him these lists."

Zak lifted an eyebrow. "Happy? Why do I think I'm missing something here? I can't imagine they'd be happy to give up anything?"

"It seems, for them, nobody's scarier than the big bad Immigrations and Customs Enforcement Agency. You mention ICE and people literally freeze. They don't want deportation to the Motherland. Somehow, they got the idea that Larry and his partner were from ICE."

"Surely they wouldn't impersonate federal officers," Zak joked.

Jay laughed. "Surely not. I told Larry hardly

anybody is scarier than the Russians. ICE must have some real badasses in their ranks."

"So it seems. What happened?"

"Larry leaned on the so-called owner, and he nearly wet his pants. Came unglued in seconds. Told him some big shot who was funding small businesses helped him get here and gave him money to start this business. Want to know who the friend is?"

"Caz Morgan," Zak guessed.

"Shucks, boss, you spoiled my big surprise."

"Sorry. But did he actually say Morgan was part of the *mafiyah?*"

"The car service owner thought I already knew or he wouldn't have spilled his guts in an unholy mixture of English and Russian. Anyway, a few ominous hints here and there and he was more than anxious to produce whatever we wanted. They get the lists because they have to check people in when they arrive. They also man the gate, so people get checked twice. No crashers at a Dunning party." He chuckled. "Larry says they all look like defrocked Russian KGB."

"Is anyone noticing the same thing I am?" Nina asked, her gaze running down the sheets of paper.

"You mean the recurrence of people from a number of Third World countries that DI isn't known for doing business with?" Jay said. "And Middle Eastern countries on the United States watch list?"

"Uh huh. They've had representatives at all the events we have lists for."

Zak frowned. "Something's off here. If Nate was pirating the Lombardo computer games, these aren't the countries he'd be selling them to."

"Here's another goodie for you," Jay continued.

"Larry showed them Miss Lombardo's picture, and they definitely remember parking her car."

Zak leaned forward, trying to control his excitement. This could be good or bad. "They recognized her?"

"Uh huh." Jay referred to his notes. "She's been at most of the functions so they remember her face. One of the valets time stamps each car as it arrives—Dunning's orders, although I think most likely Caz set it up to keep track of people—and when she arrived at eight o'clock, she gave them her car to park." He grinned. "Just like she always did."

"Hot damn." Zak looked at him. "Why didn't they tell this stuff to the cops? Or haven't the police gotten there yet?"

"Oh, yeah. The cops. They were there. Within the first twenty-four hours. But these people are more scared of Morgan than the cops. Only ICE carries more weight than Caz Morgan and the *mafiyah*."

"You better hope this guy doesn't run to Caz with news about his visitor," Zak warned him.

"Believe me, that last thing he wants is for Caz Morgan or anyone in his family to find out he's been talking to an Immigration agent."

"All right, then. Dean." He turned to look at the man next to Jay. "You want to take on the chore of finding out the flight plans for the last few trips Nate Dunning took in his personal jet? And we need the information yesterday."

"Sure." Dean nodded. "You want to know if he flew anywhere in these countries, right?"

"Give that man a cookie. DI usually concentrates their international business in Europe, certain South

American countries, and the Far East. I want to know any place he's been that's not on his usual itinerary."

"Can't we hack into someone's computer setup and find out?" he asked.

Zak gave him just a ghost of a smile. "Why, Dean. I'm surprised you'd suggest such a thing." He shook his head. "We're already into Dunning's files too deep. You need to grease someone's palm for this, and be sure it's someone who can keep his mouth shut."

"Got it. I'll get on it right away."

As he rose from his chair, Zak reached into a drawer, pulled out a cell phone, and tossed it to him.

"Disposable," Zak told him. "Tell Carol to call supplies and have them give you half a dozen more. And I'll need some for everyone else. These people triangulated on Zoe's phone by locking onto one number. Who knows what kind of sophisticated equipment they've got. I'm not taking any chances. We'll change these every couple of hours."

"I'll send someone up with a boxful before I leave." Dean opened the rear door, closing it softly behind him.

Zak turned back to Jay. "Keep digging for whatever information you can get on the major players. I don't care how small the item is. Whatever you get, I want it."

Jay nodded, then he, too, was gone.

"What about me?" Nina asked. "What's next on my list?"

"Zoe's still trying to figure out what kind of computer code was used to manipulate her simulations and why. If all someone's doing is pirating programs, they don't need to monkey with the code. You still have the files you pulled before everything got wiped?"

"Yes, but don't you think the person who wrote these programs could do a better job than I could?" she asked, her skepticism showing.

"I think you are an unbeatable expert at this kind of stuff, no matter how good Zoe is, and sometimes a fresh pair of eyes can spot something."

"Shall I call her and tell her what I'm doing? See if she wants some feedback?"

"No." Zak knew he was biting off a big chunk of trouble here, but he wanted Zoe to focus without interruption. And without her ideas bleeding into Nina's and muddying the waters. "Let's see what we get first."

"On my way." She gathered her papers and headed for the rear office door.

"So I guess that leaves just you and me." Keith shifted in his chair.

"I want you out on the street with your ear to the ground, asking the right questions."

"About what?"

"Who gets Nate's shares of Dunning International? Who'll be running the company? Stuff like that."

Keith frowned. "I appreciate the fact you think I can even find out secrets from the White House, but wouldn't this be more along the lines of something you can do?"

"Actually, no." Zak began flipping his pen back and forth. "I don't want the visibility. Besides, no one's going to talk to me. This has to be done under the table."

"That's me. The under the table man."

"Besides," Zak pointed out, "I might be tagged. The cops and the Russians probably have people with eyes on everything I do, which is why I have to make so many switches when I go to the ranch. The cops will be keeping too close an eye on me. I can play games with the helicopter and sneak around, but anything else I do is just too risky."

Keith exhaled slowly and scratched his head. "Okay. This may cost some bucks."

"Have Carol sign a voucher for you, fill in the amount, and take it to accounting. Tell George to take it out of the safety stash. I don't want a check you'd have to cash at the bank. No footprints here."

"On my way."

"And Keith?"

"Yeah?"

Zak tossed him the last phone from the drawer. "Press one to call me. Don't use this for anything else, and don't call me from any other phone."

"You think the cops are tapping you?" His eyes widened.

"No. I think the Russians might be."

As soon as the office was empty, he called Larry Blake.

"I know you're just back from an assignment and due some rest. And I can't tell you how much I appreciate your little operation with the valet service, but I need one more thing from you."

"Sleep is highly overrated, anyway," Larry joked. "What's on the menu?"

"Wherever you can find it, however you dig it up, I want to know everyone Dunning's had a personal or private visit with in the past six months. Also Morgan and Detwiler. And I need it—"

"I know, I know. Yesterday. I'm on it."

He'd barely hung up when his Intercom buzzer sounded, startling him. He pressed the Speaker button. "Yes, Carol?"

"The explosion you heard was one of your clients being escorted to a meeting room."

Demoff was here.

"And Detective Morales says he's coming in right now whether you want him to or not."

"Tell Joe it's always a pleasure to see him and send him right in."

He had barely finished speaking before Joe Morales opened the door from Carol's office. Stress had carved deep lines in his face, and he looked unbearably tired. He didn't need Zak's invitation to sit down, dropping into the closest chair and pinching the bridge of his nose.

"Okay, I give up," he said at last. "I want a truce."

"What are you talking about?"

Morales raised his face and stared at Zak with bloodshot eyes. "First of all, my lieutenant doesn't know I'm here. If he did, he'd cut me off at the knees."

Zak studied the man. "Then exactly why *are* you here? What do you want?"

"We've known each other a long time, Zak. I've watched you grow your company from nothing to a major player in the security game. I was at the announcement party when you merged with Guardian. You've never cut corners, always played straight with everyone while still protecting your clients and their interests."

"That's a nice testimonial, Joe, but I still want to know what you want."

"This morning, while I was driving to work, it hit

me. You wouldn't be playing a shell game with Zoraya Lombardo, hiding her wherever you've got her, doing whatever it is you're doing for her, if you didn't truly believe in her innocence."

Zak stared at him. "Wow! Color me shocked."

"Don't be a smartass. That's as much of an apology as you're going to get. I want to know what you know that we don't. And see if we can pool our information."

"For one thing, I didn't automatically assume she was guilty and shut my mind to other possibilities. I—"

"You've been around long enough," Morales interrupted. "This thing was a political shit storm from the minute we got the call. Nate Dunning has plenty of money and plenty of clout. He supports political campaigns and charitable causes. If you ask these people, he's practically a saint."

Zak fisted his hands. "Oh, yeah, Saint Nathan."

"I'm not kidding. Everyone from the governor on down wanted it wrapped up and tucked away before breakfast. Nobody was supposed to sleep until we got it taken care of." One corner of his mouth turned up. "We didn't count on you."

Zak pressed the Intercom. "Carol? Bring Detective Morales some refreshments while I take care of the *client* that's waiting." He looked at Morales. "This will only take me a minute. If you're serious, we can do each other some good."

\*\*\*\*

An unusually subdued Ivan Demoff sat in one of the large arm chairs in a client room, drinking coffee and nibbling on a sweet roll. He looked up when Zak entered the room, and Zak tried not to show his shock at the strain on the older man's face. Ivan looked as if he'd aged ten years in twenty-four hours.

"Sorry to keep you waiting." He closed the door and sat down near the man. "What can I do for you, Ivan?"

"I have come to offer whatever help you need from me for Zoraya." He sighed. "I'm sure you know my position in the community, Mr. Delaney. Whatever resources I have are yours, if it will help."

Zak studied the man, his posture, the lines that had deepened on his face. He almost—*almost*—believed the man's sincerity. If he wasn't such a suspicious bastard, he'd probably be all in. But he'd gotten where he was by never trusting anyone, except those closest to him

"I appreciate the offer, but I'll tell you again, Ivan. Wherever Zoe is, she isn't with me."

Ivan looked at him with sad eyes. "The police have been to my office three times today. They are camped out at my sister's house. And they are getting impossible to reason with."

"Somebody's put the fix in," Zak told him.

"I would hate to believe that, but I do not know what else to think." He studied Zak for a long moment. "You have no idea what's going on here, young man. The repercussions. Like a pond with ripples that keep reaching out farther and farther. There are bad people after her, Mr. Delaney. Very bad people. They would like nothing better than to hurt me and my family. Zoraya is a key member of that family. It's up to me to protect her and everyone else."

Zak lounged back in the chair, crossed one leg over the other, resting an ankle on the opposite knee. "I assume you're referring to the Russian *mafiyah*, the organization everyone avoids mentioning. Had Nate Dunning been involved with them? And if he was, why did you introduce him to Zoe?"

"I have spent years distancing myself from any contact with these people. I like to think I'm smart enough to avoid any traps they might set for me. But this one was very well camouflaged. Nate Dunning's family have been clients of my firm for a long time. No way did I think he was mixed up in something this nasty."

"I think we both know Zoraya is no murderer. That someone set her up. Why? And what did Nate do that got him killed?"

"I wish I had those answers."

"If you really want to help, then find them. Get me the information. Maybe we can get her out of this situation."

"I know I could have done this on the phone, but I always think things like this are better discussed in person. And perhaps I could persuade you to share with me whatever you know about this. We could combine our resources." Demoff pushed himself from the chair and held out his hand. "Let's keep in touch. I'll keep my ear to the ground if you do the same."

"Count on it," Zak told him.

The man walked from the office, and Zak wondered just how much of what Demoff said was the truth. He was either a man caught in a trap or the world's biggest bullshit artist. Zoe's life could well depend on which one it was.

## Chapter Twelve

Zoe had hoped to see Zak before he left in the morning, but even though she was out of bed by seven, he was long gone. Frank was in the kitchen filling a thermos when she wandered in there, looking for some sign of Zak's presence.

"He had the helicopter pick him up at six, Miss Lombardo. Said he needed to get an early start."

"Please call me Zoe." She found a glass in the cupboard and poured some orange juice from the refrigerator. "Did he say anything before he left? I mean, about what was happening?"

"No, ma'am. He sure didn't. I know he made a bunch of calls on his cell while waiting for Marty to get here. That's all I know."

"Is... Did he... Do you think he'll be home for dinner again?"

Frank's smile was so kindly she wanted to cry. "I'm sure he will unless he gets caught up in something. He's got good people working for him that he can leave in charge of things."

"Well, then." She dredged up an answering smile from somewhere. "I think I'll get back to the computer."

"Serita will be here in a few minutes, so you can count on her forcing food on you."

Zoe gave him a half-smile. "I'll be a blimp if I stay

here too long."

Frank's gaze appraised her. "Not meaning any offense, but I think you've got a long way to go before approaching blimphood."

Zoe felt herself blushing as she carried her juice to the den and booted up the laptop.

She was missing something, and she just didn't know what. It felt like the answer was sitting at the back of her mind, waiting for her to knock it loose, but the harder she tried, the more difficult it got.

Today she started again with the very first simulation she'd written after Nate came on board. She had gone over it so many times she'd didn't think she'd ever forget the strings of code. Yesterday's efforts hadn't produced anything, but maybe if she looked at each strand from a different angle and compared it with the ones pulled off the Lombardo simulation computers, she might figure out what she was missing.

Her problem, she decided after the first hour, was that she was too distracted by thoughts of Zak. She had no idea how to bridge the gulf that had opened up between them again. Last night, although he'd been completely circumspect and neutral, she'd seen a flash of feeling in his eyes. Then he'd tamped it down and the moment was gone.

Once she solved the problem with the programs, once she was out of this hellhole of a predicament she'd fallen into, her major project would be to restore Zak's faith in her. And hopefully revive the love they'd shared.

She heard Serita moving around in the kitchen. Not that she was hungry, but a bite of food could clear her head. And maybe Serita could give her a clue to the riddle that was Zak Delaney.

****

Zak and Morales had been at it for two hours when they finally took a break. The detective had been as good as his word, sharing what he had with Zak, which admittedly was very little. Once the police had received the tip about Zoe, they hadn't bothered to look at anyone else.

"No one wanted to poke around in Nate Dunning's life," he told Zak. "Too many people owe him favors. And those same people don't want the world to know they're connected to him if there's something that proves he wasn't what he appeared on the surface. You have no idea the pressure we're under to close this and make it go away."

"She's innocent," Zak told him in a flat voice. "I have proof."

Morales's ears perked up. "Yeah? What kind of evidence? And where did you get it?"

"You want to know what I've got, or you want to play twenty questions?"

"Okay, okay, okay. Let's have it."

So Zak told him about the rohypnol, the nitrate test, everything.

"Why didn't you come to me with all this? Why didn't you tell me about it when I came to your house?"

Zak made a rude noise. "You're kidding, right? All you wanted was to put a noose around Zoe's neck. You wouldn't have listened to a thing I said. And even right now, you don't have anything to go on except hearsay. You're not in a very good trading position."

"I'll give you that. That's why I'm here. So what do we do now?" Morales asked. "I know you've got her stashed. You can't hide her forever. My boss wants her, and truthfully, Zak, I don't want to turn her over to him. It's like you said. They want the easiest solution, and she's it."

"We need to figure out who really wanted Nate Dunning dead," Zak told him. "I'd say it's the same people who blew up her house and her business, wouldn't you?"

"I guess I have to agree. Do you have anything on Dunning himself? We've been told hands off as far as prying into either his business or personal life."

"Well," Zak said, smiling, "fortunately, I don't work for the police, nor do I have to play the political game. I've had my people digging up everything they could find. Let me tell you how Dunning International came into being, and two men who played a major role in Nate's life."

Morales listened while Zak gave him chapter and verse on Caz Morgan and Max Detwiler, along with his suspicions about the people on the party guest lists.

"That could be why some guy from Homeland Security was locked up with my lieutenant and the chief this morning."

"Yeah? Well, he's coming here this afternoon. Want to hang around? Maybe he can answer some of the questions I can't."

Morales's eyes widened. "You want me to sit in on your meeting with this guy?"

Zak gave him a humorless grin. "Better than letting you go back to your office and get squeezed by the brass."

Carol brought sandwiches and soft drinks in the middle of the afternoon, and Zak and Morales were in the act of eating when the phone on Zak's desk rang.

"Delaney."

"I didn't use the Intercom," Carol told him, "because I wasn't sure if you'd put me on speaker and I'm not sure you want to broadcast everything to your guest."

"Good thought. What's up?"

"I have Jay on one line for you and Larry Blake on the other. Who do you want first?"

"Give me Larry and tell Jay to hold on." He waited until he heard his agent's voice. "Got something already?"

"It was easier than I thought, once I figured out who to ask. Dunning's list of visitors is pretty innocuous. At the top of the list are Morgan and Detwiler. Most of the others come from the big parties he throws and an unbelievable succession of women. The guy must drink testosterone."

"So nothing there," Zak guessed.

"Not at the house. But Caz Morgan has a ranch south of San Antonio, one that he doesn't invite his usual friends to visit. I asked Jay to pull up what he could on it. I hope that was okay."

"Whatever will get us the answers we need."

"It's a huge spread, and the house is set about a mile in from the road. Nice and private. And I guess he needs it."

"Why?"

"Because Morgan's visitors include people whose faces are on the national watch list. In some cases, the international list." Larry's voice hardened. "People from countries we're not even supposed to talk about, let alone meet with their representatives."

A sick feeling grew in the pit of Zak's stomach. "You're kidding, right?"

"I wish I was. Want me to keep digging?"

"Yeah. Get as many names as you can, then call Jay on a secure line and feed them to him. Tell him to pull up profiles on every one of them."

"Consider it done."

As soon as he disconnected Larry, Carol switched him over to Jay.

"I may have something for you." Jay Browning's voice was edged with controlled excitement. "Want me to send it to your computer or bring it up?"

"Both. I may have questions."

"Okay. See you in two."

Zak had barely finished explaining things to Joe when the door to the office opened and Jay slipped in, a sheaf of papers in his hand. He looked at Morales and frowned.

"It's okay," Zak assured him. "We've got a new team player."

"You're the boss." He took the chair next to Morales. "I've got the Demoff profiles for you, but either they're very good at hiding things or they're just pawns in the game Detwiler and Morgan are playing."

"What did you find?"

"Sergei is fourth generation. Studied law at Columbia like his father did and went right into the firm. Likes women and gambling, but both in moderation. They handle all the business for Dunning International, but DI is only one of about two hundred clients." He cleared his throat. "But Sergei belongs to a private club, and guess who he hangs out with?"

"Caz Morgan and Max Detwiler?"

Jay nodded. "And some other Russian characters. Here are their names." He handed the list to Zak. "I'm running profiles on them right now. This is all connected, boss. I'm just starting to pull the threads together."

"Let's see what happens when Keith and Nina report on their assignments. And Larry's working on this same project. In fact, you should be getting some information from him to look into pretty quick."

"Okay. I'm back to it."

"What was the call you got before Browning showed up?" Morales asked.

Zak watch the blood drain from the detective's normally ruddy face when he summarized Larry's report for him about Morgan's visitors whose names were on the watch list.

"Holy crap. What was Dunning doing with these people?"

"My guess? Something that involved Lombardo Simulations. And definitely something they didn't want Zoe to know about. But again, what do they want? Selling pirated computer games is a big business, but not big enough to play footsie with these folks."

"And why kill off the golden goose?" Zak wanted to know. "Dunning was a great front man."

"I think somehow he suddenly turned into a liability. I think they discovered they needed to get rid of both Zoe and Nate and figured out a way to get it done." He fixed his gaze on the detective. "Don't get me wrong when I say this, Joe, but they set this up and the cops bought it hook, line, and sinker."

"I told you the kind of pressure we're getting," Morales began.

A knock on the door interrupted them, it opened, and Carol slipped inside. She walked over to Zak and handed him a white business card.

"Allen Fairchild, Homeland Security. Right on time for his appointment."

"Should I leave?" Morales asked. "You must have someplace you can hide me."

Zak shook his head. "No, I think it's better if you stay. I have no idea what he's going to say, but you might be able to fill in some blanks."

Morales grunted. "All I've *got* is blanks, but I'm happy to do what I can. I just want this whole business over with."

"Fine. Send him in, Carol."

Allen Fairchild was definitely no nonsense. He handed his card to Zak, frowned at Morales, but the frown disappeared when they were introduced and he handed a card to him, also.

"I'm sure you're very curious about why I'm here," he said to Zak, taking the chair next to Morales.

"You could say that." Zak kept his voice even and uninflected. But curious didn't begin to describe how he was feeling. "Do I need to get my partner into this meeting, too?"

Fairchild shrugged. "If you think it's necessary."

"I think he'd also want to know what Homeland Security wants from Guardian." He picked up the phone and dialed Reno's direct extension. When his partner answered, he said, "How about coming down to my office. You can help me enjoy a visit from the government."

"The government? Didn't you pay your taxes?"

"Very funny. I think it has to do with my current

situation. If I've brought something down on the agency, I want you to be briefed all the way."

"I'll be right there."

"This really isn't about Guardian," Fairchild told him when he hung up. "It's about Zoraya Lombardo."

Zak made his face a carefully bland mask. "What about her?"

"Let's not play games, Mr. Delaney. Just because the two of you broke off your relationship some time ago doesn't mean she wouldn't call you if she was in trouble. But that's only part of it. Let's wait for your partner so I only have to do this once."

\*\*\*\*

Serita knocked on the study door about one o'clock to tell Zoe she had some lunch ready for her and ask if she wanted to eat at her desk.

"No, actually, I think I'd like to eat on the back porch if that's okay," she told the woman. "I saw a little table with two chairs out there."

"Good, good." Serita smiled at her. "You need some fresh air."

The back porch was wide and ran the length of the house, with a wide railing and colorful pots of flowers at either side of the steps. Serita's work, Zoe was sure. The two hands were working the cutting horses in the corral again, and in a fenced area of pasture just beyond them, about a dozen horses pranced and loped, their coats glistening in the sun. A soft breeze carried the scents of fresh cut hay, horseflesh, and sycamore trees.

If things were different, she could be happy here for the rest of her life. But first she had to break down the wall that Zak had built up again.

Lunch was a delicious salad, with a tall, frosty

glass of iced tea and warm tortillas. Zoe dawdled over it, letting her brain air out, trying not to think of anything. Hoping whatever she was grasping for would come to her.

A buzzing noise caught her attention, and she looked up to see a black speck in the sky. Was that the Guardian helicopter? Had Zak decided to come home early for some reason? Her stomach flopped as the thought of bad news struck her. Why else would he be heading for the ranch this early in the day?

She started to walk to the railing and wave when Frank came across the yard at a dead run.

"Get back in the house," he yelled. "Hurry. Right now?"

Zoe stood for a moment, puzzled, then jerked herself out of her trance and hurried inside. After her stupidity with the telephone, she wasn't about to ask questions about anything.

"What's the matter?" she asked Frank as he slammed the door and strode into the kitchen. "What's happening? Wasn't that Zak?"

"I don't know, I'm not sure, and no, it wasn't," he answered rapidly, adjusting the horizontal blinds on the kitchen window to block anyone's view. "Stay away from the doors and windows." He raced for the den and came back with a cell phone. "Zak keeps a lot of spares," he told her in answer to her unspoken question.

He held one button down, trying to control his impatience as he waited for an answer on the other end. Zoe leaned against a wall, nibbling on a fingernail.

"Yeah," she heard him say. "We might have trouble. A helicopter did a flyover, and it isn't one I recognize. No, no markings. Uh huh. Hold on."

He put the phone down, ran back to the den, and returned with a pair of high-powered binoculars.

"Stay way back from the window," he told Zoe again. He adjusted the blinds to give himself a narrow space through which to look.

"No problem," she told him.

He picked up the phone again and held it to his ear while lifting the binoculars to his eyes again.

"No," he said, "there's nothing out there now, but that doesn't mean anything. The only helicopters that I ever see overhead are yours and the weather chopper from the local television station. Uh huh. Yeah. Okay." He disconnected and turned to Zoe. "The boss says he's on the way and you're supposed to stay out of sight."

Serita had casually walked out to the porch and carried in the remains of lunch as calmly as if nothing was happening.

"Take her back in the study, Frank," she told him. "I'll take care of things here."

Zoe's jaw dropped as she watched Serita open the door to the big pantry closet, reach inside, and take out a rifle. With expert ease, she broke it open, shoved two bullets into the chamber, and snapped it back together.

Serita grinned at her. "When you live on a ranch, you'd better be able to kill varmints. Go on with Frank now. It'll be all right."

In the den, Frank stood by the window, the binoculars hanging around his neck, and checked the chambers on a Smith & Wesson .38. Zoe recognized it because she'd done a simulation for the Texas Rangers, and it was the gun of choice many of them still carried.

"Frank, what's going on here?" She hoped she didn't sound as worried as she felt. She seemed to be dragging trouble around with her wherever she landed and wrapping other people up in it, too. Not for the first time, she wished she'd never heard of Nate Dunning.

"Just making sure we don't have unexpected company." He unclipped the radio he wore on his belt and pressed a button. "Randy, you at the barn? Come in."

"I'm here, boss. What's shakin'?"

"How many out riding fence and how many in the north pasture?"

"Five on the fence line on horse, two in the pickup. Seven in the north pasture cutting out the calves. Why?"

"Everyone armed?" Frank asked.

A long moment passed before Randy answered. "Checking now. Hold on." Finally, his voice came through again. "They're all carrying. What's going on?"

"Watch if you see anything in the hills that shouldn't be there, but don't be obvious about it. Tell everyone to go about their business. I don't think any of the men are targets, but tell them to cover each other's backs."

"We got unexpected company of some kind?" Randy wanted to know.

"Could be. The boss is on his way in right now. Tell everyone to check in with you at fifteen-minute intervals. And if anyone sees anything, I want to know about it right away."

"What about Wade and Sam working the horses in the corral?" Randy asked.

"Tell them to come into the barn, but be casual about it. Not like they're rushing or anything."

"Got it. Randy out."

Frank stepped back from the window and looked at Zoe. "Everything's going to be fine. Whatever it is, Zak will take care of it."

"I'm sorry to bring all this trouble with me," she said. "I know this isn't exactly in your job description."

He grinned. "My job description is whatever the boss wants me to do. I can handle things. Meanwhile, how about a glass of wine to steady your nerves?"

"Th—Thanks. That would be nice."

He filled a goblet from the bottle of merlot Zak had opened the night before and handed it to her. She had an insane desire to chug it down but made herself sip slowly.

"How long until Zak gets here?" she asked.

Frank looked at his watch. "Maybe another fifteen minutes. Don't you worry. We'll take good care of you until he gets here."

She forced a smile. "I know you will. I just hate it that I've brought this all down on you."

Frank actually chuckled. "Are you kidding? How else do cowboys keep from getting rusty?"

At that moment, the radio crackled. "Frank?"

"Yeah, come in."

"The guys in the north pasture reported seeing the sun reflecting off something at the top of Cattle Ridge," Randy reported. "They wanted to check it out, but I told them to pretend they hadn't seen anything."

"Good," Frank told him. "That's the right thing to do. Tell them to make their way slowly to that big copse of trees opposite the Ridge. Drive the calves in front of them. When they get to the trees, they can check again and see if they catch sight of anything."

"Okay. Randy out."

To Zoe, the next fifteen minutes seemed an hour long. She used every bit of willpower to keep from fidgeting. Frank spent most of the time at the window, using his binoculars to peer through a tiny slit he made in the blinds.

She heard the droning of the helicopter just as Frank said, "The boss is here. He should be landing in a minute. Take a look at this."

Zoe ran over to stand next to Frank at the window, watching as the Delaney helicopter came in low over the pasture. The side door was open and Zak was riding with one foot on the skid, a rifle braced on his shoulder. As Marty brought the bird in for a landing, Zak swept the gun from side to side until Randy jogged out from the barn and waved an all clear at him.

She waited by the desk, her whole body shaking when Zak hurried through the door, wrapped his arms around her, and pulled her tight against his body. She bit her lips to keep the tears back, pressing herself as hard against him as she could.

"Zak, Zak, Zak." She couldn't stop repeating his name. If she could have crawled inside his body, she would have.

"It's all right, kitten. I promise. Everything will be fine."

His lips moved over her hair as his big hands stroked her back. He held her so tightly her breasts were crushed against the hard wall of his chest. She wondered if he could feel the hard thump of her heart nearly leaping out of her chest.

At last, he moved his hands to her shoulders and set her slightly away from him. His mouth took hers in a brief yet powerful kiss, and suddenly her world began to right itself.

"I nearly had a stroke when I saw you up there. What did you think you were doing?"

"Nothing I didn't do in Afghanistan. Most of the time I rode the gunships doing just that."

She pressed herself against him again. "I'm glad I didn't know you then. I'd have died every day worrying about you."

"No you wouldn't, kitten." He smoothed her hair. "You'd be brave just like always."

"What's going on, Zak? What's happening?"

Gently, he sat her down in the big chair and handed her the wine goblet sitting on the desk. "This yours?"

She nodded.

"Good. Drink some more, and I'll tell you what's happening. Just give me a minute here." He straightened and looked at Frank.

The foreman was still peering through the slats with his binoculars. "I don't see anything, Zak. Could you tell anything from the air?"

"No, unfortunately. Whoever's up there, I think I scared the hell out of them coming in low as we did."

"It's not the cops, is it?" Frank asked. "That's not their style. They'd come up to the front door with enough men to arrest an army."

"I'd actually rather have the cops than these guys. Even *I'm* afraid of the Russian *mafiyah*. Frank, when you called to tell me about the flyover, I just happened to be in a meeting with someone who's looking for these people, someone who can give us some help."

"I thought I was safe here," Zoe said, bewildered.

"So did I. I thought for sure no one could find you.

But maybe it's just as well to see if we can end it here and now. As long as my reinforcements get here in time. Frank?"

"Yeah, Zak."

"Make sure everyone's on their toes. Marty will be back in a few with more company and another helo bringing reinforcements."

"From the company?"

"No. Homeland Security."

Zoe didn't know who was more shocked, her or Frank. She stared at Zak. "Are you going to tell me what's really going on here?"

"Right now, Frank, I need to talk to Zoe in private. We'll be quick about it. "

"Got it."

Zak took her arm. "Come on. Bring the wine with you."

"Where are we going?"

"The den. No one will bother us there, and you may need to lie down when I'm finished."

"Just tell me, Zak. Please."

"Let's sit down." He led her into his den and seated her in a chair across from him. "It's a little known fact that the Russian *mafiyah* has been working to get a foothold in this area. They've been doing this for decades, very quietly establishing themselves and consolidating their position. I wasn't shocked to learn that Caz Morgan and Max Detwiler were involved, but I was stunned to be told they were major players in the core group."

Zoe stared at him. "Are you telling me the truth?"

"I have no reason to lie, kitten. I was as astounded as you. They've been fooling a lot of people."

"And Nate?" she asked. "Was he part of their group or whatever?"

"Only in as much as they needed a pawn. Someone to get close to you and get part of the business. They watched you, watched you build and develop Lombardo Simulations. And when you were hungry to expand they jumped."

"So Nate was really just a figurehead? Is that what you're saying?" She wished he'd put his arms around her again. She needed his warmth and his strength. "But why?" She held out her hands, palms up. "What's so important about a little simulation company? Selling the programs on the black market?"

He shook his head. "Pocket change. But this came mostly from the research my people have just given me. The rest came from Homeland Security."

"Homeland—" Her jaw dropped.

"Yes. Zoe, your company is right in the middle of supplying terrorist groups with valuable information."

"What?" She blinked, sure she hadn't heard right. "How—What—"

Zak sighed, sat down next to her, and took one of her hands in both of his. As he talked, he played with her fingers the way he used to. "The Russian mob and various terrorist organizations have been in bed together for a long time. The *mafiyah* raises money through its various enterprises like the businesses they were buying up here. Then they use the money to buy arms, sell the arms to the terrorists at an exorbitant price, plow the money back into their various *enterprises*, and the wheel keeps on a-turning. Dunning International was being used to funnel money through dummy corporations to sell guns and other arms to terrorist. And often to foment revolution if it would help their economic interest in a Third World country."

"But that's…I mean…"

"Yeah, I agree. Two things make it even worse. One, in many smaller or unstable countries, they use their money and influence to control the government, which gives them free reign for their illegal activities. And two, with a base here in the United States, they can fund attacks on this country. Think how much control they'd have if enough attacks occurred to create total chaos."

Zoe truly felt sick to her stomach. "Again, why San Antonio?"

"A city big enough to blend into, only ninety miles from the water. Easy access for smuggling. And the drug cartels get most of the publicity so it is a good cover for everything else going on."

"But Zak, they didn't just open an atlas and pick out this city. Something triggered it for them. Or someone. And why my company? That same situation landed Lombardo Simulations on their radar. They needed my company for a reason."

She swiped her hair back from her face and tucked it behind her ears. "I don't believe this I don't *want* to believe it. Nate Dunning involved with *terrorists*? And my uncle got me into this?"

She had long since finished the wine in the goblet. Now she was wishing she had an entire bottle. "And you still haven't answered my question about why me?"

"You write training simulations for companies, right? A lot of security companies? These sims teach people hostage rescue, how to thwart hijackers, how to war game a company to make sure its security is intact.

Now. What if those procedures were reversed?"

Zoe thought about it for a moment, then as the realization dawned, she blindly reached out a hand for Zak.

"Take a deep breath," he told her.

"If the process were reversed," she said slowly, "terrorists would know how to get around these procedures and could train their people accordingly. And the teams sent on missions based on these sims would be killed and the mission thwarted."

"Exactly." Zak held tightly to her hands, his warmth comforting even if his words weren't. "Additionally those kinds of sims would fetch astronomical prices on the open market. I'm willing to bet every terrorist organization in the world has been courting the Russians once the word got out. And if they could pirate the games along with it?" He shrugged. "Well, that's just a few more pennies in already bulging pockets."

"My god." Zoe had to grip her hands together they were shaking so badly. "You mean...that is...oh, sweet lord. What have I done?"

"Not you, kitten." He tightened his arm around her. "People who took advantage of you and perverted what you did."

"No wonder they blew up the company building and my house." She shook her head. "It's like you thought. I might have stored everything in the cloud, but they didn't know what I might have kept on the hard drive of my computer. They had to destroy any hard evidence that was put there." She scrubbed her hands over her face. "How did I ever get myself into such a mess?"

"Don't blame yourself for this. You were managed by master manipulators."

"You think it was just Caz and Max?" She frowned. "They ran the whole thing? These two men who were pillars of the community here and in the state?"

"A lot of pillars are made of salt," he pointed out. "But you're right. It would take more than just the two of them. I'm hoping when Allen Fairchild gets here, he'll fill in the blanks for us. I wish I had time to move you someplace else, but…"

"If I'm not safe here, where can you possibly take me? We're out in the middle of nowhere."

"I thought the same thing." He shoved his hands in his pockets and paced. "I even set it up so Arrowhead Ranch is owned by Arrowhead Corporation. I didn't want my name on any deeds or property lists so I'd have someplace to hang out where no one can find me."

"So how *did* they find us?"

Zak peered through a tiny space in the slats at the window, then turned back to her. "I'm guessing the same way I tracked down everything about them. They know how to dig. They were casting a net for every relationship you had that might factor into this, so it wasn't too big a stretch to find my name. Plus, they use threats and intimidation when nothing else works. And believe me. You don't want to be intimidated by the Russians."

A tap sounded on the door, and Serita's voice called, "Zak? Zoe? Marty just landed again and there's another helicopter coming in right after them."

"We're coming," Zak called. "I'm hoping that my people will have the answer to that last question any time now."

"These people frighten me," she said.

"With good reason." He stood and pulled her to her feet. They stared at each other for a long moment. "We don't really have time to indulge ourselves right now, but I can't wait any longer. Before we finish this discussion, I have to clear the air between us." He sucked in a breath and let it out. "Kitten, I've been a real ass."

Zoe raised her eyebrows. "Are you speaking in general or something specific?"

"We aren't the same people we were two years ago," Zak went on. "That should have been obvious to me. Kitten, the fact that you came to me, not anyone else, when you were in trouble means a lot to me. A lot. I'm sorry I acted like a jerk."

"I'm sorry I did, too."

"I was mad about the phone call you made. It endangered a lot of people, not the least of which was you. I convinced myself you hadn't changed. That you were just as stubborn and hot-headed as you were two years ago, not listening to me. Not—"

She pressed her fingers against her mouth. "Hush. You're right. I wanted to call my mother, and I didn't pay enough attention to what you said. I know that's why you pulled back from me. But it's okay. I've more than learned my lesson. Believe me. I'll apologize forever if it will help."

"No." His hands slid up and down her arms. "I think we've both made mistakes, and we've both learned. I was stupid myself not to realize how important it would be for you to let your mother know you were all right. I should have figured out how to handle that, but all I wanted to do was keep you safe while we got to the bottom of this."

"I know." She blinked at the tears pressing against her eyelids. "I understand. Truly I do. I just wasn't thinking."

"This isn't the time for this, but I can't help myself." He cupped her cheeks with his gentle hands, holding her gaze with his whiskey eyes before he bent his head toward hers. The kiss this time was anything but brief.

When his tongue pressed against the seam of her lips, she opened for him and the hot whip of his tongue swept inside. His fingers tangled in her hair as he held her head steady, his mouth ravaging hers. Heat traveled through her body, firing her blood and warming her down to her toes. Her nipples hardened, and her pulses throbbed. She held on for dear life as a whirlwind of emotion raced through her.

When they broke apart, they were both struggling for air. Zak recovered first, tracing the line of her jaw with his fingertips. "Okay, then. Now that we've got that out of the way, let's get back to business."

"Or the business of business," she said, trying to make a little joke. Anything to lighten the tension of the situation they were facing.

He pulled Zoe into his arms for one more quick hug, then looked hard at her. "Too late to take a chance on moving you now. They could have eyes on the roads leading in here, and we'd be sitting ducks. Besides, I don't want a shoot-out on a highway."

She swallowed, then stiffened her body. "Neither do I. I just want this over, and I trust you to make sure I don't get hurt. Or killed."

"When this is over, we have a lot of time to make up for," he told her.

"I can't wait." She stood on tiptoe and brushed her lips against his. "Now let's go see about your company."

## Chapter Thirteen

The kitchen was full of people when they walked into it. Zoe had trouble adjusting to the site of the slender Serita stirring pots on the stove, the rifle propped against the wall, ready at hand. Every seat at the kitchen table was filled with men she'd never seen, poring over what appeared to be an aerial map of the ranch. Marty and another man leaned against one wall, drinking coffee, with Keith and Dean against the opposite one. And all the men were armed.

A man looking distinctly out of place in a sport coat, slacks, and tie looked up at their entrance.

"Well, Miss Lombardo, it's nice to finally lay eyes on you," he told her.

Zoe looked at Zak, unsure of what to say.

"Meet Detective Joe Morales of the San Antonio Police Department," he said.

Zoe's knees wobbled, and she gripped Zak's hand more tightly. "You brought him here?"

Was he going to arrest her after all? Had she been foolish to trust Zak in this? No, that couldn't be right. No one else seemed to be concerned.

"Don't worry," Zak told her. "He's here at my invite. He's on our side. Finally."

"Oh," was all she could manage.

A man with a lined face and chocolate brown hair, who looked to be in his forties, was directing the conversation at the table. Zak touched his shoulder, and he looked up.

"Allen Fairchild, meet Zoe Lombardo."

The man reached up and shook her hand. "I'm happy to finally get to meet you, Miss Lombardo. We hope to get you out of this and shut the operation down at the same time."

Zoe looked from one man to the other with curiosity.

"Allen's with Homeland Security," Zak explained. "He and I had an interesting visit today. That's how I learned about the arms trade and a few other things."

Allen turned his attention back to the table, pointing at various places on the map spread out in front of him, asking questions that Frank answered clearly and concisely.

"Okay." Allen leaned back in his chair. "We know they're out there. When Zak told me what was happening, I called Washington and got the satellite imagery for the area, real time."

"Did it show anything?" Zak asked him.

"Sure did. We know that a helicopter dropped them at the back end of this property. Probably right after the flyover. We just aren't sure exactly how many there are. We think they'll wait until the hands that are out there head back to the barn before moving in. That way they can get everyone at once."

"You mean they plan to kill everyone here?" Zoe couldn't quite wrap her mind around such a horrendous thought.

Allen Fairchild's face was grim. "Unfortunately, to these people, human life has little value."

"You don't think they know we've got

reinforcements?" Frank asked. "What with the Guardian helicopter and yours coming in just a little while ago?"

"They can make a guesstimate. Also, we don't know if they've got more men coming in from the highway. But I'd say that's a good possibility. I'm willing to bet when they saw us land they called for reinforcements."

Zoe leaned against Zak, twisting her fingers together. "Isn't this a little overkill just to get rid of me?"

"I think this is as much about the files you saw as anything else. Nate got careless, you got inquisitive, so you both had to go." Fairchild looked at Frank. "Call your man down in the barn, tell him to have the hands start back here but at a steady pace. If they've been cutting calves out of the herd, they can drive them down here and nothing will look out of place. Bring in some of the ones riding fence, but have a couple of them conceal themselves strategically so we get some advance warning when our friends start to move in."

"Is it safe for them to be moving?" Zak asked. "Shouldn't they just find someplace to hide?"

Fairchild shook his head. "We can control things better if everyone's here in the same place. They'll be okay riding in. The Russians won't pick them off one at a time. If one body falls, the other hands will radio in what's happening, and they don't want that advance notice going out."

"I'll do it right now." Frank rose from his seat, went to a corner of the kitchen, and called Randy on the radio. Zoe could hear him repeating Allen Fairchild's instructions.

"All right, children." Allen pushed his chair back from the table. "You all have your marching orders. Zak, where can you and Zoe and I talk privately?"

"My den, where she's been working on codes."

"Excellent. And Miss Lombardo, you can tell me what exactly you're looking for in those files and how far you've gotten."

Serita followed them in with a tray of coffee and pastries. Zoe thought if she got cut of this alive, she might never drink coffee again.

"Okay." Allen took the chair at one corner of the desk and cradled his mug in his hand. "Miss Lombardo, why don't you go first? Zak tells me you've been trying to decipher what someone's done with the programs you wrote for the simulations and the games adapted from them, but you're having a problem."

"Yes, and it's giving me a headache. I do this for a living." She pushed her hair behind her ears. "You'd think it would be a simple matter since I wrote the original programs, but I get just so far and I'm stuck."

She told him everything she'd been working on since Zak brought her the laptop. Trying to take apart the few programs Nina had been able to download. Recreating from memory some that she'd written.

"You can do that?" he asked. "Without notes to refer to?"

She gave him a tiny smile. "My codes are my babies. They're usually branded into my brain. Plus, when I discovered I had an aptitude for this kind of stuff, I also realized I had...not a photographic memory but an extremely retentive one. I could remember what worked and what didn't and what strings of code could be repeated from program to program. It's why I was able to grow Lombardo Simulations to the point it was at when I met Nate Dunning."

"I'm impressed." He gave her a tired smile. "If you ever want a job with the government, just give me a call. Zak has my card. We can use people like you."

Heat rose in her cheeks at the compliment. "Thanks, but I think, after this, I'd like to go back to what I do best. Running a small company and handling one client at a time. Big business and the limelight haven't proven to be advantageous for me."

"Okay," Fairchild prodded her. "So you've tried to crack the new codes someone inserted into the programs you wrote, without success. Do you have any idea why?"

She shook her head. "The problem is, there are symbols in there I don't recognize so I don't know how to get past them."

"Probably because they are characters from the Cyrillic alphabet the Russians use instead of what you're used to. It makes the program very specific and proprietary."

Her jaw dropped. "They've had Russian programmers rewriting my codes?"

"Since this whole operation is run by the Russian mob, I'd say that's a good bet. I'd have to have one of our guys look at it to be sure, but that's the easiest answer."

"But why? For what reason? Zak said he thought Nate wanted my company to launder money through. They don't have to rewrite programs to do that."

"The money laundering was only a small part of it," Allen said. "Zak told me your arguments with Nate began over the names of clients and suppliers you'd never heard of. That was the mechanism for the laundering. But if you made an issue out of that, everything else would have fallen apart."

Zoe sipped at her coffee. "And if Nate was just a figurehead, like Zak said, and he called too much attention to the situation by arguing with me instead of giving me a plausible answer…"

"He became a liability that needed to be removed at once. The company was operating efficiently. He was replaceable."

"So what *were* they doing with my company and my programs?"

Allen crossed his legs, took a long swallow of coffee, and gave her a searching look. "Has Zak told you about the people Nate and Caz Morgan have been meeting with at Caz's ranch? People from countries on the international watch list? People running vast terrorist groups?"

Allen nodded. "They could hack into your computers and erase everything on them, but they needed to physically retrieve or destroy hardware, like your laptop and your notebooks. That's why they set the fire at your company, too."

Zoe raked her fingers through her hair. "I just can't believe this. It's…it's my worst nightmare come true. This looks like I was helping terrorists, doesn't it?"

"It did at first," Allen agreed. "But then I had a long talk with Zak and discovered the *mafiyah* had set you up as their fall guy. In more ways than one."

"Did… Did Zak tell you about my being drugged at the party and waking up with the gun in my hand?"

"Yes, and I'm not surprised. Rohypnol is used in great quantities by the Russians. They drug the girls they buy for use as prostitutes and to sell in the white slave market. Anyone at that party could have slipped it into your drink, walked you into the den, and waited for you to pass out."

"I've tried to remember who I was near, who I talked to," she told him, her voice hitching with frustration. "But I just can't. Oh. Wait." As if someone had briefly opened a door, pieces of images flashed through her brain.

"Remember something, kitten?" Zak asked, his arm still reassuringly around her.

"Yes. I spent some time talking to Caz, which surprised me because he usually just gave me his glamour boy speech, then spent his time on the clients. The money people." She looked at Zak. "I can't believe I was caught up in something like this. I must have a stupid sign on my forehead."

"These people are pros," Zak told her. "This is a big operation. Caz Morgan and Max Detwiler are just the tip of the iceberg. The problem is, the trail stops with them no matter how hard we look. We're hoping the head honcho will show up today to finish the job himself. Usually, they don't, but this is an exception."

"You think he'd do that, whoever he is? Expose himself like this?"

"You're the last piece of the puzzle to get rid of. He won't want to take the chance of anyone screwing it up. So yes, I think he'll be here today. If for some reason he doesn't show, then we can at least get information out of the people we capture."

"You think you'll be able to do that?" she wanted to know. "Get them to give up the name?"

Allen's smile was pure malice. "Oh, yes. No

question about it."

Frank chose that moment to come in with a report. "Randy radioed that the boys will be here with the calves in about twenty. And all the fence riders but two are back in the barn. They took it nice and easy, so they didn't arouse any suspicions."

"Good, good. And everyone else?"

"Ready for whatever happens. The rest of your men are here, too."

A tall man dressed all in black, wearing a bulletproof vest with the strap of a semi-automatic weapon slung on his shoulder, appeared behind Frank.

"We're good to go, Allen," he said. "I thought we'd pair each of our guys with a ranch hand."

"Fine." Allen looked from the tall man to Zak and Zoe. "Meet Dyson Trumbull, the team leader. I don't doubt that we're all safe in his hands."

Zak shook hands with the man.

"Nice to meet you," Zoe told him.

"I'll set a perimeter and deploy everyone where I think they'll do the most good," he informed Allen.

"You don't think they'll try to attack from the helicopter, do you?" Allen asked.

"They might, although I think this time they'll want to get up close and personal to make sure no one escapes. Besides, if they do decide to try, we can blast them out of the sky in a heartbeat." His grin had little warmth to it. "We have shoulder fired missiles with us just in case."

"Okay. It's in your hands then."

At that moment, the phone hooked to the landline rang, and everyone in the room stared at it.

## Chapter Fourteen

Zak finally reached out and lifted the receiver. "This is Zak Delaney."

"Ah, Mr. Delaney. I am so glad you answered the telephone yourself."

The voice was definitely Russian, although the accent wasn't terribly thick. Someone who'd been here a long time, then. And muffled to disguise it.

"I assume it's your men who invaded my ranch," Zak said. "What do you want? Me? Come and get me."

"Such a brave man." The chuckle was pure evil. "But no, you are not the treasure we seek. And there is no need for you or any of your people to get hurt."

"Yeah? Then back off my land, and we'll talk."

"I'm afraid I can't do that. But if you will send the charming Miss Lombardo outside and have her stand in the middle of the clearing by the barn, we will pick her up and all of us will be gone."

"Sorry," Zak told him. "No can do. I guess you'll have to try and take her."

"It would be a shame to have to destroy your property for the sake of one worthless woman, Mr. Delaney. Surely you're smart enough not to endanger everything for her."

Zak gripped the phone so hard his knuckles were white. The man was baiting him, and he couldn't afford to let his temper take over. "I think we might have a few surprises of our own."

"Then, how is it you say? Game on, my friend."

He broke the connection, leaving a seething Zak holding dead air.

"Our friends?" Allen asked.

"In the flesh. I suspect they think, as a last resort, they can launch another explosives attack and get rid of us all at once. Unless, of course, I send Zoe out to them."

Fairchild grunted. "Their last two attempts at that didn't turn out too well for them. It drew attention they didn't want, and Zoe's still alive. But all the same, I'd better tell Dyson to get ready with the big guns."

He excused himself and went in search of his team leader.

Zak started to reach for her, but she stood and went to stand by the window.

"Zak." She spoke without turning to look at him. "I really don't want to die, but I don't want everyone else to die, either. Maybe... Maybe I should do as they ask and turn myself over to them. Maybe I can convince them they have nothing to fear from me. Maybe..."

"Maybe nothing." He moved up behind her, wrapping his arms around her waist, holding her softness to his body, inhaling her essence. "No way in hell am I allowing you to be a sacrificial lamb. And trust me. They don't want to listen to any argument you might have. So no, I'm not even listening to such an idiotic idea. We have plenty of people here that know what they're doing. Let's let them do their jobs."

She took a deep breath, obviously trying to pull herself together. He knew the last thing she wanted was to turn into some sniveling female in front of everyone and embarrass both of them. That just was not Zoe.

He nudged her hair aside with his cheek and pressed his lips against a sensitive spot on her neck. "I'm going to go check on what's happening, but first I have something to tell you."

"And what's that?"

He wasn't surprised at the tension in her voice. He hoped what he had to say would ease that a little. "I love you. I don't know when I'll get to tell you again, so I wanted to be sure to tell you now."

"Oh, Zak." She turned in his arms. "I love you, too."

He brushed his lips against hers. "When this is all over, I'm going to take the time to show you properly."

He meant every word of that. He was done trying to protect himself, and from what? A woman who loved him as much as she did? He was ready to do anything to keep her safe. Too bad he couldn't take back all the time they'd wasted being apart. It was as much his fault as hers, and he was done with it. He wanted a life with her. If he had to die protecting her, he would, because she meant that much to him, but he sure hoped it didn't come to that. Not when he finally realized what they had together.

The sound of the door opening startled them, and Zoe jumped backward.

"Sorry." Allen Fairchild stood in the doorway. "Dyson said they've spotted a helicopter coming in low over what Frank says is Cattle Ridge. I believe they're going to try some kind of one-two punch—men on the ground and an attack from the air."

"What should I tell my people?" Zak asked.

"Not a thing. We've got it covered. Dyson and the

team have a little surprise for our friends. Just wanted to keep you in the loop."

"I feel as if I should be out there with everyone," Zak told him.

"Your job is to take care of Miss Lombardo. Leave the rest to us."

"I'm coming into the kitchen, just the same," he told the older man. "It's just as safe as this room and at least we won't feel so isolated."

"Come on, then. You'll be just in time for the fireworks."

Zoe shuddered and gripped Zak's hand tightly as he led her into the kitchen.

The scene had changed slightly. Serita was standing in the doorway to the pantry, rifle held loosely in her hands. Three men, all wearing bullet-proof vests and loaded with paraphernalia Zoe couldn't even identify, were stationed at the windows, holding what looked to her like very lethal weapons. The air was thick with the tension of the moment.

Allen Fairchild, who stood near the window, plucked a radio from his belt. "Dyson, anything yet?"

Static crackled in the air, then the rough voice answered. "Not yet. I just— Wait. We've got something in our sights. It's a plain black helicopter. Where's Frank?"

A second passed, then Zoe heard Frank say, "Here. This is the same one we saw before."

"Okay," Dyson told him. "Everyone get ready. Shooters, get set."

Zoe waited, every muscle and nerve in her body vibrating with expectation. She wished she could go to the window and peer through the tiny space between slats, but she wasn't about to break protocol again. Ever.

The radio sputtered again, then Dyson said, "It's over us, over the empty pasture. Here we go, guys. On my count. Three, two, one."

She heard a loud explosion, then shock waves that reverberated through the walls. She looked up at Zak. "Was that them or us?"

Then she heard Dyson saying, "One bird down."

Zak grinned. "Us. I'd say someone on Dyson's team just shot their helicopter out of the sky."

The man with the radio looked over his shoulder. "They downed it in the pasture, Mr. Delaney. Your people will have some work to do after the DHS cleanup crew gets through."

"No problem," Zak assured him.

The landline rang again, and Zak reached for the instrument on the wall. "Lose a few people?"

"A slight miscalculation on our part," the Russian said, his voice still muffled. "But only a tiny setback. Rest assured. Miss Lombardo will not leave this place alive. How many people die with her is up to you." Abruptly he hung up.

Zak looked at everyone in the room, then repeated the conversation.

"They'll wait for dark now." Allen pressed the Talk button on the radio. "Dyson? Is Morales with you?"

"Affirmative," came back.

"Put him on the radio."

More static, then Morales's voice. "What do you need?"

"Did you take one of those disposable phones we

were handing out?" Allen asked.

"Sure did."

"Call your lieutenant and have him brief the chief. Also the sheriff of this county. But be sure they don't come in with guns blazing and lights flashing. We're okay here."

"He'll be grateful for the heads up. This Dunning thing has him tied up in knots. I'll let you know what he says."

"Copy that." Allen looked at Zak and Zoe. "Now we wait."

"What about food for the men?" Serita asked.

Zoe couldn't help smiling, even in the seriousness of the situation. Serita would definitely think of everyone's stomach.

Allen shook his head. "Not until this is over. They're good."

"I'll keep the coffee pot full," she assured him and proceeded to work on it.

Silence settled over the room as everyone stood watchfully alert. In case the Russians didn't wait until dark to try and move in, they didn't want to be caught off guard. When the radio crackled again, everyone jumped.

"It's Morales," said the voice. "I spoke to my boss, and he put me on a three-way with the county sheriff. The lieutenant is good where he is as long as I keep in contact with him. But the sheriff says he can be a help. Three of his deputies are Native Americans, and he says they can move into places we can't even see. If someone will fax him the aerial map of the ranch and a phone number, he'll get right back to you with his suggestions."

Allen rubbed his chin thoughtfully. "All right," he said at last. "Only let me call him directly. Give me the number."

He picked up the folder from the kitchen table, unclipped another piece of equipment from his belt, and headed for the den with it.

"Satellite phone," Zak told her. "These people won't have equipment with them to track it."

Allen Fairchild was back in less than ten minutes. "I told the sheriff to get his men moving. We can use them, especially as it gets darker. And they can get into places we can't because they know the terrain. They know what to do, and they won't be contacting us by radio or phone unless it's absolutely necessary. But they'll be the advance guard."

After that, there really was nothing to do but wait. Zoe didn't know how the men, Zak included, managed it. She was ready to jump out of her skin, yet they stood silently, immobile, moving only when necessary. Every so often they accepted coffee that Serita handed to them, nodding their thanks. But no one said a word.

Through the tiny spaces in the slats, Zoe saw the sky darkening and night slowly closing in on them. The darker it got, the more uptight she became. Numbly, she washed mugs and set the clean ones out again, wiped the counter and sink so many times Serita finally took the sponge from her hand, smiled kindly, and made her sit down.

"No more coffee," she protested when the woman tried to hand her a mug. "Do you by any chance have tea?"

"Of course. Just give me a minute."

The tea, when Serita fixed it, had a slight orange

tang to it and soothed her as it slid down her throat. Zak had left the room for a couple of minutes, and when he returned, he had a gun tucked at the small of his back. She tugged on his hand, and he looked down at her. Her eyes slid to the gun and back to his face.

"I feel better having it," he told her. "All these other people are great, but your safety is my responsibility, and I take that very personally." Despite the roomful of people, he bent down and placed a hard kiss on her mouth. "Trust me, Zoe. I'm not going to let anything happen to you."

Only Allen Fairchild happened to see the kiss and hear the exchange. He smothered a grin and turned back to business.

"It's full dark," one of the men said. "There are spotlights out there that came on automatically. Should I tell Frank to turn them off?"

"Absolutely," Allen answered. "We don't want to make this too easy for them."

"But don't you want to see them move in?" Zoe asked. "Wouldn't it make it harder for them to get close to the house?"

"We want them all where we can get at them," Fairchild explained. "If a few of them try to break through and they see us pick them off, the rest will scatter and regroup. Maybe for another time."

More time passed. Then a voice from the radio. "We picked up some movement through the night vision goggles. These guys are good, I'll give them that. If we weren't looking for them, we might miss them completely."

"Are they out in the open yet?" Allen wanted to know.

"Negative. Still in the trees at the edge of the nearest pasture. Wait a minute." Silence. Then, "We see movement along the fence line on the right. If we didn't have good eyes, we'd think it was an animal moving there."

"Okay. Keep on it."

Zoe dug her fingernails into her palms to keep from screaming with frustration. She just wanted this to be over. Now. Her nerves were stretched to their limit. Even Zak's reassuring presence no longer had a calming effect.

"I think our folks from the sheriff's office are doing their job." There was a hint of humor in the voice on the radio. "Whoever was moving along the fence just had his throat slit in the neatest movement I've seen in a long time. Thank the lord for NVGs."

"But won't that warn the others, like you said before?" Zoe asked.

Fairchild shook his head. "Apparently they aren't wearing NVGs so they can't see in the dark and there was nothing for them to hear." He lifted the radio to his mouth again. "Anything else?"

"We've got movement out of the trees, some of them coming along the same fence line, others on the opposite side of the pasture."

"They think they can avoid being seen that way. Shadows. No one will notice." The Homeland Security man relayed new orders, then dispatched two men in the kitchen to the front door. "Let's not leave our backs exposed," he told them.

More waiting. Then the voice on the radio whispered, "Damn! I want to learn to do that."

"Do what?" Allen asked.

"Someone tried to rush the barn, and one of Delaney's men roped him like a calf, tied him up, and shoved a gag in his mouth."

The laugh the image inspired briefly broke the pressure in the room.

Just at the moment Zoe was ready to scream, shots erupted outside, men shouted, more shots were fired. Someone yelled, "Hold your fire. Hold your fire."

Everyone waited. Then the voice on the radio spoke again. "Allen, it's Dyson. We've got all but two. Don't anyone in there move. We have two intruders approaching from the front. Weird. They don't seem to be together, and the one in front is apparently oblivious to the one several steps behind him. They think the dark covers them, but we're on their tails. I'm on my way to the house now."

"Copy that."

Zak and Allen moved in front of Zoe, guns drawn, just as the front door crashed opened and a man stood there, big and angry, holding a gun. Zoe covered her mouth to hold back a scream at the sight of Sergei Demoff pointing the gun at them, eyes blazing, face twisted with anger.

"Put the gun away, Demoff, or I will shoot you," Allen told him in a hard voice. "You're done here."

"Not until I take care of business." Sergei spat on the floor, ignoring the weapons aimed at him, and glared at Zoe. "I should have found a way to kill you before, you stupid little bitch."

"*You* had me run off the road? *You* broke into my house? *You* killed Nate and framed me? And all the rest of this has been so you could kill me? Why? What did I ever do to you?"

"You ruined everything." His tone was so vicious she recoiled.

"Get down, Zoe," Zak told her in a controlled voice. "I've got this. If his finger tightens a millimeter, he's a dead man."

"Everything," Sergei growled. "All the things I worked so hard for. Destroyed because of a nothing like you. You couldn't stop asking questions. Sticking your nose where it didn't belong. You made Dunning a liability. You deserve to die. I am ashamed that I have failed."

Zoe stared. "*You're* the one who did all this?" She could hardly believe he had the brains for this.

Then a voice came from behind her cousin. "No, my dear. Sergei couldn't even do the simple tasks we gave him. Very unfortunate for him."

A shot echoed in the hallway, and Sergei fell, face down, revealing Ivan Demoff standing behind him. And right behind Ivan was one of Fairchild's men, his weapon at the small of Ivan's back.

"Sorry, chief," he told Allen. "I was too many steps behind him to take him out before he got a shot off."

"No matter." Ivan raised his hands, the gun dangling from one finger. "I did what I had to. The boy destroyed us all."

The agent relieved him of the gun, forced him to his knees, and pulled his hands behind his back to cuff him. The man offered no resistance, just did as he was told.

Zoe stared at Sergei's body on the floor and her uncle in restraints.

"Uncle Ivan?" She dug for some measure of control, but she couldn't stop shaking or keep the shock from her voice. "You?"

"Sorry, Zoraya." Sorrow actually lined his face. "We all made a lot of mistakes here. It's over, and even though it hurt me to kill my own son, it had to be done."

"But why?" Nausea rolled through her, and she forced it back. "Your own son?"

"A son I am ashamed of. But his mistakes destroyed all we've worked for."

She had to swallow twice before she could speak again. "All *you've* worked for? My God. I can't believe you're part of this…this…abomination. Nate is dead. I was almost killed. Would you even have shed a tear?"

He shook his head. "You were never meant to be in harm's way. I'm so sorry."

"But I'm your niece," she cried. "Your flesh and blood."

"And you just saw how much that means to these people where their crimes are concerned." Allen Fairchild took her arm and guided her back to the kitchen. "My men will take out the trash. Let's get you a drink. Or coffee. Or whatever you prefer."

"I think a drink would be wonderful, please," she told him in a shaky voice. When she was seated at the table with a glass of wine in her hand and her nerves settling a little, she shook her head. "I can't believe my uncle was involved in this. That he was part of this vicious group of people. It just doesn't seem possible. Zak never really trusted him, and I should have listened to what he said."

"He put on a good front," Fairchild told her. "And he was more than involved. He was the head of the *mafiyah* in this area. The structure of this new generation of *mafiyah* was hatched over a holiday weekend at the estate of one of their families on Canyon Lake. They were all aware the wealth of their families came from less than savory means. They thrived on that and wanted to grow it even more. As attorneys they could find ways to cover themselves legally."

Zoe couldn't stop looking at him. "But these are some of the oldest and wealthiest families in Texas."

Fairchild nodded. "Yes, they are. And all Russian, only with their names changed to disguise who they really were. Their offspring, all partners in the law firm, decided they could do it larger and better and even cloak it in legitimacy." He shrugged. "Of course, when that didn't work, wasting someone like Nate Dunning cleaned up the mess."

"And their clients?" Zak asked.

"Some legitimate, enough to keep their standing in the community and their places in the country clubs and to cover their illegal activities. Truth be told, they're all damn good attorneys who knew exactly how close they could skirt the law. They created social positions where they were virtually untouchable while establishing a strong branch of the Russian *mafiyah* here."

One of the DHS agents came back into the kitchen. "All clear."

"Good," Allen acknowledged. "Dyson? How about your end?"

Dyson's voice came through the radio. "All clear back here."

Everyone in the house breathed a collective sigh of relief. Except for Zoe. She was still grappling with the truth of everything.

## Chapter Fifteen

"I need something stronger than coffee or tea," Zoe told Zak. "And maybe even more than wine."

"Coming right up." He started for the den, then came back and pulled her into a strong hug.

"You can leave her for a minute," Allen assured him, a teasing note in his voice. "There are enough guards around her. Go on while I take inventory."

Zak returned in seconds, holding a cut glass tumbler filled with a gold liquid. He fished ice cubes from the freezer, dropped them into the glass, and handed it to her.

"I remember how much you like bourbon," he said, "but drink it slowly. Your adrenaline is running high right now, and the liquor will just jack it up more."

"I will." She took a small swallow, feeling the familiar burn as the liquid slid along her throat. As soon as it hit her stomach she began to settle, to feel better. "You always were suspicious of him," she reminded Zak. "Even when we were engaged, you never quite trusted him."

"He wasn't family. I could look at him through a professional's eyes and see there was something off kilter about him. But I didn't want to ruin your illusions unnecessarily, in case I was wrong."

"I still find it hard to accept that he is part of such a vicious group of people."

"Not just part of. The head of it. He was the quiet brains behind everything."

Zoe sipped some scotch, hoping to calm her nerves a little more. Everyone was either talking on radios or moving to the backyard. She knew Zak was itching to find out what was going on, but he stood valiantly next to her, his hand on her shoulder, assuring her with his presence that it really was all over. Watching through the window, he told her there were three black vans with the side panels slid open. DHS agents were moving their prisoners, properly cuffed and restrained, and loading them one at a time.

Allen Fairchild came in through the back door, still holding his radio.

"We've got the live ones in the vans," he told them. "There are six bodies, which we'll transport in the helicopter. Miss Lombardo, I'd stay inside for a bit if I were you. Just until we get everyone out of here." He looked at Zak. "I'll have a team out here in the morning to clean up the mess from the downed copter as best we can."

"If you can just get the debris out of the way," Zak told him, "my men will handle the rest."

"No problem."

"I can't believe Uncle Ivan and his partners were behind all this," Zoe said, not for the first time. "That a member of my own family would actually want to kill me. God, my mother will have a heart attack."

"And their parents before them. This has been going on into the third generation."

"My mother—"

"We have someone with her, trying to explain everything. And a doctor on standby if she needs medical attention."

"We're all she has," she told him. "My uncle and my cousin. My father is dead, and so is Uncle Ivan's wife. I don't know what she's going to do now."

"We'll see that she's taken care of," Zak assured her, squeezing her shoulders. "Not to worry." He pulled a cell phone from his pocket. "I think it's safe to call your mother now. She probably needs to hear from you."

He was so right. The minute the woman heard Zoe's voice, she burst into tears.

"Zoraya, Zoraya, Zoraya," she kept saying over and over. "What has happened to our family?"

"I don't know, Mama, but I promise you everything will be all right. Please don't cry. The worst is over."

Eventually, she was able to calm her mother down and promised she would be at the house the next day. They would sort everything out then.

More than an hour passed before all the thanks had been said, the sheriff and Morales's lieutenant brought up to speed, both Allen Fairchild's boss and Reno Sullivan given a short briefing, and everyone was finally gone. Frank insisted on having one of the men stand guard with him during the night, and Keith and Dean added themselves to the mix. Zak had someone drive Serita home, refusing to let her leave by herself and telling her Frank would send someone to pick her up in the morning.

When Zoe glanced at the clock again, it was after three o'clock. With her adrenaline crashing she was so exhausted she could hardly make herself move. Stretched out in the big chair in the den, she waited for

Zak to finish taking care of whatever business he had.

The reality that Sergei had such a major role in this whole mess still shocked her. *You think you know someone, and then they turn out to be a stranger.* Her mother, especially, would be a long time getting past that. Zoe dreaded seeing her the next day, seeing the shame and pain on her face, but Zak would be with her so she'd be able to get through it.

"Ready to hit the hay?"

She looked up to see Zak standing in front of her, his face lined with exhaustion. "Is everyone gone?"

"Yes. We have the house to ourselves again, and our guardian angels are patrolling outside."

She sat straight up. "You don't think…I mean, there's no one left out there, is there?"

"No. They're all gone. And I'd venture to say by the time DHS finished, the last traces of the Russian *mafiyah* in San Antonio will be gone, too."

"What about Caz Morgan and Max Detwiler?"

"Picked up at Caz's ranch where they were waiting for a report on Sergei's success. Tomorrow, we need to go into the city and meet with Allen for a final wrap-up, but right now, I think it's time for us to go to bed."

"I vote for that," she agreed.

Zak scooped her up in his arms and carried her through the kitchen, down the hall, and into his bedroom.

"This is where I should have put you in the first place," he told her. "This is where you belong." He held her gaze with his darkened eyes. "Right?"

"Right."

"Okay. A shower to wash off the filth of those people and to relax us, then sleep."

She was sure she'd fall asleep standing up, but the moment they were in the shower together, every nerve in her body woke up. She as sure that Zak's swollen erection and the hunger in his eyes had a lot to do with it. She closed her eyes and hummed with pleasure as he glided his soap-slicked hands over her body, squeezing her breasts, pinching her nipples, and letting his finger trail down the hot crevice between the cheeks of her ass.

"Feel good, kitten?" he murmured in her ear.

"Mmm," she hummed. "More than good."

He slid his hands over every inch of her naked skin, rubbing and caressing before rinsing her off. Then he leaned her against the shower wall, lifted one of her legs to wrap around his hip, and as he slid his tongue into her mouth, he thrust two fingers into the hot well of her sex.

"Oohhhh." Heat flared through her, making her nipples ache and her sex throb around his touch.

While he fucked her with his hand, he mimicked the motion with his tongue in her mouth, licking every inch of the inner surface. She hadn't thought she'd be able to do more than stand there, but his touch lit her up like the Fourth of July and made every nerve spark and flare.

He kissed her until neither of them could breathe, then drew the tip of his tongue across her lips and along her jaw line. She tried to rock back and forth on his hand, but he held her in such a position it was nearly impossible to move. Her inner walls gripped down on Zak's hot fingers, and with each slide and retreat, her need grew.

"I have to touch you," she murmured. "Don't let

me fall."

Pressing the one leg around his waist and wrapping an arm around his neck to balance herself, she slipped a hand between them and closed her fingers around his throbbing shaft.

"Jesus!" The word came out on a breath of air.

"Feel good?"

"So good," he murmured.

They maneuvered themselves so that as he stroked in and out, she matched the movement of his hands with hers on his cock.

"I have to be inside you," he rasped, setting her away from him.

"What—" She looked at him from beneath her eyelashes, caught up in the sensuality of the moment and the pulsing desire in her body.

"Just hold on." His voice had a raspy quality. "Just—hold on."

He slid open the shower door and reached for something on the counter.

When she saw what he had, she gave him a half-smile. "Anticipating, were you?"

"Hopeful." He rolled the condom on with one hand, then lifted her leg again to wrap it around his hip, spread the lips of her sex, and drove into her.

"Oh, God!" The words whispered from her lips as he filled her completely.

Zak held them like that for a moment before taking her mouth in a voracious kiss, and then he began to move his hips. Thrust and retreat. Forward and back. In and out. Slower, then faster, his mouth still glued to hers, feeding from her like a starving man.

He slid a hand between them and found her clit,

rubbing it in time with their movements. The pressure built inside her, stronger, higher.

He tore his mouth from hers. "Now, Zoe. Right now."

He gave her clit a pinch, and she went right over the edge. The spasms of their release shook them both, easing at last and leaving them limp and spent. She had no idea how long they were like that, bodies glued together in the aftermath of their passion.

Finally, Zak eased her leg down and gave her a soft kiss. "I love you, Zoe. I never stopped."

"Me, either," she whispered.

I have one more thing to say," he murmured as his kips touched hers again

"Mmm? What's that?"

"The water's cold, and I'm freezing my butt off."

She burst out laughing. "Me, too."

He turned off the water, and when they stepped out on the bathmat, he dried them both off. Then he carried her into the bedroom and held her while he slid them both between the covers. When he pulled her against his body, spoon fashion, she curled herself so she fit perfectly against him.

"Mmm," she murmured. "Good."

Nestled against him, she fell asleep with his arm across her waist, his hand cupping her breast, and his warm breath in her ear.

\*\*\*\*

Zak woke her shortly after seven, waving fresh coffee under her nose. "Marty will be here with the helicopter at eight."

"You're kidding, right?" She sipped the coffee gratefully. "It feels like we just went to sleep."

"We're due at Homeland Security at ten, and I thought you might want to do a little shopping first, unless you want to go to the meeting in jeans and a T-shirt."

"Shopping? At this hour? No one's open except Walmart. Although," she grinned at him, "after looking at the lingerie you got there I'm sure I can find something."

"No Walmart today. Guardian Security has a client that owns a string of boutiques in Texas and Arizona. I called the owner, and they'll have one of the shops open just for you."

"Can you do other magic tricks, too?"

He kissed the tip of her nose. "Try me, only when we've got more time."

Marty dropped them at the Guardian offices so Zak could pick up a vehicle. Lainie Coyle, the owner of *Texas Smart,* was waiting for them at the boutique in one of the new high-end shopping centers.

"You're so kind to do this for me," Zoe told her. "You have no idea how much I appreciate it."

"I owe a lot to Zak," the woman said. "Come on into the dressing room. Zak gave me the sizes and described you. I know you're short on time so I picked out a few things for you. I hope you like them."

"Are you kidding? At this point, I'll be ecstatic with anything. I love your clothes."

Half an hour later, Zoe was dressed in a short-sleeved summer silk suit in navy with a red, white, and blue print shell and navy heels. Her hair was brushed back and held in place with a heavy gold clip from the accessories department, and Zak had insisted she take the other three outfits as well.

She was embarrassed when Lainie wrote out the slip. "I'm afraid Zak has all my identification and credit cards."

"Already taken care of," Lainie assured her.

"Oh, but—"

"I can't have my future wife walking around naked, now can I?" he teased.

Heat crept up Zoe's cheeks. "You haven't actually asked me," she whispered while Lainie pretended not to hear."

"That's next," he assured her. "After the meeting."

She had to admit clothes made the woman. She felt human and confident in her new outfit, ready to hear anything and deal with it.

Zak parked in the underground garage where DHS had its offices, and they rode up in the elevator to the twentieth floor. Allen Fairchild came out to meet them when the receptionist buzzed him.

"We have quite a crowd this morning," he told them, leading them into a conference room. "I thought it would save time if we only had to go through this once."

Zak nodded in agreement.

The first person they saw in the room was Reno, who came forward to give her a hug and shake hands with Zak.

"Good job. And nice work getting us a pat on the back from Uncle Sam."

"I agree," Zak told him, "but the important thing is Zoe's safe now."

Reno nodded. "The client always comes first." Then he winked at her before he took his seat again.

As Zoe surveyed all the faces, the only other one

she recognized was Detective Morales. She began to tremble, and Zak took her hand, squeezing it.

"Don't worry," he whispered, bending to her ear. "It's almost over."

Allen sat down at the head of the table and introduced everyone. Sitting with Joe Morales was his lieutenant, Keith Colson; three men Allen introduced as DHS department heads, an agent from Immigration and Customs Enforcement, and the head of the local Drug Enforcement Agency office.

"I think we're all here," he said at last. "I'll make this as brief as possible and still cover all the details."

Zoe listened carefully, trying to absorb everything. She heard again how the five men, sons of established local *mafiyah*, concocted the idea to take things even further. Branch out even more. Going to law school and getting their degrees put them in a better position than their fathers to control what they wanted. They created a network of businesses that fed into each other, drew up papers to legitimize activities that skirted the law, and drew on the muscle they inherited from their fathers to squash anyone who dared go against them. Meanwhile, they lived at the top of society, pulling strings, and manipulating people who didn't even know what was happening.

"They had their sights set on Lombardo Simulations," Fairchild explained, "because they wanted to be able to sell the programs for exorbitant prices to drug cartels, Third world rebels, criminals of every kind, but most especially to terrorists.

"Whose idea was it to find someone like Nate Dunning?" one of the men asked.

"They needed a good front man, and after

chumming the social waters, there he was. Rich, good social standing, with an unbearable ego but without a lick of common sense. He was the DI figurehead." He turned to Zoe. "And all that stuff he spouted to you about expansion and growing the company? It was being spoon-fed to him."

"They built the organization one block at a time," he went on. "First a couple of legitimate businesses, with public success and recognition for Dunning. By the time they had prostitution, then drugs, up and running, Nate was in so deep he couldn't get out. So he played his part and got richer and richer."

"I had a hard time getting my head around his relationship with the cartels," the DEA man told him.

"Caz always preached it's better to keep your enemy close than anger him," Allen said. "And he felt he could actually use the cartels without them realizing it." He paused to take a sip of water. "They had contacts in the Middle East which allowed them to expand their flourishing white slave trade, and they used the ports of Galveston and Corpus Christi to smuggle people in with shipments of merchandise for one or more of their blind companies."

"The Russians have been making money for a long time supplying arms to terrorists," one of his own agents pointed out, "using the proceeds from drug sales and the slave trade."

Fairchild nodded. "But Sergei was aware of the importance of technology in today's world. And he had a bright, young cousin who was doing wonderful things with simulations. If you can plan how to rescue hostages, he reasoned, why couldn't you reverse the process and be prepared to defend against a hostage rescue? For terrorists, this would be a treasure, and for Sergei, a gold mine. Not to mention the fact they could add a little on the side with the pirated games."

"I think I feel sick," Zoe said, gripping Zak's hand.

"I'm a little sick myself at the way they used you," Fairchild told her. "Introducing you to Nate was a simple matter. Dinner with a charming, wealthy man. Sergei knew you wanted to expand, and Nate had ready, easy money."

"I was a damn fool," she said, embarrassed that her stupidity was out there for everyone to see.

"You were a businesswoman looking to expand and were introduced to a man who came highly recommended and who supposedly had impeccable credentials."

"But then Nate made a mistake," Zak ventured.

"Right. He carelessly left records out where Miss Lombardo could see them. Then, when she called him on them, instead of making up a plausible story, he argued with her and told her it was none of her business."

"So Nate then became a liability," Allen went on. "And so did Miss Lombardo."

"Who put the rohypnol in my drink?" Zoe asked.

"That was Sergei," Allen said. "He actually bragged about it, the idiot. How easy it was and then how he managed to walk you into the den with no trouble and talk to you until the drug took effect."

"And killing Nate?"

"That was him, too. I know that night is still a blank, but it seems you actually did argue with Dunning loudly enough so people could hear you. Sergei simply took advantage of it. When everyone had left, he took

Nate into the den where you were unconscious on the couch, shot Nate, put the gun in your hand, and called 911."

"And it almost worked." Zoe swallowed the bile rising in her throat.

"I have to take the blame for that," Lieutenant Colson said, speaking up for the first time. "You looked so good for it, we just didn't take the time to ask ourselves why. Plus, we were under enormous pressure to put it to bed."

"I'm just glad it's over." She shuddered.

"Are you through with us?" Zak asked?

"Yes." Allen Fairchild leaned forward on his elbows. "But we'll have a lot of wrapping up to do. Miss Lombardo, we'll need you to try and recreate as many of the sims as you can so we know how the terrorists figured to counteract them. Then we'll want you to rewrite them for your clients for their own protection as well as ours. And we still have questions about Nate Dunning and the others."

"Understood," she said. "I want to do whatever I can to help clean up this terrible mess."

The agent rose and extended his hand to her. "I'll be calling you." He grinned. "But I think you can take a breather for a little while."

She and Zak shook hands with him, then with everyone else in the room. Finally, they were in the elevator going down to the garage.

"I can't believe I don't have to hide anymore," she said.

"You're free to do whatever you want. Including rebuild your business if you want to."

She shook her head. "I actually don't know what I

want to do. I have enough money that I can take the time to figure it out. Right now I just want to hang out with you."

He squeezed her arm. "That sounds good to me."

"So where are we off to now?"

"You'll see."

"Ooh! I love surprises."

"I hope you like this one."

When they didn't head for the Interstate but instead drove toward the center of downtown, she looked at him. "The Riverwalk?"

The collection of colorful shops and restaurants that followed the winding San Antonio River was a world famous tourist attraction. On their first date, Zak had taken her to dinner there, and she wondered if that was where they were going again. But when he pulled off the street to the raised entrance of one of the city's newest hotels, she looked at him, puzzled.

"Are we going to eat here?" she asked.

"In a manner of speaking. Have patience." He winked at her.

He waited for the ticket from the valet service, then ushered her through the revolving door and over to the elevators. Now she really was confused, but Zak looked so pleased with himself she decided to keep quiet and let him play this out.

The elevator doors opened smoothly on the top floor, and Zak led her down the corridor, their footsteps muffled by the thickest carpet she'd ever walked on.

"Don't we have to register or something?" she blurted out.

"The company keeps a suite here for high profile clients. I marked it off on the books for a couple of days."

He pulled a key card from his pocket, slipped it into the lock, and pushed the door open.

Zoe had been in luxury suites before, but this one was beyond anything she'd ever seen. The sitting room was huge and filled with vases of fresh flowers. Partially open double doors led into the bedroom beyond, which appeared to be just as large.

Zak guided her to the glass wall and slid the doors open to the patio, which overlooked the Riverwalk. Barges of tourists glided past on the water, and from below, she could hear the music of a *mariachi* band. A table had been set for two with china and crystal.

She stared at Zak in amazement. "When did you do all this?"

"While you were still lazing in bed this morning. Like it?"

"Are you kidding? But what's the occasion?"

He reached in his pants pocket and took out a small box. When he opened it, a diamond winked in the sunlight. "Recognize this?"

She touched the diamond ring with the tip of a finger. "Is this…?"

He nodded, grinning. "The one you threw in my face? One and the same." Then he sobered. "I could never give this to anyone else, kitten, and I couldn't return it. I kept hoping that one day something would happen and we'd find our way back to each other."

"Too bad it took my almost getting arrested or killed to do it," she said with a rueful smile.

"I meant what I said yesterday. The fact that you called me when you were in trouble, that you saw me as your only chance, means more to me than I can ever tell you. It meant you trusted me. And maybe, I hoped, that you still loved me."

"Oh, Zak, I do love you. More than I ever did before."

He lifted her left hand and slid the ring onto her ring finger. Then he captured her gaze with his. "Will you marry me, kitten? Will you have my children, grow old with me, and live a wonderful life with me?"

"Yes, yes, yes."

She stood on tiptoe and threw her arms around his neck, pulling his lips down to hers.

With their mouths still fused together, he lifted her in his arms and carried her into the bedroom. As he'd done the other night, he stripped back the covers, stood her on her feet, and undressed her as if she were a precious prize.

As each part of her body was revealed to him, he worshiped it with his mouth. His tongue traced circles at the hollow of her throat, and his lips closed over each pointed nipple. She clung to him as he caressed her hips, the curve of her buttocks, then probed at her already drenched sex.

"I can't wait," she whispered.

"I think that's supposed to be my line."

"I don't care. I want you. Right now."

He tossed his clothes aside, then carried her down to the bed with him, nestling between her thighs.

"I love you," he repeated, tracing her mouth with the tip of his tongue. "I will always love you."

And as he slid home into her welcoming body, he showed her exactly how much.

## About the Author

Known as the oldest living author of erotic romance, Desiree Holt has produced more than two hundred titles in nearly every subgenre of romance fiction. Her stories are enriched by her personal experiences, her characters by the people she meets.

After fifteen years in the great state of Texas, she relocated back to Florida to be closer to members of her family and a large collection of friends. Her favorite pastimes are watching football, reading, and researching her stories. She lives with her three cats, who love to sit with her when she writes.

~*~

Desiree loves to hear from readers.
www.facebook.com/desireeholtauthor
www.facebook.com/desiree01holt
Twitter @desireeholt
Pinterest: desiree02holt
www.desireeholt.com
www.desiremeonly.com

~*~

To chat with Desiree Holt and other Wild Rose Press authors of erotic romance, join us at
www.groups.yahoo.com/group/thewilderroses.

Also Available

# Killing Lies
*Guardian Security Book Three*
## By Desiree Holt

*http://a.co/8actflx*

After her husband was killed and she lost her unborn child, Sarah Madison believed she'd never find love and happiness again. Instead, she has channeled all her energy into her job as assistant to the sexy CEO of Guardian Security. When he proposes a marriage of convenience, the chance to become a mother is tempting, and so is her new prospective husband. His only flaw—the distance he keeps between himself and his sweet little daughter.

Reno Sullivan's life is a mess. His first marriage was based on a lie, and the fiery death of his wife left him to raise a baby—a constant reminder of his wife's deceit. He desperately needs someone to mother the child and take charge of his personal life, and his no-nonsense assistant is perfect for the job. Unfortunately, the alluring woman in the bedroom next to his chips away at his determination to maintain the hands-off clause in their agreement and the ice around his heart.

A near-tragedy and Reno's fear of love could kill Sarah's hopes of turning their fake marriage into happily ever after…

Also Read

# Big Bad Easy
## By Ursula Whistler

*http://a.co/iJf2GuE*

A grueling unsolved murder case is the tipping point for detective Jameson Kelly. He's ready to hang up his holster for early retirement when Zara Robinson walks in to his precinct, the victim of a car break-in. She's everything Jameson likes in a woman—tall, blonde, beautiful, and athletic. More than enough woman to take him down and make him beg for more. One more case can't hurt to help pass the time, especially one he knows he can solve.

Zara is a woman who knows what she needs, and top of her list is closure on this spree of car break-ins. And there's Jameson—he's big with an air of bad despite being a cop and all man. Man enough to easily make her feel soft and womanly. But when clues to the theft lead to something bigger, she's glad to have his brains as well as his skills on her side.

www.ingramcontent.com/pod-product-compliance
Lightning Source LLC
Chambersburg PA
CBHW060522260626
47161CB00003B/723